Polar Shift

Nowhere to Hide
And
Nowhere to Run

Anthony Fox

Published by

Chipmunkapublishing

United Kingdom

http://www.chipmunkapublishing.com

Front cover design by Antonia Keen

Acknowledgments

I wish to thank my daughter Colleen and my son Jamie for their encouragement over the course of this

book project

Polar Shift

Summary

Most of humanity had failed to see the warning signs. It had happened before in earth's history, but a long time ago before the civilization of man. Archaeologists had unearthed whole mammoths frozen solid with food still in their mouths, but no one paid attention as to why this was the case. It was a mystery as to why this had happened in the past, but the majority of the scientific community had failed to provide answers, they preferred to ignore the possible reasons.

Chapter 1

"It looks like rain."

"We do need it."

Dr. Isabella Garcia and Dr. Joseph Goldstein had both just finished teaching at the University of California for the summer holidays when they started to plan their summer adventures. Isabella wanted to pursue her pet theory and gather more evidence. While Joe was willing to tag along to just about anything Isabella had in mind.

"The clouds are building up for a storm tonight," Joe remarked.

"At least, out here in Sonora, we don't have wildfires to contend with," Isabella remarked.

"Although, they did get close one year…"

"That was a few years back…"

"What plans do you have…no school," Joe said with a twinkle in his eyes.

"None, at the moment, but I'm packed and ready to go anytime soon," Isabella replied, smiling.

"Oh, really!"

"I plan to visit Rebecca in Boston and see some sights."

"Is that Rebecca Steel whose brother has just recently retired from the CIA?" Joe asked candidly.

"Yes, but shush, we're not meant to know that, but Rebecca mentioned it the last time via email, and mind you keep it to yourself," Isabella said harshly.

"Okay…"

"Good."

"Have you heard about Murphy's Law or Sod's Law or whatever you what to call it? What will happen often when you haven't prepared for that event? Those little gremlins appear to spoil your day, and when that happens what you should have prepared for often does, otherwise, the gremlins will win. I often hear my students say they've lost their coursework on their computer and they hadn't bothered to think about having backup strategies."

"Of course, I have…"

"When you tempt fate it often happens…"

"It brought us together…didn't it?"

"Yeah, it did…"

It reminded Joe and Isabella about the first time they had met at a symposium conference in Salt Lake City, Utah during the summer of 2011, shortly before the 9/11 attack on the twin towers in New York City. The symposium was well attended partly due to the far-reaching brief the conference catered for. Joe had attended because he was interested in the theory of Panspermia and Isabella had attended because she was interested in some of the other theories being discussed concerning evolution. It was on the first day of the three-day event that Joe first saw the attractive blond standing in the lobby of the hotel they were both staying at in the city. From that first meeting, a friendship developed, and eventually a relationship began when they returned to California after the conference.

"We were both in the lobby."

"Yeah, I remember staring at you because of your dark good looks, in the lobby, we were lost, in our own little worlds," Isabella said.

"I asked you if you were attending the conference," Joe said, smiling.

"Not exactly the best chat-up line," Isabella said, smiling.

"Well, it started the ball rolling…we're together now."

"But, we haven't tied the knot, yet," Isabella remarked.

"It's on my radar…"

"We don't have the paper but we're a couple in love," Joe said.

"Now, you're starting to get romantic, Joe."

"Let's sit on the balcony and watch the sunset, it's nice and cool out there this time of day," Joe said happily.

"Look!"

"Bats…"

"Yeah, out to feed…at least, they keep the insects' numbers down," Isabella said.

"What was that about Murphy's Law you said earlier, tonight?" Joe asked.

"Just pointing out the chances that another scientist will be on the same endeavor as me," Isabella said.

"It's Murphy's Law...as soon as you start something...then something else will happen," Joe said.

"Like my pet theory."

"Yeah, your pet theory," Joe said, smiling.

"It could have happened...a polar shift...causing wide-scale climate changes, in the recent past," Isabella said.

Isabella went on to explain to Joe that around twelve thousand years ago, the earth was plunged into a catastrophe that reshaped some parts of the world. Some scientists had theorized that an extraterrestrial force may have been involved, which causes the polar shift, although no evidence had been produced to support this theory. She also explained about the anomaly of maps of Antarctica showing it ice-free and accurately drawn without the aid of modern technology, how was this possible? The map is thought to date from the sixteenth century, but based on earlier maps perhaps many thousands of years ago, she explained to Joe. But could a polar shift have occurred overnight, without warning? She continued to explain to Joe and want answers from him.

"I don't have the answers, you just need to find the evidence," Joe said.

Isabella continued to explain that a slight wobble of the earth's rotation could have caused the polar shift. An asteroid strike could have caused the wobble in the earth's rotation, she thought. Only a slight shift in the earth's rotation would be enough to cause a polar shift and major climate change, she stressed.

"The more I learn about it the more it seems likely."

"It sounds like science fiction, but the truth is something happened and a polar shift is the likely answer. Could it happen again, of course, it could," Isabella stressed again.

"For such a claim then it will require extraordinary evidence," Joe said, lightheartedly.

"Yeah, I know…"

***

"Have you heard about the 'Havana Syndrome' and the mystery of the microwaves?" Joe asked.

"Not another of those strange stories you read," Isabella replied.

"Don't you remember those news stories about US government officials working in Cuba who reported feeling ill with a wide range of symptoms such as feeling dizzy and experiencing fatigue," Joe said.

"When was that?"

"It started in 2016 and has continued in many other countries since then," Joe replied.

"Did you say microwaves?" Isabella asked intently.

"Yeah, they reckon microwaves were used to affect the people in those government buildings in Cuba and other places around the world. The article said that it could be the

Russians or the Chinese, but there was no definite proof as to who it may have been or indeed if it was the use of microwaves, but the evidence suggests it may have been the cause," Joe replied.

"What do you think after reading the article," Isabella asked intently.

Shrugging his shoulders, Joe replied, "From the evidence that many scientists have conducted into the use and the effects of using microwaves on animals it suggests that you can also interfere with our brains, so it's possible some rogue government is using them to cause harm to some people."

"It's possible that our government knows what's happening and is choosing to keep the truth from the public as it does for so many secrets because they believe the public couldn't handle the real truth," Isabella said.

"Yes, I agree…anything is possible. When you consider that we have gone from using windmills to Nanotechnology in the space of less than two hundred years," Joe said.

"Hmm, yes, it frightens me…the power science has given to some people who don't have the best interests of the public in their hearts. Who knows where it will all end," Isabella said sadly.

"At least, we have good intentions with our current interest in polar shifts. It's a worthy cause to help unravel certain events of the past and present evidence to back up our claims without causing anyone any harm," Joe said.

"Yeah, you're right, Joe…I wouldn't want to get involved with anything that caused anyone harm. It's just not me or you," Isabella remarked.

"Your late parents taught you to respect everything and everyone the same as mine, we're much like two peas in a pod," Joe said, smiling.

"That reminds me…the wildfires are more frequent and this story is related. This guy I knew told me about this fellow called 'Harry the Hat' who was a gambler and spent most of the time gambling and not being productive. You asked me the other day what was the most destructive vice to have and that is gambling. Most people lose whatever they are doing because the stats say only three percent are winners. Now, Harry had spent his life as a merchant seaman visiting all parts of the world. He was paid a good salary, but he thought he could supplement his income through gambling, but he lost and he became like every other gambler a loser."

"What happened next?"

"He continued to lose more than he won until eventually after losing a small inheritance he had spent the lot mostly on his gambling addiction. He even used borrowed money with loans and credit cards, but still lost the lot. He had got down to zero, that's what it said when he looked at his bank statements."

"He was at the bottom of the barrel."

"What happened next?"

"He decided to change his life around and to never gamble again."

"Did it work?"

"It's only been seven months…he still has a way to go, but he now enjoys the extra takeaways he treats himself with every week and compares it to the money he would have lost in ten minutes. He gets far more pleasure from his takeaways than he did gambling, he told friends"

"Why are you telling me this?"

"You were worried about my recent investments in the stock market…you said I may have a gambling problem," Joe replied.

"I was just kidding, but hoping that you would be careful with your money," Isabella said intently.

"Yes, of course…I have a strategy."

"That's what they all say…didn't you just say only a small percentage actually make money?"

"Yes, that was about gambling and I'm not gambling. My strategy is to only invest what I can afford to lose and no more. I will match my research and intuition to a company that has the potential to rise in value."

"Don't become a groundhog and spend all your free time immersed in stock market reports," Isabella remarked nonchalantly.

"I don't intend to get greedy…it's just some fun and we will see how it goes. I don't intend to chase losses."

Chapter 2

Harry Steel could hear the sound of bells ringing from the local church tower as he strolled back from the outdoor market to his home situated on a quiet street in an outer suburb of Omaha, Nebraska. He was no longer a Central Intelligence Agency (CIA) agent and he was glad he had taken early retirement from the organization when he had the chance. He had become cynical of the government's intelligence organizations and the petty rivalry between the Federal Bureau of Investigation (FBI) and the CIA. He was also tired of killing people even though it was legal and warranted, at the time. The CIA had made him cynical of their true intentions when most of the time he was never told the truth and this made him angry involving him in missions where the real truth had been hidden from him from the beginning of many of his last missions. This had endangered his life and the closest people around him such as his future wife Susan Ginsberg, to whom he was now happily married. She still worked for the CIA, but she never spoke about what she was doing and he wasn't about to ask her. She worked full-time as a biologist for the local Nebraska state food and land department, which was cover for her nefarious or not CIA activities. They had discussed her early retirement, but no final decision had been yet made. Susan wasn't about to retire without knowing what she would do next, she had said this to Harry many times over the previous year since their marriage.

It was early summer, and it had just rained for the first time in months. The birds were chirping away, at least they were happy, he said to himself. There was a freshness in the air as he breathed it all in. As Harry walked along the street to his home his mind drifted back to his time in the CIA. He

15

had spent over twenty years in the CIA serving his country, which had made him cynical of the government. Some people in government had too much power and chose to keep too many secrets from the public. They in government believed the public couldn't handle the real truth about the state of play as he saw it. Even the commander and chief the president of the United States was unaware of much the CIA got into, he said to himself.

During his time as a CIA agent, he had toed the line many times when he thought about revealing what he knew to the public, but he didn't he just carried on serving his country and the government. He thought there was too much power in the hands of a very small group of people, who often had a different agenda than the president of the United States.

On his last mission before he retired he was forced into a month-long sabbatical because he hadn't followed CIA protocols and procedures deciding instead to use his own judgment about how to proceed on a case and not to risk the lives of innocent people who were present at the time. He was not a psycho or a manic just a cynic. He had accepted the month-long holiday from the director of the CIA, but not the retraining he had to do afterward before being allowed back on active duty because of his actions of not following CIA procedures. He had forcibly explained to his boss the reasons why he took the actions he did and why he wasn't willing to risk the lives of innocent people who had been present at the scene. As far as he was concerned he had made the right decisions under the extreme circumstances. At the time, his sister and his future wife were present at the scene and he wasn't about to risk their lives for the sake of CIA protocols. And now he was just cynical of how the CIA operated without due concern for other people's lives. When he had the opportunity to retire he took it with both hands and was glad, but still angry about how he was treated considering his long and commendable service in the organization. But he knew too much and too many secrets for some people, but he wasn't about to reveal anything to anyone he would take it all to the grave rather than risk reprisals from the CIA or anyone else. Every day he still carried his trusted Glock-19 handgun in his shoulder holster ready for any terrorist or anyone else willing to get even. But even now, he said to himself, he had to be careful there was always that chance even in retirement that someone would come looking to kill him. He didn't trust anyone outside his family or close friends, but this had kept him alive over the years.

Harry was now living in his wife's home having rented out his Washington, D.C., home to a young couple working for a government department. He still had the log cabin in the foothills of the Appalachian Mountains, which he had decided to keep just in case he needed somewhere else to stay, which no one else knew about but him and Susan. He had a decent pension from the CIA and had saved much of his income over the years so he wasn't short of cash. He was enjoying his retirement, spending time fishing in the Florida Keys and hiring a boat, and sailing down the Mississippi River with Susan on days when they could relax together. He thought about his sister Rebecca in Boston and wondered about what she was doing. The last time they spoke was a brief phone call he had with her about three months ago when she was telling him of her latest paranormal adventures. She had the same determination that he had and the last time he had spent time with her shortly before he retired from the CIA, he had tagged along with her on several of her paranormal adventures, and for the first, he had begun to believe in the paranormal. It was while he was on one of these paranormal cases with his sister that he came aware of the 'mad cow' disease from one of her clients. He had become intrigued and then undertook his own research into the subject. His research into the subject led him to believe that some of the evidence of the 'mad cow' debacle didn't stack up in his view. There were too many anomalies and because of his move to Nebraska, he had to leave the investigation for another day. But he still had qualms about it and would continue his research when he had more time to devote to the subject, he thought.

There was now a new president in the White House, and what his agenda would be, only time would tell, he said to himself.

"Morning Harry," said the old man behind the counter, who ran the small local convenience shop located on the edge of the town.

Good morning, Stan."

"Just the paper…"

"Oh, I need some milk, as well."

Bellevue, Nebraska was indeed a small town compared to living in his previous home in Washington, D.C., but times had moved on and he was now retired and married. It was the two things in the previous year when he married Susan and moved to Nebraska, which he would never have guessed happening. But that's fate, he would say to himself. Don't bet against it, because it's liable to bite you in the ass when you're not looking. Yes, fate or chance, call it what you like it was an unseen force guiding people's lives, he believed that most people were not aware of.

Harry had not voted in the last election, deciding politics wasn't for him. In his view, while he was a CIA agent it was best not to take sides, and that's what he did. Now, that he had retired his option to cast his vote he would freely take it. All people should, he would say to his friends and colleagues when the subject came up in conversation. Many people fought and died for the right to vote, so you should respect that right by honoring the fallen by casting your vote, he would say to them.

It reminded him of his first taste of the reality of the brutality of war. He had joined the Marines and shortly after finishing his training, he was deployed with the rank of sergeant to the war in Iraq. It came the first week he arrived in the war zone. His commanding officer had said don't worry you are unlikely to see any of the enemy as most of the enemy had retreated to Baghdad to make a stand there. And there was Harry, thinking don't tempt fate.

The mission involved around twenty soldiers on a reconnoiter mission. They were to head for this small village on the outskirts of Baghdad to make sure it was clear of enemy combatants and report back. It was early in the morning, but it was hot and sticky from the early morning sun as they headed towards the village. They had stopped just outside the village and proceeded on foot checking each dwelling for possible enemy combatants, but from first observations, it was clear the village appeared empty. It was eerily quiet not a sound from a howling dog or a chirping bird did they hear from inside the village. They were almost about to relax when the first rattle of machine gun fire hit them like a rocket from hell. Most of them had made it to the nearest building for cover, but unfortunately, two of their fellow soldiers lay on the ground wounded and groaning in agony. There wasn't anything they could do. They were caught in a trap and surrounded by the enemy. They returned fire the best they could, while our commanding officer a young lieutenant decided on what to do. Our radio communications lay outside with one of the dying soldiers in the street. The enemy had decided to let the soldiers in the street die in agony rather than finish them off; it was their way of delaying the agony for us. They heard the moans and screams of the dying soldiers for what seemed like hours. Harry could hear the orders in his head as if it was yesterday. He had never forgotten that day.

"Sergeant, take three and get those soldiers, we will give you cover," the young Lieutenant Shiver said.

"Yes, sir," Harry replied.

Harry thought about arguing against the action, but considered not, during the heat of the battle. They tried their best to give them covering fire, but it wasn't enough the enemy was firing at them from all directions as soon they made their attempt to recover their fallen comrades. One of his best mates died almost instantly they made for the open street. His name was Willy Spencer, he had made plans to marry his childhood sweetheart. He planned to take over the family farm and raise a family back in Tennessee. Many of his fellow soldiers were mainly from the southern states. For many young men, it was the only viable job prospect in that part of America. Harry guessed he was the joker in the pack. He had just finished university and was living in Washington, D.C. when he decided to join the Marines looking to serve his country.

They took cover behind a burnt-out car and pulled Willy to cover, but he was already dead. He had died serving his country in a war started by false pretenses as they were later to learn.

20

Harry's other two mates had fared a little better, one was also dead and the other was injured but alive and was now under the cover of a low wall of a bombed-out house. The two soldiers they were meant to recover were still in the middle of the street. Harry could see one had stopped moaning and was now dead and the other was still alive, which the enemy had decided not to kill. They wanted to torture his comrades with his calls for help. He was dead the second he hit the ground when the enemy had decided to let him groan until he died or they decided to kill him. They used him as bait. They made a second attempt to rescue the soldier but by that time he had lost too much blood and died during our escape from their holdout, which was a bombed-out house with a central courtyard. Part of the house still remained intact but about a third lay in ruins from a previous mortar shell most likely hitting it.

"We will make our escape as soon as it gets dark. Be ready, sergeant."

"Yes, sir!"

Finally, the young lieutenant was starting to think straight, and they were getting the hell out of there, he said to himself. Harry had considered the orders from the lieutenant foolhardy at best but didn't choose to raise his concerns. They didn't know from where the enemy was firing, so our ability to give cover was weak. To most observers, it was doomed to fail but probably allowed in the heat of battle, when the head is not always giving and making logical decisions. But the lieutenant had risked not only Harry's life but the lives of the other soldiers, for an action that was suicidal in nature.

The young lieutenant at the time just happened to be a replacement for our previous lieutenant who had his head blown off by a M662 Calibri round from a sniper's rifle. It was only his second day in Iraq, when they were sent out on patrol, in a small town with only a few miles of desert separating it from the outskirts of the ultimate prize the city of Baghdad.

They had captured the town if that's the right word only a few days before and now they were trying to bring order to a chaotic landscape of peoples and cultures with religion in the mix, as well, he said to himself. It was when their lieutenant decided to pop his head over the turret in their armored vehicle that a bullet sheared off his head like cutting a melon in half. It scared the shit out of him and his men. The lieutenant had decided to view the gathered crowd at an open-air market on the right side of the road as they slowly made their way down the street avoiding the craters and rubbish scattered in every direction. The town had been captured several days before, but it was still chaotic with many factions not fighting us but among themselves. It was a civil war and they had let the dogs of war out to play. They never found the sniper, the lieutenant just happened to be in the wrong place at the right time. Sometimes you are unaware how close you are to Damocles's sword, thought Harry as he crossed the road towards his home.

It reminded Harry of reading about the life of the Buddha, when for the first time the young prince tasted what life was like outside the walls of the palace where he was confined to, since his birth. His father the king had decided to hide life and death from his son. The prince grew up knowing nothing about the frailty of man. When the young prince decided to leave the palace, he saw how his people really lived. At first, he was in shock at what he saw, but then he gradually understood the ages of man and began to understand after a period of reflection. Upon a long period of meditation, the Buddha achieved spiritual happiness in his life called nirvana.

To Harry marriage hadn't changed how he felt about Susan. Their relationship had got stronger. He had gotten used to being at home and not chasing spies all over the world.

He could hear only the sounds from the flag post rattling in the wind in the center of the town square, and apart from that it was eerily quiet, he thought.

Harry's thoughts turned back again to the lieutenant's decisions that proved to be costly for his friends and comrades in arms. All of his fellow soldiers had never seen any action, and that included the young lieutenant. The lieutenant had ordered four of his group to rescue the fallen soldiers in the street, which only resulted in another two soldiers losing their lives for nothing, he said to himself. It was a desperate attempt of rescuing the soldiers and the radio communications, which were on the back of one of the now-dead soldiers. They didn't even know if the communication equipment was still working, it seemed pointless and yet it could be their only chance of getting much-needed help, at the time, he said himself.

As the enemy moved in closer for the kill they caught sight of their uniforms and recognized they were surrounded by the Republican Guard the elite forces of the Saddam Hussein regime.

The Republican Guards were the Marines of Saddam Hussein's regime. They were highly trained and well-equipped forces and not the regular army and willing to die in their endeavors if they had to. Because the battle for Baghdad had just begun in earnest the theater of war had got chaotic and it was assumed that they had been forgotten about. It was about to get dark and their only means of escape would be if they could get back to their vehicles and drive the hell out of there. But they didn't know if their vehicles were still drivable and had not been disabled by the enemy such was their predicament, he said himself.

The lieutenant had posted guards with our vehicles but he didn't know if they were still alive or not. So their position was untenable, without communication. The lieutenant decided it was best to make a break for their vehicles from their position using the cover of darkness to aid their escape. As they tried to make their escape from building to building they were met with a hail of enemy fire from all directions, and that is when the first bullet caught my jacket just inches from my heart, luckily it just skimmed through his jacket without piercing his body, but the bullet caught the soldier next behind him. It was a friend and fellow soldier who died instantly. It shook him up for a few seconds before returning fire at the enemy. Harry felt like stone, at the time, feeling nothing just reacting instinctively firing back, he thought. His fellow soldiers had given him the nickname Stone, as everyone used a nickname other than their real names.

Eventually, they fought their way back to the vehicles losing several of our group in the process. Luckily, the soldiers guarding our vehicles had held off many attempts by the enemy to get at our vehicles. They eventually called in air support and the village was blown to pieces and we were then able to recover the bodies of our fallen comrades. It was a lesson in death and how close it came for him, he said to himself.

Polar Shift

Harry didn't have time to mourn his fellow comrades, it wasn't until their bodies were stacked in a shed waiting to be flown back to the States that his emotions got to him and he had shed some tears over their caskets. It was for the first time that the reality of war struck him as if he had been struck by a car. At first, everyone in their group was gun-ho about going to Iraq and killing the enemy as if the enemy never hit back. It wasn't considered they were like little boys pretending they were safe and could kill without seeing the other side of the war. It was a wake-up call for Harry, from that moment onwards he treated the war with respect and he believed the other soldiers who had made it through the first few days did the same as him.

Somehow, Harry had survived, by a miracle or just plain luck, and so he had decided not to fear death and that there was no point in worrying about it either. After a while, he began to respect their replacement lieutenant even though he still had thoughts about his orders that day that bordered on suicide, but decided to keep it to himself rather than seek justice up the chain of command.

Ever since, that episode with death there have been other occasions where death had been a close call. Harry would tell friends and colleagues about his brush with death on the battlefield. But, he told them from that moment onwards he never spent any time worrying about it. If it had its calling card then there wouldn't be anything he could do about it. Catching a bullet when the time came was something he didn't spend time worrying about because worrying never stopped a bullet.

***

As he turned the street corner on his way home he could hear the birds tweeting in the tree-lined avenue as he approached his house and his life was about to change dramatically, but he was unaware of the events, at that moment, that would alter his life for good. The first thing he noticed was the black sedan car parked outside his home with what looked like two men inside. Harry had his gun in its shoulder holster should he need it.

"It's too quiet...I don't trust the motherfuckers," Harry said to himself.

"Are you Harry Steel?"

"Yes, who are you?"

The two men flashed their CIA credentials and Harry let them into his home wondering what they wanted, now that he was retired from the CIA. The CIA agents explained the need for their visit, and not discussing it 0ver the telephone.

"And now, you're asking for me to come into the CIA fold as a sub-contractor for special operations in which you need my skills. This is something I will have to think about before I give you an answer. Will, tomorrow suit you, because I have to discuss this with my wife before I make a decision. I don't know if I want to step into my old shoes again, regardless if my country needs me or not. But, if I decide to come back then the CIA is going to have to re-hire me as an employee and an agent with full benefits, so you can tell my old boss Michael Kurious that's the only way I'm coming back to the CIA. In the meantime, you can get the hell off my couch and tell Michael what I want before I consider coming back," Harry said to the two agents.

Chapter 3

Meanwhile, in the northeast of Russia, in what is part of Siberia, in an area known as Yakutia two men are about to set off on a journey. From a small town called Namtsyr, about 500 miles east of Moscow these men set out in their old rusty brownish pickup truck and drive along the dirt track that ran almost parallel to the local river that ran north of their town along the Russian northern steppe. Both men were from the local Yakust tribe, in their mid-fifties, and married with children. They had recently retired due to ill health from the local oil exploration industry, which employed most of the local population in the region. They were both overweight and drank too much alcohol, which was brewed locally by many in their village, which helped them through the harsh Siberian winters. They had eked out the winter months living on hunting and ice fishing. It was now early summer and they were eager to get to the river after recent storms before other locals started searching for mammoth tusks. It was a race against time during the short summer season when the permafrost melts and conditions allow for the search for mammoth tusks. Dmitry and his friend Yuri had waited through the harsh winter to make money during the summer selling what tusks they could find to the Chinese market for ivory.

Since the woolly mammoth had died out around 5000 years ago all across the Russian steppe the locals had referred to the area as the 'Mammoth Steppe' because of the hundreds of thousands of mammoth bones (Kost) found in the region.

As Dmitry and Yuri traveled north towards the river they could smell the smoke of a forest fire inside their vehicle and see in the distance the dark gray and black murky clouds above the lower slopes of the local Kisilyakh mountain range. Forest fires were not unusual in the Yakutia during the summer months, but the fires were starting earlier each year and getting bigger and harder to control. The smoke now covered a vast sway of the horizon. The wind was blowing in their direction and they could smell the larch and pine trees burning even though they were many miles away from the forest fire.

As Dmitry and Yuri's vehicle came to the end of the track they stopped on the bank overlooking the river. Both men put on their mosquito head nets to protect themselves from the relentless mosquito attacks on the tundra. It would be hard enough work dredging through the muddy shoreline of the river in the heat and humidity without the added problem of millions of mosquitoes constantly attacking any bare skin. Each carried a backpack of essential supplies, tools, and a rifle for protection. Such was the rivalry between mammoth tusk hunters because of the money involved many had resorted to carrying weapons for protection.

The men carefully made their way down the sloping bank onto the river shoreline and the only sound they could hear was the fast-flowing river and a raven in the distance screeching. In previous years, Dmitry and Yuri had never been as far up the river before searching for mammoth tusks. They both noticed the absence of any human footprints in the mud, so they hoped for rich pickings. Both men were already perspiring in the early morning sun as the day began to heat up. They had decided to split up with one searching along the river bank and the other along the muddy shoreline. During the spring rainy season when the river flooded and cut away more of the river bank, it exposed many mammoth tusks for the first time in thousands of years. They hoped they had chosen the right time to begin their search after a recent storm had made its way through the region.

"Look! I've found one. It needs to be dug out from the bank," Dmitry said excitedly.

"Great!"

They could see only a small portion of the mammoth tusk poking out from the river bank waiting to be unearthed. The top part of the tusk had broken off, but it was still worth the time to retrieve the rest from inside the permafrost in the river bank. Most collectors wanted whole complete tusks, but partial tusks were still valued by carvers who would use the ivory to carve intricate trinkets to sell into the Chinese market.

"At least, this will pay for our expenses, so we better get started and pull the rest from the permafrost," Yuri said. They both knew broken or partial tusks were worth their weight nearly in the price of gold such was the demand for ivory and the lack of elephant tusks available to service the demand in China.

"Get the tools out, we will have to hack this out without causing the river bank to collapse on us," Dmitry said. They carefully hacked around the tusk for an hour before they finally retrieved the mammoth tusk from the river bank. The tusk was about as tall as a man and would easily pay their petrol and expenses for that day. They were well pleased with their efforts and carefully wrapped the tusk in canvas to carry the tusk back to their truck and afterward, they continued their search for more.

After several more hours, they had found many shorter pieces of the tusk but still worth picking up as they scanned the river bank and shoreline for longer complete tusks. It was late in the day when they were about to head back to their truck when they came upon a section of the river bank that had completely collapsed onto the muddy shoreline revealing a block of permafrost that was gradually melting away in the heat of the sun. As they drew closer to the giant slab of ice they could see the outline of a mammoth frozen inside. They recognized it was a baby woolly mammoth perfectly preserved with all its hair as if it had only died relatively recently. They were amazed at what they could see. Dmitry and Yuri had never seen a real woolly mammoth they had only seen pictures of what these animals looked like when they roamed the steppe.

"What are we going to do? We can't handle this…it's too big to cart back to the truck," Yuri said dejectedly fearing losing a big payday.

Shrugging his shoulders, Dmitry said, "Eh, yes I know. Let me think. We will have to tell the authorities about this…it's the only thing we can do."

"What about other hunters they may find this before we get back again?" Yuri asked disappointingly.

"It's the risk we have to take, otherwise, we risk the authorities coming down on us like a ton of bricks," Dmitry replied. Continuing, he added, "Besides, I believe this find may be too important for us to ignore. We may get rewarded in some way later, who knows."

Both men wondered if the find would make them some money, but it would be a race against time because if it rained in the mountains the river would flood and the baby mammoth would likely wash away downriver and perhaps be lost forever. After an hour of trekking back to their truck laden with tusks, they loaded their spoils for the day and headed back to their town. It was another hour before they finally reached their town late in the evening, but it was still light.

"I'll phone a friend, he will know who to contact," Dmitry said optimistically.

"Who's that?" Yuri asked.

"You know, comrade Papalov, he's the local communist party official. That big ugly turd of a fellow," Dmitry said, laughing.

"Oh, that big shit, who is always trying to steal favors from just about anyone," Yuri said.

"Yes, that's the man. I won't tell him where we found the mammoth until he gives me the official to contact. That way we can preserve our find from other eager hunters. Luckily, at the moment, most of the able men in town that are not working in the oil industry are being employed by the authorities to help fight the local forest fires," Dmitry said. Continuing, he added, "This should provide us some time before the whole town finds out about our mammoth."

***

Later that evening, Dmitry went looking for Gordi Papalov the local Communist party official at his favorite bar in the town. Dmitry had arranged a meeting with the party official earlier that evening in the bar room hoping Papalov would be able to put him in contact with the appropriate person who would be able to rescue the frozen baby mammoth.

"Good evening, comrade Papalov, I need your help," Dmitry said.

"Sit and tell me more my friend," Papalov suggested. Dmitry noticed the smirk across the fatty face of Papalov has he was expecting to benefit from their meeting in some way. Stroking his fat belly he ushered Dmitry to sit down and talk.

"Earlier, today, Yuri and I found a completely intact frozen baby woolly mammoth along a river bank not far from here.

"Where?"

"Not so fast comrade Papalov. First, I need to contact the person who can deal with this baby woolly mammoth, before it disappears down the river in the next flood," Dmitry replied.

"Keep your voice down, before the whole village knows about this find," Papalov suggested.

"Just give me the contact and I will tell you more," Dmitry said.

"Okay, but you know this may be important to the party, so don't try to keep me out of the picture. The person you need to contact, Igor Stravinsky, a scientist working in the city of Yakutsk," Papalov said.

Immediately, Dmitry was on his mobile phone hoping to contact Igor Stravinsky before it was too late. Looking around the bar there were only a couple of teenagers playing pool and one other patron sat at the bar room counter. But, Papalov was right it wouldn't take much loose talk before the whole town knew about the find and then anything was possible, he said to himself.

"Hello, is that Igor Stravinsky?"

"Yes, Dr. Igor Stravinsky here how can I help?"

"My name is Dmitry Yanakuta."

"Yes, comrade…"

"Right, I understand you are the person to talk to. Today, my friend and I while looking for Kost, we found a complete baby woolly mammoth preserved in a slab of permafrost," Dmitry said excitedly.

"You say a complete mammoth?" Dr. Stravinsky asked in a skeptical tone of voice.

"Yes, a complete baby woolly mammoth encased in a slab of permafrost along the river shoreline. It has everything…its hair the whole animal is there," Dmitry said quietly. Continuing, he added, "But it won't be there for long if it rains and the river floods…it will be washed down the river and lost for good."

"Yes, I understand. Where is the mammoth situated?" Dr. Igor Stravinsky asked.

"It's about an hour's walk from the end of the dirt track that runs parallel to the Omolon River going up the river. We will have to meet you there to show you," Dmitry replied.

"I will arrange a helicopter and some help to hoist this mammoth back to our museum. It's best if we start at first light, tomorrow. Is that okay with you?" Dr. Igor Stravinsky asked.

"We can meet in Namtsyr village and plan our route from there. We have a pickup truck so we could transport the mammoth once it's hoisted into our truck," Dmitry replied. Continuing, he added, "Say we meet at six in the morning in the town square."

"Yes, okay…see you, tomorrow."

***

The following day, at around six in the morning, Dmitry and Yuri stood waiting in the village square for the helicopter to arrive. A blanket of mist cloaked the village and obscured the early morning sun.

"They won't be able to land in this," Dmitry said.

"No shit!"

"I'll phone the doctor to let them know, we've gone ahead and how to reach us," Dmitry said.

"Yeah, let's get going!"

"Hello, Dr. Stravinsky."

"Hello, what's up?"

"There's a blanket of mist on the town…you won't be able to land there…so we've gone ahead and will meet you on the river," Dmitry replied.

"Where on the river is it?"

"Yes, it's just past the giant elbow in the river…you will see our pickup truck parked there. It's about an hour's walk through the mud for us. You should see a giant slab of permafrost below where a large section of the river bank has collapsed onto the shoreline. That's the spot!" Dmitry said excitedly.

After around an hour's walk through the mud and up the river, Dmitry and Yuri approached where the baby mammoth lay and they could see the doctor already viewing the mammoth. They could see Dr. Stravinsky with another person trying to secure a harness around the slab of permafrost. The slab of permafrost had already lost about half its thickness during the time they had last seen the frozen mammoth.

"You were right, to let us know about this find...it truly is a great find," Dr. Stravinsky said cheerfully.

"Do you need our help rigging that harness?" Dmitry asked.

"Yes, we do. Oh, by the way, this is my assistant Dr. Alana Petroskov," Dr. Stravinsky said. Continuing, he added, "We need to get these straps under the slab of permafrost."

"We have shovels so we can dig under the slab of ice and feed the straps under the permafrost without disturbing the mammoth," Yuri said matter-of-factly.

"Good."

After digging under the slab of permafrost for nearly an hour, Dmitry and Yuri were able to feed through four straps to support the weight of the slab of ice without damaging the precious mammoth. As the helicopter carefully hoisted the slab of ice back to the pickup truck, Dmitry and Yuri watched as the slab of permafrost was safely lowered onto a wooden pallet in their pickup truck. They then covered the slab of permafrost with a canvas sheet to protect it from the sun.

"We will see you back in Yakutsk at the museum. Try to drive as carefully as you can…we don't want to damage the specimen before we get a chance to examine the mammoth," Dr. Stravinsky said. Continuing, he added, "The museum is signposted once you get into the city."

"Yes, of course."

It was almost two hours before, Dmitry and Yuri arrived at the museum in Yakutsk. They had carefully avoided any bumps and potholes in the roads as they made their way to the museum. As they arrived at the front of the museum building they could see the crowd of news media waiting with their cameras for their arrival, which they had not expected.

"Go around to the back entrance," Dr. Alana Petroskov shouted out to Dmitry and Yuri above the noise of the news melee. They quickly drove around the back of the building where Dr. Stravinsky was waiting to open and shut the gates to keep out the news media people. Inside the gates, a forklift was waiting to lift the pallet and take it into a loading area where the mammoth could be safely lifted onto an examination table.

"Good! I can see no damage to the permafrost, but it has already lost its thickness along the journey to get here. There is no time to wait, we will thaw out the rest of the permafrost and see what we have," Dr. Stravinsky said hurriedly.

"We would like to wait and watch while you examine the mammoth," Dmitry said.

"Yes, we want to be here to see the mammoth for the first time," Yuri said excitedly. On the long journey to the museum, Dmitry and Yuri had discussed the prospect of seeing the baby woolly mammoth in the flesh. The mammoths had reigned supreme until a man or climate change had seen their extinction on the tundra. Dmitry and Yuri had also discussed the possibility of making some much-needed cash from their find, but couldn't see how this would work out. Perhaps, they could charge the news people for the story they had considered.

"Yes, of course…but it will take time for the rest of the permafrost to melt away. I suggest, you visit our small canteen and take a rest. And come back in an hour," Dr. Stravinsky suggested.

Meanwhile, Dr. Stravinsky and Dr. Petroskov began the laborious task of carefully releasing the baby woolly mammoth from its frozen tomb. Using hand-held air driers they both removed the ice from the mammoth in large chunks as the permafrost began to melt in the warm temperate of the laboratory. The first thing they noticed was the smell of the creature as it was finally being released from its frozen tomb.

"Can you smell that?"

"Yes, it's an earthly smell, but not unpleasant considering it's been thousands of years since it's seen the fresh air," Dr. Petroskov said.

"Yes, I agree, but it does smell like shit to me, but then I'm always on the wrong side when shit happens. Like when the communist party decides this and that when you know heads will fall," Dr. Stravinsky said dejectedly.

"Keep the politics out of this…we have a job to do, it's as simple as that," Dr. Petroskov said.

"You're right about that," Dr. Stravinsky said lightheartedly.

"It looks to be completely intact, comrade Stravinsky," Dr. Petroskov said, laughing.

"Seriously, you're right, it is and will be a fine specimen to our collection here in the museum," Dr. Stravinsky said.

"That's if the party doesn't what to cart the mammoth off to somewhere else in Russia," Dr. Petroskov said.

"I hope to stop that if I can," Dr. Stravinsky said intently.

"The body of the mammoth is nearly thawed out. You can feel the elasticity of the flesh. This baby mammoth didn't die from a predator…there are no visible wounds that I can see…although we haven't seen the other side of the animal, yet. What do you think, Igor?"

"Well, Alana, we need to see the other side…the way the mammoth's head is orientated, at the moment, hides the animal's mouth. We will have to hoist the animal and rotate the animal to the other side before we can make a full examination of the animal. Connect those straps to the hoist and we'll lift the mammoth off the table," Dr. Stravinsky said intently.

"Arrgh! You're back from your rest, comrades," Dr. Petroskov said cheerfully.

"Yes, I see the mammoth has completely defrosted," Dmitry said.

"Wow! What a sight!" Yuri said excitedly.

"Yes, it is…gives a hand lifting this mammoth back onto the table…we were just about to examine the other side of the animal.

As Dr. Stravinsky and Dr. Petroskov were just about to start their examination of the mammoth a young male assistant came into the laboratory with news from the communist party officials. The officials had seen the news about the mammoth and wanted the news media to have access to the animal. They wanted the world's exposure to the story, it was seen as a national pride story to show the world the first baby woolly mammoth in the flesh and they wanted plenty of pictures taken of the animal with them.

"Oh, we'll have to let the hoards in for a brief time…to keep the party officials happy," Dr. Stravinsky said.

"Let them wait until we've made our examination…the officials can wait…let the bastards stew," Dr. Petroskov said.

"I hope you're right, otherwise, we could end up in trouble. But to hell with them…they can wait…let's continue," Dr. Stravinsky said.

Dmitry and Yuri heard the conversation between the doctors, but they made no attempt to interrupt or say anything. They knew the communist party was no friend of theirs and it often made life harder and more expensive for them. There were more rules and permits needed just to make a living on the tundra and sometimes party officials to pay off. The whole system was corrupt, they said to themselves.

"That's strange," Dr. Stravinsky said out loud.

"What is strange?" Dr. Petroskov asked intently.

"This baby mammoth's mouth is filled with food…it thought it didn't have time to digest its food before being frozen. It must have happened in seconds before it was frozen solid. It didn't have time to even digest its food before whatever happened…happened. It was happily grazing on the tundra and then was suddenly frozen where it stood on the tundra. I can't see any wounds or injuries from a predator…it just died where it stood and frozen for millennia," Dr. Stravinsky said intently.

"Yes, that is strange…when do you think this happened?" Dr. Petroskov asked curiously.

"It's hard to say, at the moment…we will have to see if we can get a carbon date from the organic material this mammoth was eating, until then we won't know for sure," Dr. Stravinsky said intently.

Then suddenly, the door flung open to the laboratory and a rush of news media people with their cameras rushed into the room with communist party officials in tow. A look of shock and horror lit up the face of both Dr. Stravinsky and Dr. Petroskov, as they witnessed the pushing and shoving of people trying to get the best advantage to take their pictures of the baby mammoth. Communist party officials were doing their best to have their photograph taken with the mammoth and in some way take credit for the historic find. Dmitry and Yuri for a short while were pushed to one side during the melee as cameras flashed constantly for what seemed like it wouldn't end for them. Eventually, Dr. Stravinsky calmed the situation by announcing to the news media people that the real story was Dmitry and Yuri, who then suddenly found they were the center of attention.

Dr. Stravinsky winced and suggested, "Dmitry and Yuri take yourselves outside this room and tell them your story."

"We will release a press statement later today," Dr. Petroskov said shouting to the gathered press core. When the press core was ushered out of the laboratory the scientists continued with their examination of the mammoth.

"Let's continue with our examination of the animal."

"Yes, of course."

"We will make an incision into the mammoth's stomach and take several samples of what this animal was feeding on. Then we can be certain through carbon dating when this mammoth died," Dr. Stravinsky said intently.

"Yes, of course," Dr. Petroskov agreed.

Later that day, the scientists released a press statement to the gathered media detailing what they had found out about the mammoth. The news of the historic find then soon circulated around the world.

Chapter 4

Meanwhile, research into past polar shifts had intrigued Dr. Isabella Garcia since gaining her PhD in Biology at UCLA in California. According to her research, there had been many polar shifts over the eons of time of the Earth's existence. Her research into polar shifts didn't directly relate to her field of study. The environment directly changed by a polar shift did relate to her field of study. How did early maps of Antarctica showing it ice-free, which had been produced in the past, puzzled her, she said to herself? These anomalies had bugged her since she first heard about them at university. Mainstream science had ignored them, for reasons unknown. Now, in her early thirties, she had the time to devote to her studies. Isabella's boyfriend Dr. Joseph Goldstein had also studied at UCLA gaining a PhD in Astrophysics and was also in his mid-thirties and was willing to go anywhere Isabella went.

Isabella could hear birds squawking in the trees that surrounded her house as she gazed at the view from her balcony. The view of the Sierra Nevada Mountains in the distance with snow covering their peaks looked calm and inviting that morning. There were blue skies in every direction and it was already hot and sticky, with little wind to cool the skin. The air felt fresh and clean as she stood on the balcony breathing in the morning breeze. She could hear Joe, shouting.

"Joe, what's up?" Isabella asked.

"It's amazing…"

"What is?" Isabella asked with excitement.

"It's on the news channel, it's a big story!" Joe said excitedly.

"Don't keep me in suspense, what is it?" Isabella asked again.

"They have found a complete baby woolly mammoth in Siberia. There's more. They found the mammoth frozen with a mouth full of food. Like it was frozen before it had time to digest its food," Joe said. Continuing, he added, "It's a big story on all the news channels!"

"Frozen solid…"

"Yeah, that's right…"

"When did they find this mammoth?" Isabella asked excitedly.

"Only a few days ago, a couple of tusk hunters found the mammoth on a river bank and now it's on display in a local museum," Joe said.

"You say it was frozen solid with food undigested in its mouth? Isabella asked.

"Yes, that's what the news story said. They believe the baby mammoth was frozen solid standing up, which is very unusual, to say the least."

"That is strange. We need to get out there and check it out, I can't wait to see the specimen and find out when the animal died," Isabella said.

"When do you want to leave for Russia," Joe asked.

"First, we need to find out if we can view the mammoth. The Russian authorities may have restrictions on who can view the mammoth. Remember, that group of scientists from UCLA that went there recently for a research project and found there were lots of restrictions on their movements around the country? It was a complete debacle and we don't need that sort of hassle, especially, in a place like Russia where anything can happen," Isabella said.

"Yes, of course…"

"Okay, then contact them…"

"I'll contact the museum in Russia and ask if we can see the mammoth and see what sort of response we get from them," Joe said.

"Make sure you stress the reason why we are so interested in seeing the mammoth in person. Tell them about my theory about polar shifts and how this evidence could be very important to solving the riddle. Oh, also tell them we would cover any expenses, Joe," Isabella said.

Later that morning, Joe contacted the scientist in charge at the museum in Russia and asked if he and Isabella would be able to view the mammoth. Dr. Stravinsky the scientist in charge at the museum told Joe that the mammoth was likely to be moved to another museum within the next few days and that it would probably end up being placed at different museums around the country for public viewing over the summer, such was it prized as a national curiosity.

"We would cover any expenses on your part," Joe said to Dr. Stravinsky on the phone.

"Yes, of course, but it's not the money…the party will have control of the mammoth within the next few days and then there is not anything I can do about it. So, at the moment, I am very busy making a thorough examination of the mammoth before it's out of my hands for good," Dr. Stravinsky said.

"The party…"

"Yes, the communist party. They have their hands on everything here, you will see that in this country," Dr. Stravinsky said.

"Oh, I see…"

Joe explained to the Russian scientist their interest in seeing the mammoth before the animal was transported around Russia for public viewing. He outlined Isabella's pet theory about polar shifts in the past and wondered if the mammoth had succumbed to such an event. The Russian scientist was intrigued by what Joe had to say and was eager to see them both and discuss the possibility of a polar shift. The Russian scientist had told Joe that it was likely the mammoth would be moved to another location in the very near future and said that it was imperative that they come to Russia as soon as possible.

"Thanks for your help…and we look forward to meeting you and viewing the mammoth," Joe said. Continuing, he added, "I will contact you via email with our flight plans and what time we shall arrive."

***

The following day, Isabella and Joe took a flight to Moscow and then a connecting flight to Yakutsk. Finally, a taxi ride to their hotel before heading on to the museum, where Dr. Alana Petroskov was there to greet them and to show them down to the basement laboratory where Dr. Igor Stravinsky was waiting.

"Thank you, for seeing us on such short notice and letting us view your baby woolly mammoth," Isabella said excitedly.

"Yes, thank you again," Joe said.

"It's perfectly preserved!" Isabella said inquisitively as she walked around the animal lying on the table for inspection.

"As you can see the mammoth looks to have been frozen solid in an upright position. You can tell from the position of the mammoth's legs this looks to be the case," said Dr. Stravinsky authoritatively. Continuing, he added, "You can see from the position of the head that it looks to have been frozen in an upright position."

"You haven't found any injuries from a predator then?" Isabella asked eagerly.

Shaking his head, Dr. Stravinsky said, "No, none at all."

"Nyet, we have found none," Dr. Petroskov said in a commanding tone of voice, in Russian and broken English, and was looking astonished at the questions from Isabella and Joe.

"Could it have been caused by a sudden drop in temperatures in literally seconds…a polar shift?" Joe asked politely as he viewed the faces of the Russian scientists hoping for answers.

Shrugging his shoulders, Dr. Stravinsky said, "It's possible…and I don't see any other explanation, at the moment."

"Look!"

Dr. Stravinsky then showed Isabella and Joe a series of photographs of the other side of the mammoth on a projector screen in the laboratory and he pointed out that there were no predator attacks visible on the animal. The Russian doctor stressed that it was a mystery how the mammoth had died and that he thought it may have been caused by a polar shift sometime in the past. Both he and Dr. Petroskov were perplexed at when this may have occurred and had not had any confirmed dates at when the mammoth had died. Dr. Stravinsky explained that carbon dating samples had been set off for analysis, but the results were at present unknown.

"There are no marks…no predators attacked this animal. We wait to see the carbon dating results. But, in Russia sometimes things don't move that fast," Stravinsky said.

"Yes, I can see…"

"Nyet, no marks," said Dr. Petroskov.

Dr. Stravinsky said, "Look here, pointing to a small plastic container full of what looked like mashed-up dirt, on another table. Continuing, he added, "Look, at what we found inside the mammoth's mouth. It is the grass the mammoth was eating when it died. It didn't have time to digest its food before it was frozen solid."

"Can we meet the men who found this animal?" Isabella asked eagerly.

"Yes, of course, their names are Dmitry and Yuri," Dr. Stravinsky said.

"Great!"

"Yes, here is their contact phone number. We have already told them of your interest, so you can meet them later today or tomorrow," Dr. Stravinsky replied.

***

The next day, Isabella and Joe were taken to the river by Dmitry and Yuri who had offered to drive them there if the Americans paid for their time and expenses. After agreeing terms, they went on their way. After a long drive to the river and driving along its banks they finally stopped the vehicle before they got stuck in the boggy terrain and began walking the rest of the distance to the spot where the baby mammoth was found by following the contours of the river upstream. Isabella and Joe noticed how boggy the ground was since leaving the dirt track. After an hour's walk along the top of the river bank, they came to the place where the mammoth was found. It seemed a barren place, just tundra, and Isabella wondered how the environment would have changed over the thousands of years since the mammoth had died, she said to herself. Isabella imagined the mammoth grazing on lush vegetation along the Russian steppe before it mysteriously died. Meanwhile, Isabella was anxiously waiting for a confirmed date when the baby mammoth had died before she could confirm the evidence important enough for her pet theory.

Isabella and Joe were amazed at the amount of the river's bank that had been dislodged when the permafrost gave way and released the mammoth from its encasement. All four of them carefully made their way down the river bank without dislodging any more of the river's bank to get a better view of where the mammoth had been entombed. They could clearly see the U-shape the mammoth had made in the five to six feet high river bank where it had lay hidden for thousands of years until a recent storm had flooded the river and eroded the bank of the river sufficiently enough for the frozen mammoth to slide down onto the shoreline.

"It's good you came, today," Yuri said in broken English.

"Why?"

"Storm," Yuri replied pointing to the black and grayish overcast clouds.

They all saw the flock of cranes and could hear them screeching as they flew overhead on their way due south avoiding the approaching storm. Apart from the birds and the rushing river water the tundra was a barren place, it felt cold and uninviting, Isabella, said to herself. The environment must have changed a lot since mammoths walked this land, she thought.

"Yes, a storm is due, any day now," Dmitry said. Continuing, he added, "This part of the river's bank would likely wash away."

"Oh, I see…"

"Storm…coming," Yuri said.

"Yeah, leaving no trace that a mammoth had been found here," Joe remarked.

"What's that black smoke I can see in the distance below those mountains?" Isabella asked candidly.

"Oh yes, it's a wildfire…burning the forest. Many men in our town are helping to control the fires. In recent years, we have had more fires than we did before. Climate change, I guess," Dmitry said calmly.

"Hmm, I see…"

"Do you…"

"Anyhow, you can see from the photos we took on our mobile phones how the animal was encased in the permafrost," Dmitry said with enthusiasm for the photographs he had taken of the scene. Yuri just looked on with amazement at the American's keen interest in the photos.

"Look!"

"You can see in the photo the shape of the permafrost, it looks very much like it was frozen upright, Joe," said Isabella pointing at the photographs the men had taken of the river bank.

"Yeah, I can see…"

"Look! If you look at the river bank and the shape of debris that has been dislodged it very much looks a U-shape like the shape of a bell curve on a graph," said Joe intently.

"Yeah, I can see…very unusual," Isabella said matter-of-factly. Continuing, she added, "From the evidence I seen so far…it's conclusive to me."

"Yeah, I've been trying to imagine what may have happened because it looks pretty much conclusive. The mammoth must have been frozen solid in seconds and the animal stayed upright frozen to the ground. And then ice and snow covered the mammoth keeping the animal in its upright position for thousands of years until the river cut its path through the tundra and Dmitry and Yuri found the mammoth," Joe said matter-of-factly.

"And from that point onwards the climate must have changed quite dramatically...staying cold throughout the year not allowing any ice to melt," Isabella said.

Later that afternoon, they thanked Dmitry and Yuri and paid them for their petrol and time, and made their way back by taxi to their hotel. Later that day, in the evening, they met with Dr. Stravinsky and Dr. Petroskov again, at the laboratory, for a drink to celebrate their historic find.

**

"Before you leave I have something you should hear about to spur your research on," the doctor said curiously. Continuing, he added, "This will open some doors for you in your quest."

"It's not really a quest...it's just something worth understanding before I'm too old in my ways to get out and about," Isabella said.

"I concur with that," Joe remarked.

"You have heard about the Piri Reis Map no doubt?" the doctor asked curiously.

"No, tell me more," said Isabella intently.

"Yes, tell us more, doctor," Joe also asked intently.

"It's the oldest map in existence as far I know. First discovered in Spain, I believe, by a Spanish explorer in the eighteen hundreds. It was produced by a pirate turned cartographer who was apparently meticulous in his work, but as cartography goes it is well drawn and fairly accurate for the times it was created this is what I have been told by other scientists," the doctor said.

"How old is the map?" Isabella asked curiously.

"Archaeologists and historians agree it was created in the early fifteen hundreds because Peri Reis signed the map fifteen thirteen, but they believe a rendition of the map was in circulation during the time of the Vikings, which goes back to about eight hundred A.D. until around the late twelve century, between that age range. They believe the Piri Reis Map is a copy of a much older map that must have been in circulation in those times but has not survived to the present day," said Dr. Stravinsky.

"Where is this map now?" Isabella asked in excitement.

"I believe the original is displayed in the national museum in Istanbul, Turkey. But, what will intrigue you as it did me when I first saw it? You can see the digital version online. Anyhow, the continent of Antarctica is shown on the map as ice-free with mountain ranges and river systems. How this was done is beyond me, but it intrigues me. And it should be yourselves. And the mountain ranges and river systems that are drawn on the map match up with what we currently know about Antarctica, which is intriguing and a mystery. As I said, the original is in Istanbul and worth a visit just in case you can find out any more clues for your quest. Let me know how you get on and if you make any progress with your research. It is now a mystery that will plague my mind until I also find answers," said Dr. Stravinsky.

"Yes, no problem. When I find out more information I will certainly keep you updated on my progress," Isabella said cheerfully.

"From what you are saying, doctor, it is certainly a mystery and one worth pursuing when we get back to the States," said Joe intently.

"When do you leave?" the doctor asked.

"Tomorrow, we have a connecting flight from Yakutsk to Moscow and then have to wait for a flight to LA, later that day," Joe said succinctly.

"Until then, let's celebrate the Russia way with some vodka and toast your good health on your journey," the doctor suggested.

"Yeah, let's do that," Isabella said cheerfully.

"Okay, sounds like a good idea to me."

"I'll be glad to see the back of those mosquitoes…the little bastards are ferocious," Joe said philosophically.

"Let's drink to our friendship," said Dr. Stravinsky.

"Yes, let's drink," said Joe enthusiastically.

"Yes, of course…"

"And you, Alana…"

"Da, it's true…"

"Yeah, let's drink!"

"Da, I love my country," Alana said. Continuing, she added, "From Russia with love."

"We have a saying in Russia…the bear and the tiger live in the same land, so beware of what may be around you, otherwise, you may end up being their lunch," Dr. Stravinsky said, laughing.

"Da…"

"Drink..."

"Be happy…"

"Tomorrow we have to…"

"Don't worry about tomorrow…it's another day." Dr. Stravinsky said, laughing.

They all laughed and toasted the evening with plenty of shots of vodka until they all had had enough. Even Dr. Petroskov did her best to relax with the Americans once she got drunk.

The following morning, Isabella and Joe awoke with headaches after their drinking session the night before but were looking forward to going home later that day.

Chapter 5

Isabella and Joe were still weary and groggy from their drinking session the night before, but glad they were on their way home. It had started to rain heavily and a cold wind blew across Moscow like it was a winter's day, but it was still late summer and to them, it was uninviting. The air terminal building was busy as they boarded the airplane. On the flight back to LA from Moscow, Isabella and Joe discussed what they had found out and how it related to Isabella's theory about a polar shift in the past.

"I still have a nagging doubt," Isabella remarked as she looked out the window of the airplane.

"What's that?"

"Well, animals die all the time suddenly. I grew up on a farm where I experienced cattle suddenly dying with undigested food in their mouths. So, it's quite common," Isabella remarked.

"Would you like a drink?" the air stewardess asked.

"Just some water for me," Isabella replied.

"The same for me," Joe reiterated.

"Okay, what did you think about the Russians finding a complete baby woolly mammoth?" Joe asked curiously.

"It's truly amazing!"

"Yes, it is…"

"Why it's unique is not that it died with a mouthful of food undigested, but that it died standing up. Nearly all animals that suddenly die fall over and in this case, if it's true, then we have a special event."

"Yes, I understand."

"The animal either died standing up or was frozen solid while it was eating, that's the long and short of it, Joe," replied Isabella calmly.

"You saw what I saw and those Yakutian hunters who found the mammoth were certain the animal died standing up the way the permafrost had formed around the animal. And the way the accumulation of tundra and dirt had thousands of years to accumulate like a bell curve on a graph. The doctor also pointed out how the animal's legs were positioned on the ice suggesting the animal was in an upright position when it died. And the doctor could see no injuries from a predator on the body of the animal," replied Joe emphatically.

"I agree!"

"You, agree!"

***

"I'm glad to be back in the States, and now it's a long drive back to Sonora," Joe said, smiling.

"We're not stopping off at your apartment in LA?" Isabella asked irksomely.

"No, I thought we go straight to Sonora from here," Joe replied briskly.

Shrugging her shoulders, Isabella agreed reluctantly with Joe's decision to head straight home for Sonora.

"Changing the subject…you agree with the doctor in Russia that the baby woolly mammoth died in an upright position then," Joe asked intently.

"Yes, but without an autopsy on the animal shortly after death you are only making assumptions. But, I believe you're right, and I agree the animal died standing up and was frozen in that position until a man came along many thousands of years later and relieved it from its frozen coffin. The Russian doctor stressed that point, in the way he pointed to how the animal was articulated. It points to a weird conclusion. The animal died almost instantaneously and was frozen in situ for thousands of years, just waiting for some 'kost' hunters to retrieve the animal," said Isabella authoritatively.

"But, you're still waiting for the carbon dating results, yes?"

"Yes, until a date is confirmed, then it's difficult to add it to our evidence," Isabella said emphatically.

"There is no other conclusion you can draw, but mainstream science will find other possibilities, like a flood, which could account for the way the body was in position and then frozen solid. It all depends on which way you see it…assumptions are nearly always wrong. But, this time it would seem the logical conclusion, but some would say you are fitting a story that best suits your theory," said Joe emphatically.

"I don't think that's fair…I thought you were on the same side?" Isabella asked irksomely.

"Yes, I am…but this is what they will say on the other side of the argument or debate. I agree, but many will not. You will have to have irrefutable proof and then your theory will become the norm and accepted as the truth. You know what scientists are like, we're never satisfied," Joe said, smiling.

"Oh, come on…"

"Well, it's true. Consider how history is always changing. We now accept that it wasn't Christopher Columbus who founded the Americas but the New World was settled by the Vikings possibly five hundred years before. Our education system still teaches kids that Christopher Columbus found the New World in fourteen ninety-two. But, most scientists agree that the Vikings settled these parts around five hundred years before. So, it takes a lot for the norm to become the established truth. I agree with you, but as I said before there will be many who have other ideas to stew," said Joe philosophically.

Smirking, Isabella agreed, "Yes, you're right."

"Do you know the story about…the curse of treasure seekers?" Joe asked, smiling.

"You've probably told me this before…"

"It goes something like this…"

"For some, it will be a reminder for others hearing it for the first it will be a warning! Beware of the deadly sin of greed. It is demonic greed that some people fall foul of and like snakes and ladders slide back worse off than when they embarked on their greedy path. The curse of the treasure seekers is present in the men and women who once bitten by the lure of treasure can never leave it. They cannot stomach the thought of someone else finding the treasure. Whether it is gold, jewelry, or other desirable they will spend most of their life searching for that treasure at the end of the rainbow." said Joe calmly.

"Keep your eyes on the road!" Joe said sternly.

"I am, don't worry about that," Isabella said calmly.

"So, I hope you haven't caught the dreaded curse of the treasure seekers. Have you?" Joe asked curiously.

"No, I understand what you are saying. Don't worry you'll get a cut if I find any treasure," Isabella said, laughing and cheekily in a soft tone of voice.

"What do you think about that?" Joe asked curiously.

"Was that meant to be a warning?"

"No, just don't get too carried away about your pet theory. It's a mystery for sure, but so is life, you are under the sword of Damocles as if I were the king. It's just how you see it," Joe replied, laughing.

***

On the drive back to their home in the town of Sonora, in the foothills of the Sierra Nevada Mountains, Isabella, and Joe reflected on their journey. Joe explained that the dates had to match up, for the theory of a polar shift to have occurred in the recent past. Isabella insisted the evidence looked positive that a polar shift may have occurred as the Great Flood, in the recent past.

"I understand your view, but it all depends on the evidence!" said Isabella calmly.

"Yes, of course, continuing, he added, "That car is still following us!" said Joe anxiously.

"If it's the government, then they have a long journey ahead of them before we reach Sonora," said Isabella calmly.

"We're being followed!"

"No fucking way! Stop fooling around, Joe."

"I'm not. Just keep going and we'll see what they do," Joe stated.

"The car following us has government plates...that much I do know," said Joe.

"Shit! What do they want?"

"How the hell do I know? I'm not a psychic," said Joe.

"I wonder what they want."

"Just keep heading home."

"If they wanted to arrest us they would have done so by now," said Joe lightheartedly.

"Yeah, you're right."

"You are a treasure seeker for sure!"

"What do you mean?"

"I once knew a treasure seeker. Do you want to hear his story?" Joe asked inquisitively.

"Alright go ahead..."

"I met this young man by chance. He was an African from Senegal, who had spent ten days in an inflatable dingy with other migrants adrift in the Mediterranean Sea before being rescued and housed in Spain. He had left if wife and two young children to go searching for prosperity. He said he was a fisherman but the fishing wasn't like it was and so he risked his life to make it to Europe. Because of the influx of migrants into Europe, they are not particularly loved in many places and so, he had many periods of sleeping rough on the streets, until, when I met him, he was being housed by a local charity but he was still waiting for his papers from the government about his claim for asylum in Britain.

I met him on the Southbank in London when I was living a party lifestyle after just graduating from university. He was watching the birds along the Thames shore grouping together and so was I. We got talking and that's when he told me his story. So, you see he was a treasure seeker. He had been told stories about how he could make it rich in Europe by the people smugglers and other people probably paid to spread the word, much like the disinformation that is spread on social media these days. Many of them have a different brew to stir. And he found out the hard way that what was once a golden goose and being allowed once your asylum claim was accepted is not the same in Britain. You can't just bring your family and expect the state to look after them on taxpayer dollars. So, you see for him he is still chasing that dream. But found the reality totally different," Joe said light-heartedly.

"It's good to have dreams," Isabella said cheerfully.

"Yes, when they are real," said Joe.

"Have I told you about the curse of the treasure seekers...It goes like this, when some people start their

61

treasure quest for gold and precious items they get sucked into an everlasting effort, which they cannot relinquish without first finding their treasure until they either find it or they die trying, that's the curse of the treasure seekers. It's a form of greed, yes, well it is greed because you cannot stop…you never see sense, and continue spending your money and time in the quest for riches…instead of standing back and observing your behavior and making drastic changes," Joe said.

"I understand how you feel, but no, I haven't become a treasure seeker," Isabella said calmly.

"Greed is one of the seven deadly sins…and when you are in the arms of greed you are on your way down the slippery slope to disaster. Greed catches the so-called smart people and the stupid ones who have put everything into greedy action and when it turns sour and they lose everything. Greed comes in many different forms, but whatever form it takes don't get into bed with it or you will see your disaster, faster than a speeding bullet. I always remember the story about one of the Rothschild family members in the banking dynasty, when asked how he made his fortune, he would say that he always sold too soon, but that he always banked a profit," said Joe.

"I can see the lesson from the Rothschild's story," Isabella said.

"People change when they don't see the sun."

"Yeah, I have read about that in places like Norway when they have no sun for months. It really affects people's minds…not in a good way," Isabella said.

"Yep, it's true…"

"Is the car still following?"

"Yes, like shit to a goat's ass?"

"What are your thoughts about a trip to Turkey?" Isabella asked.

"It sounds like a plan."

"The one thing that the Covid pandemic taught me was that our government was not prepared. It's like leaving the fate of the nation under the sword of Damocles. If we haven't got a disaster committee with strategies to deal with such issues as food safety and food supply then we are doomed, because soon or later our luck will run out," Joe said emphatically.

"It's not a long list of car parking penalties, is it?" Isabella asked, smiling.

"No…of course not."

"Go on."

"It pays not to speculate, humans are terrible at predicting events," Joe said, laughing.

"If the 'Great Flood' was caused by a comet strike twelve thousand years ago, then it's possible a polar shift occurred. And through mythology and lore, it was an event that changed the world spurring the migration of people due to the comet strike itself and changing climatic conditions that followed the comet strike. Impact results and computer calculations suggest millions of people will have died and the world is thrown back to the Stone Age again," Isabella said emphatically.

"Remind me when the Stone Age occurred?" Joe asked candidly.

"It lasted around three and half million years and ended between four thousand B.C. and two thousand B.C. when the ability of metal-working replaced stone tools," Isabella said emphatically.

"I always wondered, why the Stone Age lasted so long, it doesn't make sense. They used stone tools for such long periods without any development in that time frame," Joe said intently.

"Well, it happened, and you're right it doesn't make sense because around forty thousand years ago we were making sophisticated wooden tools," Isabella said emphatically.

"You could be right!" said Joe excitedly.

"What do you think about the Piri Reis Map?"

"It's an interesting diversion for your research."

"Yes, it seems so."

"It's great to be back in Los Angles even with the earthquakes to contend with and the threat of wildfires increasing every year," said Joe philosophically.

"I fancy a trip to Turkey, what about you, Joe?" Isabella asked eagerly.

"Yes, why not?" said Joe rhetorically.

"Are they still there?

"Yes, but farther back and keeping their distance," said Joe.

"I wonder what they want with us," Isabella asked apprehensively.

"Don't include me…in your plans. I've done nothing to have this hassle. Perhaps, it's your ecological protests or something similar, which has prompted their interest," Joe said hard-heartedly.

"I hope not."

"Whatever it is don't fuck with the government…it's the last thing you should do," said Joe, laughing.

"It's not funny, Joe."

"Yeah, just kidding, Isabella!"

"The Piri Reis Map is an interesting artifact but not evidence just conjectures as you can't apply any empirical studies and compare the science. But, as I said before, an interesting artifact and a mystery for us to try and unravel if we can," Isabella said philosophically.

***

"Dr. Isabella Garcia and Dr. Joseph Goldstein, I'm special agent Thompson and this is special agent Chavez of the FBI. Can we come in…we have some questions we would like answers to."

"Yes, what's this about?" said Joe irritated by the whole episode. He wasn't getting answers. He was bemused by the government's attention.

"Did you sell shares in SkyCloud.com recently?" said Thompson who seemed to be leading the interrogation.

"Yes, I did."

"We're investigating wire transfer fraud," said Thompson sternly.

"Oh, my god," Isabella cried out.

"Yes, sold the lot and made a decent profit," Joe stated.

"What was the reason for selling?" Thompson asked.

"The shares had gone up a lot in the previous days and so I figured it was a good time to sell before prices lowered again. I needed the money for other projects," Joe replied.

"You didn't have privileged information from inside the company, did you?" Thompson asked strenuously.

"No of course not, that would be illegal," Joe replied sternly.

"Did you, Dr. Garcia?" Thompson asked again.

"I didn't even know he had the shares. We're a couple but we don't live in each others pockets. He doesn't need me to tell him unless he's asking for advice. And he doesn't need my advice, he's a big boy. He can make his own mistakes without me," Isabella replied strenuously.

"You could have stopped us at the airport arrivals and not followed us all the way back here. Why was that?" Joe asked suspiciously.

"Yes, we wanted to find out how you would react under pressure. Sorry, about that. You will need to come into the local FBI office for further questioning. We will inform you later," Thompson said matter-of-factly.

"It must be a coincidence that I decided to sell my shares just as the FBI decides to investigate," Joe said sarcastically.

"We will need access to your email, social media accounts at a future date," Thompson said.

"I know, I have not spoken to anyone about the selling of these shares or received any information concerning the selling of these shares," Joe said anxiously.

"What about your trip to Russia?" Thompson asked.

"What about it, it was purely business, I didn't speak to anyone concerning the shares, besides I had already sold the shares before we left LA for Russia," Joe replied succinctly.

"That's it for now, we will be in touch when we want you to attend an interview at the office, you may decide to engage a lawyer in the meantime, thank you for your time," Thompson said.

"What was that all about?" Isabella asked as the two FBI agents returned to their vehicle and went on their way.

Shrugging his shoulders, Joe said angrily, "Shit, how the hell do I know."

"Oh, I see…"

"I bought and sold the shares without anyone's guidance but my own folly," Joe said emphatically.

"What's the name of the company again?" Isabella asked candidly.

"It was the SkyCloud.com computer company in the cloud space, I figured they looked a good bet to get bought out at some stage so I bought some shares and took the risk. I didn't have any advice from anyone, and that's the truth," Joe replied strenuously.

Isabella grimaced and asked, "So, it's just a coincidence that the FBI is now investigating the company and its shareholders, then?"

"Yes, you know me I wouldn't get myself involved in any insider trading or anything illegal...it's just not me," Joe said intently.

"Well, that's what I thought...but you better hire yourself a lawyer just in case the FBI takes it further," Isabella said.

"Yes, I will...now let's settle in and talk about something else!"

"Oh, what did you need money for...you said to the FBI agents you needed the money?" Isabella asked sheepishly.

"It was meant to be a surprise...so I plan to keep it that way until I'm ready!"

"Changing the subject...do you agree with me that the baby woolly mammoth is a good piece of evidence for my pet theory, would you agree to this or not?" Isabella asked intently.

"Yes, as I said before…it's an excellent piece of evidence but you still need more to back up your theory," Joe replied.

"That's why I've decided we should go out to Turkey as soon as we can arrange flights and visit the museum and see the original Piri Reis Map," Isabella suggested.

"Sounds like an excellent idea…when do you plan to leave?"

"Within the next few days while we've got the opportunity to have some time off from our normal teaching work," Isabella replied.

Chapter 6

The world in most places was still dealing with the aftereffects of the Covid-19 pandemic. Many countries were having financial and economic wobbles they had never experienced before.

Meanwhile, Dr. Benjamin Denarii and Dr. Shelia Attworth both graduate geologists are on the jetty on the Negros River with four other scientists waiting to board the barge, which was hired by their oil exploration company to journey up the Amazon River.

"What do you think about the expedition?" Ben asked.

"We should find out if oil or gas is present, which I think we will because previous surveys nearby that area have had good results in the past. The company pays the bills and our salaries," said the scientist.

"Yeah, I know, but it's the first time for Shelia and me," said Ben.

"Yes, it's our first expedition, virgins you could say," said Shelia, smiling.

"Yeah…"

"Well, there's a first time for everything, don't worry," said the scientist.

"My name is Dr. Charlie Simmons lead scientist on this expedition, but feel free to do your job and voice your observations," said Dr. Charlie Simmons.

"Everyone here uses first names, it saves all the fuss."

"Captain, can you get your crew to help load this equipment and supplies?" Charlie asked.

Ben's thoughts, now, had drifted back to when he was studying to be a geologist at UCLA and was intrigued by how the science of geology had progressed from its early formation as a science in the 1800s. The use of sophisticated technology had now made what was below ground a lot easy to see.

"The jetty is busy!" said Shelia as she watched the crew help the scientists load their equipment and supplies onto the barge.

"Yeah…"

"What are you thinking about?" Shelia asked.

"Oh, how the science of geology has progressed from its early days," Ben replied. Continuing, he added, "I had many debates while I was at university."

"It's a bit of a tight squeeze, but we have enough bunk beds," the captain said.

"Good…"

"The crew will sleep in the bridge while you're on board, you have their accommodation," said the captain.

"So, did I, on the same issues we discussed before," Shelia said.

"Still a bit anxious, though…I bit nervy…you know the jungle and its many predators," Shelia said.

"Don't worry…"

"I'm not worried…just concerned that's all…and we're not a couple just friends and colleagues."

"Yes, I know…"

"We have Charlie the boss, Tex from Texas the wildcatter, Slim our doctor, and Henry the wizard at analyzing data to guide us through the jungle and they're all experienced explorers. So, we shouldn't have anything to worry about. Plus, we have two Indian guides to translate should we need them," Ben said.

"Don't forget the two donkeys for company," Shelia said, laughing.

"Yeah, hee-haw, hee-haw…"

"Captain, can you make sure your men handle those explosives, carefully," Charlie said calmly.

"Enzo, take care with those boxes of explosives, and you also Manuel. Load and secure those explosives carefully in the hold," the captain shouted.

"Yes, boss…"

"Tex, do we have enough fresh water supplies?" Charlie asked.

"Yes…I brought extra purifying tablets just in case," Tex replied loudly.

"When do we sail?" Ben asked casually.

Shrugging his shoulders, Charlie said candidly, "As soon as we are loaded."

"Is all your equipment loaded?" Shelia asked.

"The last few boxes are being loaded, now."

"The jetty is almost clear," Tex said.

"It's a start of a whole new adventure," Ben said excitedly as he waited with the other scientists on the old wooden jetty to board the barge that would be their home for the coming days and weeks.

"When those mosquitos start biting…you'll wish you were somewhere else…mark my words…it's no holiday, but a grind out in the jungle," Tex said.

"They don't seem to bother with me as much," said Slim, who was as thin as a rake.

"Not enough meat on the bone," Henry remarked.

"I lose so much weight while on these treks through the jungle that I don't have to diet, the humidity and the heat it just pours out of me like a sprinkler," said Henry.

"Yes, you have to be careful about dehydration, Henry," said Charlie.

"Yes, I know…"

"What about you, Ben?"

"I hate the thought of biting mosquitoes, but if that's all I have to worry about I'll be glad," Ben replied.

"You can all board, now!" the captain said to the scientists waiting on the jetty. The six explorers boarded the barge in anticipation of a good and fruitful expedition.

"We've cast off…"

"Our journey starts here on the Negro River and then into the mighty Amazon River," Charlie said excitedly.

"At least, we have this canopy for cover while we sit under the sun and view the river's shoreline," Ben remarked.

"Is this the best the company could hire," Tex asked sarcastically.

"Sorry, folks, but yes it seems so," Charlie replied.

"It figures!"

"It's only a few days…and then into the jungle."

"I'm excited about finding oil…and who knows what," Ben said.

"We're just about to enter the Amazon River."

"This barge is not that fast, almost a snail's pace," Shelia said, smiling.

"Well, at least we get to see the wildlife along the river's banks."

"Conserve your energy for the trek into the jungle, you'll need it," Tex remarked.

"How did you get into the oil business, Tex?" Ben asked intently.

Tex shook his head and laughed, "It's a long story…it started in Texas on the oil rigs back in the day when the technology was primitive compared to what we have now. I started out as a wildcatter on the oil rigs. And then found myself, in Africa searching for oil and spent many years there, in places like the Congo. Eventually, I ended up working on oil and mineral exploration expeditions for various companies in South America. Finally, I ended up working here with our company in the Amazon. That's pretty much my story."

"Interesting mix…"

"Look!"

"There's a panther sunbathing under that overhanging tree on the river bank," Shelia said.

"You've got good eyesight…"

"It's a beautiful animal…"

"Yes, it is," Charlie said.

"He doesn't look like it's hungry, at the moment," Ben said, laughing.

"Don't laugh…"

"Sitting here with all of you all day, we have to have some laughs, otherwise, the day will seem too long," Ben said candidly as he sat with the other five scientists under the canvas canopy at the stern of the barge.

"You have to worry more about a snake bite…it can kill you in minutes if not seconds. But, just in case we carry a snake bite antidote, which will save your life. But, you will most likely have a painful experience, which could last for several days even with the antidote," Slim remarked.

"Oh, by the way, everyone around here calls me Slim, but I am Dr. Willian Folds, and I am paid as the expedition's medical doctor. So, be careful where you place your feet."

"Oh, I see…"

"Do you…"

"Unless you're unlucky, you won't come across a snake," Charlie said.

"Just be careful that's all," Slim uttered.

"I will…"

"Yes, me too…"

"Listen!"

"To the sound of the jungle, the birds squawking and the monkey calls," Charlie said.

"Why is the barge slowing down?" Shelia asked sheepishly.

"The captain will want to stop for the night…it's safer than traveling during the night. Too many fallen trees in the river to watch out for," Charlie said.

"Yeah, too dangerous…"

"Get the fishing rod out!"

"Hopefully, I can catch something worth cooking!" Charlie said excitedly.

"The Indians will be scavenging the jungle for monkeys, bats, or anything they can find," Tex said.

"No doubt about that...but I much prefer the fish from the river...ideal over the grill," Charlie said.

"We have supplies, but it's worth fishing for your meal than using up our supplies, you never know when you may need more," Charlie said.

"I agree..."

"Yeah, me also..."

"It's started to rain, Shelia said, "You can hear the rattle as the rain hits the canopy."

"Good..."

"Better fishing..."

"I've been sniffing for oil most of my adult life, in one capacity or another. Since I joined our present employers I had traveled most of the world searching for oil deposits mostly, but also mineral deposits. I often find my gut instinct carries a lot of weight. There have been plenty of times when my instinct for oil has paid dividends for the companies I have worked for and there have been many. In many ways the industry has got a lot simpler, because of the new technology we have at our disposal," Henry said.

"Eh, you've got a bite on the line..."

"We're not using educated guesses anymore...we now have the ability to know for sure what's beneath our feet," Charlie said.

"Wow, that's a nice fish!"

"Yeah, a couple more and we have our meal tonight!" Charlie said.

"The fish in this part of the river are good to eat, not much pollution up this way, too far up the river, for that," Charlie uttered.

"The fish will take a while to cook, meanwhile, tell us about yourselves," Tex said.

"Not much to say…"

"Just graduated from UCLA and found myself as a trainee geologist working for the company. I wanted to go on expeditions and this will be my first one. I'm looking forward to the experience," Shelia said.

"Me much the same, graduated from UCLA and applied for a job as a trainee geologist. Looking forward to our expedition, hopefully, we will find some oil," Ben said.

"We were friends at university and applied for the same jobs…"

"And you found yourselves here," Charlie uttered.

"Yep, that pretty much sums it up," Ben uttered.

"You're in good hands…Charlie knows his stuff."

"But, I would cover as much of your skin as possible, the insects and bugs in the jungle are just dying to meet you and give you problems."

"A tick can give you an infection and there are millions out there, so be careful," Slim said.

"Is the fish ready, yet?"

"No, they're still cooking…"

Listen!

"What?"

"The sounds of the millions of insects…it's just a constant buzzing noise!"

"Crickets, grasshoppers, frogs, and more…"

"And every creepy crawly you can imagine," Tex said.

"Without the noise of the barge's diesel engine chugging away you can hear the jungle clearer," Ben said.

"And every predator out there…"

"A good fire keeps most predators away and the rest we hope we don't meet," Slim said.

Shrugging his shoulders, Charlie said, smiling, "We have enough firearms to go around, so there's no need to worry, about that score."

"And plenty of medical supplies to keep everyone healthy," Slim said.

"When do we start again?"

Shrugging his shoulders, the captain replied, "Hopefully, tomorrow, early first light we cast off."

"Good…we have to avoid that storm, which is brewing to hit us, in the next few days," Charlie said emphatically.

"This fish is nice…what is it?" Ben asked.

"It's called 'Peixe Nobre' by the locals, not much more I know, but they are good eating, yes?" Charlie asked. Continuing, he added, "With the rice, it's a good hearty meal."

"Yeah, good..."

"It's almost like eating bass..."

"Similar..."

"When we went nuclear, we overstepped the mark, releasing the devil," Tex remarked.

Why's that?"

Don't get him started on that subject, he'll talk for hours, it's one of his passions," Henry said, smiling.

"It's the pollution, that lasts for hundreds of thousands of years and is deadly to all life on earth," Tex uttered.

"No shit..."

"It's as stupid as shooting oneself in the foot..." Slim remarked.

"Think about it...we have to look after that radioactive pollution for thousands of years before it may be safe to deal with. The real cost of what seems like free energy is long-term and unknown. Our legacy is the pollution we leave behind," Tex said.

"Well said..."

"Yeah, no shit!"

"Tex, don't get too serious," Charlie said.

"It's true though, what Tex is saying," Ben muttered.

"I agree," Shelia agreed also.

"The fish is cooked and ready to eat, so eat and enjoy!"

"It's good!"

"Hmm, yeah, very good…"

"Our job is to find oil and the rest is just politics," Charlie said.

"What do you think, Henry?" Tex said.

Shrugging his shoulders, Henry replied, "It's what pays the mortgage and all the other bills at home."

"And where's that?" Ben asked casually.

"Boy, you do ask a lot of questions…"

"Just making conversation…"

"Seattle that's my home."

"The capital of big tech," Ben remarked.

"Six months ago I was working in Canada and now here," Henry muttered.

"Tomorrow, we will be close to our first stop…the Matsés village. The Indians there rely on supplies from trading up and down the river from barges like this one," Charlie said.

"It will be good time to stretch our legs, in the village while the crew unloads supplies for the Indians," Tex said.

"Yeah, cooped up like chickens is no fun, after a few days on this barge we will all feel the same," Slim said.

"Yeah, I agree with that…"

"This boat wasn't made to walk around on," Ben said begrudgingly.

"Yep, but that's how things are out here in the jungle," Tex said.

"Everything is cramped for space…"

"No shit!"

"You got an Australian accent, is that so?" Tex asked.

"Yeah, you're right on the money…but I did an overseas education transfer," Shelia said.

"My home is in Melbourne on the outskirts of the city…"

"In Australia, we're used to a lot of creepy crawlers that can give you a serious bite or too," Shelia said.

"The mosquitoes here are bad enough, especially at night, they haven't stopped attacking my face," Charlie said.

"Me, too…"

"Yeah, I agree…the little bastards…"

"Well, at least, you have all had your shots against Malaria," Slim said.

"Yep, it wouldn't be safe out here without any protection," Charlie said.

"No shit…"

"Yeah, the company looks after us and the locals have to look after themselves," Henry said.

"Isn't it always that way?"

"Yes, you're right Shelia, but that's the beauty of business…it always looks after those that feed it," Charlie said.

"Not always…"

"Henry, don't get philosophical…"

"No, he's right, sometimes the company doesn't look after their employees, but those days are gone. These days we have health and safety rules to comply with, which safeguard every employee of the company and also the environment," Charlie said.

"Yes, that's right, Charlie…"

***

The following day, the barge raised the anchor and slowly made its way farther up the river. The smoke from the barge's diesel engine slowly drifted into the wind from the single pipe stack as it chugged along the river. It was nearing its first destination a small Indian village that also traded with other Indian tribes that lived along the Amazon River's shoreline.

"Everything was last minute, I guess, Tex," said Charlie.

"You know the company best, Charlie, they're always looking at the bottom line, if they can save a few dollars hiring this barge they will," Tex said.

"Yep, I agree…"

"I agree, it's not the best but it's getting there…all be it slow."

"What do you think, Ben?" Shelia asked candidly.

"What happens when you realize you're not the Masters of the Universe, anymore? Think about it. We could be all lab rats. That would mean a complete paradigm shift," Ben replied.

"You mean the whole of humanity?" Shelia asked.

"Yes, it would take extraordinary evidence, but just suppose if it did, it would mean a complete paradigm shift for mankind," Ben replied.

"In other words, we would be inside the fish bowl and didn't know it," Tex said, laughing.

"That's the point of crash test dummies," Henry said.

"Yeah, no point in knowing you're the dummy."

"Yep, that's the point of an experiment to keep the subjects ill-informed," Charlie said.

"Look!"

"A bunch of caimans sunbathing on that sand bank and waiting for their next meal," Tex said.

"That reminds me…what's on the menu, tonight?" Slim asked.

"Maybe monkey meat, we can trade with the Indians," Charlie said flippantly.

"Are you hungry already?"

"Yep, as soon as you started to mention food…my taste buds started to cut in," Slim said, laughing.

"Relax, relax…"

"You can buy some extra food at the village," Charlie said.

"Boss, we have plenty of supplies down below," Tex said.

"Yep, that's right…so if I don't catch any fish…then tonight you may have to starve," Charlie said, laughing. Charlie had made sure there were plenty of rations of food for their expedition, as well as enough clean water for everyone, which was now stored below deck, in the main storage hull of the barge.

"Can you hear that…"

"It's a helicopter…"

"Yes, look…it's a military one…"

"I wonder where it's going…"

"Probably patrolling their borders looking for guerrilla incursions and other illegal activity," Charlie said.

"No shit…"

"Don't worry, where we're going, we shouldn't run into any guerrillas maybe the local Indians, that's it," Charlie said.

"Yeah, I hope you're right…"

"This place is no paradise…all sorts of illegal shit goes on," Charlie said.

"Everyone in this country is trying to make a dollar…"

"And so are we…"

"This place we're heading for is uncharted…a no man's land," said Slim.

"Yeah, an area except for illegal reports we have little information on, ask Henry, he will tell you," Slim said.

"Yes, he's our leading geologist and statistical wizard…"

"And a comedian at times…"

"Yes, Henry can interpret from the graphs and tell if the below-ground strata contain oil deposits or not. He's our main man. He's the best out there," Charlie said.

"Hold on, wait my position is changing as we speak, the computer analysis available now can tell much of what a lifetime of experience can have, so hold on, don't praise me too much. I'm just as important as everyone here," Henry replied.

"Yeah, we know Henry, but it doesn't harm to raise your ego now and again," Tex said emphatically.

"But, you don't need me to tell you that life is changing fast as we speak. Artificial intelligence has moved every industry I know leaps and bounds, we are in the Age of Aquarius, the age of change," Henry said authoritatively.

"Industry should be reporting increased productivity…right now," Tex said briskly.

"Yes, the world is still dealing with the pandemic, even without the pandemic productivity should have increased since the use of artificial intelligence."

"Yes, in a major way…we are in the Age of Aquarius, the age of change. The world's inhabitants should see major changes in their lives because of artificial intelligence," Henry stated.

"Yep, that just about sums it up," Charlie said.

"From how toothbrushes are made to satellites in orbit then artificial intelligence plays its part," Henry said.

"It's involved in everything in our lives…the productivity reports should be going supersonic," said Tex.

"Yeah, why haven't they…?"

"Yes, why is that so?" Shelia asked

"It's strange that they're not," Ben replied.

"A government conspiracy most likely," Shelia said.

"The pandemic really slowed things down," Slim said.

"Yeah, no shit!"

"He's right though…"

"The governments never tell you what's happening unless they're forced to," Charlie said.

"You're just too cynical, Charlie," Tex said.

"Look!"

"Dark clouds on the horizon, it doesn't look good…"

"It looks like a storm is brewing," said Charlie.

Standing up to view the horizon from under the canopy, Slim said, "No shit."

"It meant to be the dry season, yet, more rain," Henry said.

"Yeah, climate change is what's happening," said Charlie.

"We're not far from the village…"

"Good…"

"I can stretch my legs…I need a walk around," Shelia said.

"I'm saving my energy for the trek into the jungle," Ben remarked.

"You'll need it…the humidity will sap your strength faster than a speeding bullet," Tex said, laughing.

"Water becomes a big issue out in the jungle…dehydration is a big factor to survival," Slim stated.

In the Amazon jungle, the scientists were exploring a previously uncharted region of the jungle. The only activity reported, in the area, was from indigenous tribes and recent reports of illegal loggers, gold miners, and prospectors. Most of the population of Brazil was living on just a few dollars a day, if they were lucky, so the country was rife with people taking what they could and the government was lax to control it or didn't have the resources or the will to stop it. The whole system was corrupt in one way or another.

Chapter 7

Meanwhile, Isabella and Joe were discussing a trip to Mexico as they sat on their balcony in Sonora, California. It was early summer and the breeze coming from the direction of the Sierra Nevada Mountains, in the distance, was a welcome relief from the humidity of the day.

"It's only one piece of the puzzle, there's still more to find. I've been in touch with one of my tutors at university; he's currently working in Mexico. He has invited us to come and see him, he says he has some interesting finds for us to come and see. So, a trip to Mexico would seem the right course of action, at the moment. What do you think, Joe?" Isabella asked.

"Do you plan to fly down there or we drive down there and visit a few places on the way?" Joe replied.

"Which would you prefer?"

"We have plenty of time, so a drive would be good," Joe replied.

"Yes, a few days sightseeing would be nice, now we're on holiday before we see the professor," Isabella remarked.

"What's his name and how did you become friends?"

"His name is Dr. Philippe Manuel. We became friends during the many lectures I attended during my final year at university. Although his lectures were not directly related to my studies, I chose to attend his lectures because I found his work very interesting. We had many debates and discussions about Darwin's theory of evolution. The professor taught archaeology and I was studying biology so the two different fields of study became a hotbed of discussion and debate," Isabella said.

"What is the professor like?"

"It's a few years since I last saw him, but when I saw him last he was a man in his mid-thirties and a likeable character. He was always trying not to get involved with any of his female students because he was a handsome man and many of his female students were always flirting with him, although I never fell for his charms. I never inquired as to whether he was married or not, my interest in him was purely academic," Isabella said, smiling.

"Are you sure?" Joe asked, smiling.

"Yes, of course…you know me, Joe."

"Yes, I do…"

"Anyhow, changing the subject, when do you fancy leaving for Mexico?" Isabella asked.

"Whenever you want to…it would be fine with me."

"Okay then…tomorrow would suit me," Isabella said emphatically.

***

The following day, Isabella and Joe set off from Sonora on their drive to Mexico to see the professor. They decided to take turns driving and would stay at motels along the route. Once they had crossed the border they would take the main highway down to the southern end of Mexico. The southern end of Mexico was radically different terrain compared to some parts of Mexico, which were more like deserts and not the lush and green landscape of the southern tip of Mexico.

As they crossed into Mexico at Tijuana, which is one of the busiest border crossings in the world they began their journey.

"Well, we're in Mexico!"

"Yep, it all begins now!" Joe said happily.

"Yeah, I'm looking forward and starting to relax…it feels like a holiday of sorts. We definitely needed a break from the university," Isabella remarked.

"What did you think about our trip to Russia?"

"Keep your eyes on the road…we don't want to miss the turn-off for the main highway," Joe said.

Eh, yeah…"

"Okay…"

"Yeah, I am…don't worry, Joe."

"Well, it's the early days of my research and the Russian trip started the ball rolling, so to speak," Isabella said intently.

"Yes, okay…"

"The Russian evidence was just a small piece of a very large puzzle. This area is very much like where we live…like Sonora. Don't you think, Joe?" Isabella asked candidly.

"Bush and desert with a few pines scattered here and there," Joe said briskly.

"You can see the Sierra Nevada Mountains. range that continues down the length of Mexico into South America," Joe said emphatically.

"Yes, beautiful, isn't it?"

"Look! Snow-capped mountain peaks like ice cream cones…"

"Yeah, nature at its best…"

"But it was good to get one piece of evidence that may fit my pet theory. Getting a verifiable date would be good. It's not evidence unless it fits with my theory," Isabella said emphatically.

***

Later that day, Isabella and Joe stopped for the night at a motel near the town of Tiatico. They discussed their plans for the following days. Joe explained to Isabella that another night at a motel should be enough before they would reach San Lorenzo.

"The terrain should start to change from desert to green as we are around a third of the journey before we reach the southern tip of Mexico," Joe said emphatically.

"It's a beautiful country!" said Isabella excitedly.

"I enjoyed that Mexican food we had, today," Joe remarked.

"Yes, it was good not having to cook for a change," Isabella said, smiling.

"Uh, oh yeah..."

"I'm intrigued by what the professor has to show us. I explained my theory to him some time ago. And I refreshed his memory when we spoke on the phone. So, I hope it's worth it?" Isabella said.

"Hmm, yes, I'm sure it will be."

"I hope so, you think so?"

"Just treat it as a bit of a holiday. After all, we are on summer break from our university jobs.

"Yeah, okay...it suits me."

"I'm sure it will be worth it, remember, we are also on holiday. You said earlier that you had started to relax. So, relax!" Joe replied.

"Yes, I will."

"Well, it's safer not traveling at night, especially, when you're in a foreign country, even, one as close as Mexico," Joe remarked.

"Oh, yeah...I agree!"

"You know traditionally the Mexicans use a lot more vegetables in their food than we do in America."

"Yeah, but we're changing fast, especially me, I'm learning to cook with for more variety than say my parents did," Isabella remarked.

"What did the professor say?"

"He told me he was researching an ancient civilization that should be of interest to me. He said not much was known about the mysterious culture, but he said they seemed to be an advanced civilization for the time period," Isabella replied.

"Is that all?"

"No, he said the Aztecs knew the people as 'the rubber people' of the lowlands of what we now call Mexico. They harvested the local trees for the syrup for making rubber," Isabella said emphatically.

"You said time period…what time frame are we looking at?" Joe asked intently.

Isabella explained that the civilization existed before the Maya civilization started and was thought to be the forerunner. The Maya language and writing were thought to have been derived from the 'rubber people' who the Aztecs named the Almecs. They are thought to have existed from around two to three thousand years B.C. until around five hundred to six hundred A.D. just before the Maya culture started.

"Why are they so important?" Joe asked intently.

"They came out of know where and then just vanished, overnight, it's why they are so mysterious."

"A lot of empires and civilizations just come and go. As you say overnight, which is probably due to a range of factors, until one event tips the balance and everything changes in a brief moment in time," Joe said.

"Yes, that's how I…pretty much see it happening," Isabella said.

***

Finally, Isabella and Joe reach the southern lowlands of Mexico where the mountains are covered with lush vegetation of trees and plants and fields of crops grow in the valleys.

"Hello, professor…"

"I hope you enjoyed your journey," the professor said.

"The more I see of the country the more I like what I see. It's so diverse with this region lush with vegetation, whereas up north it's more like a desert," Joe remarked.

"It was fine…so glad to see you," Isabella said.

"This is my boyfriend, Joe…this is Dr. Philippe Manuel."

"Glad to meet you, Isabella has told me a lot about you and what a beautiful country," Joe said

"Thanks that means a lot…"

"What makes the Almecs so mysterious?" Joe asked intently.

"Well, it's because they're not indigenous to this area, or indeed this continent. You see, I believe they originally came from Africa. You will see for yourself when you see the Almecs site we are currently excavating," Dr. Philippe Manuel said.

"Well, professor you haven't changed much since the last time I saw you at the university," Isabella said.

"The benefit of good food and clean air," the professor replied.

"Today and tomorrow, I have a lot to show you…we have a camp set up over here…and the Almec site is not far. But, it's difficult to access; at the moment…it's not really a tourist spot. The Almecs chose well," the professor said.

"That's just great!"

"During the day we don't get a lot of tourists, because of how difficult the site is to access the place," the professor said.

"Yes, I can see why that is," Isabella said.

"Yeah, our journey was precarious at times," Joe remarked.

"The climate and the rich soil make it an ideal place to grow food."

"It's an amazing difference from the desert of the north of Mexico."

"Where the Almecs settled was also an ideal defensive position because they would see you coming long before you reached their city," the professor said.

"Yes, an ideal location."

"The Almecs were close to fresh water and gold!" the professor said.

"What makes the Almecs so important?" Joe asked intently.

"As I said before, they emerged virtually overnight, but I believe they came from Africa and started a successful civilization and in that time they started one of the first pyramids to be built. It is called the 'Cholula Pyramid' at Cholula de Rivadabia, Puebla here in Mexico, and is the largest by volume of any pyramid built by man. It was built over the course of fourteen hundred years," the professor said.

"Perhaps, we will visit the pyramid, yes?" Joe asked.

"When Isabella told me of her pet theory, I thought the Almecs could provide some answers to her quest, although perhaps not directly related," the professor replied emphatically.

"Oh, I see what you are saying," Isabella said.

"The answers to questions we ask are not always clear as day they are often hidden within other spheres, it is up to us to figure that out for ourselves," the professor said.

As the professor, Isabella, and Joe trekked through the jungle to the Almec site and followed the path, which had been cut through with machetes and kept clear for tourists; they soon realized how difficult it was to access the site.

"Look! What do you see?"

"It's a face...of a man," Joe replied briskly.

"Yes, it's of a man, but its features...what does it tell you?" the professor asked.

"Hmm, yes of an African man...a face of an African man," Joe replied.

"Now, we may regard these giant head sculptures as perhaps their gods, but they represent an African man," the professor said.

"A completely different continent…"

"How is that possible at that time period?" Isabella asked.

"Well, it must have been possible," the professor said.

"It doesn't make sense…"

"What's that, Joe?"

"It just doesn't make sense… it's like the whole place should be in Africa and not here. I can see what you mean. The answers are not clear cut," Joe said emphatically.

"The Almecs were smart people…"

"And great carvers…"

"The symmetry on these face carvings is simple but so accurate," Joe said emphatically.

"We believe the Almecs that settled this region of Mexico, first settled in San Agustín, Columbia before coming here," the professor said.

"Why do you think they chose this region of Mexico?" Joe asked intently.

"Many factors as I said before, a ready supply of clean fresh water from the mountains and rich soil to grow crops. And of course, something to trade with…the likes of gold," the professor replied, smiling.

"Was gold so important…?"

"As it is for many cultures then as it is now," the professor said.

"Not much use if you're starving…"

"Yes, you're right, but people value gold for many different reasons," the professor said.

"Anyhow, let's sit around the campfire and have some food. We will talk more, later," the professor said.

"Yes, today, it's being used for high-end electronics where they need superconductivity," Isabella remarked.

"Yes, copper doesn't cut it in space where there is a need for superconductivity and zero issues with electrical interference," the professor remarked.

"This food is good…"

"It's the burritos I had in the cooler," Joe said.

"Wow! Tastes real good…"

"Anyhow, professor…why do you think I'll find answers to my theory here?" Isabella asked intently.

"Well, I think the most important piece is the dates…when things took place. The Almecs came here and to Columbia for a reason. Knowing the dates is important for your theory and understanding this is the most important part. And of course, I wanted to see you again," the professor said, smiling.

"You were always a charmer…"

"Listen!"

"What?"

"The sound of millions of insects and grasshoppers buzzing in the background," the professor said quietly.

"What's your point?"

"They will go on without our presence…empires and civilizations come and go in a relatively short time frame compared to the longevity of ecosystems," the professor said vigorously.

"You said the Almecs were also in Columbia before they came here, is that right?" Isabella asked.

"Yes, that's right. We now know they first started a civilization in Columbia at a place called San Agustín, before immigrating to Mexico," the professor replied. Continuing, he added, "Perhaps a visit to San Agustín will help again further your research."

"What do you think, Joe?" Isabella asked, smiling with a twinkle in her eyes.

Chapter 8

Later, that day Harry Steel receives a phone call from his former boss at the CIA headquarters, in Langley, Virginia, in the USA.

"Hello is that Harry?" asked Michael Kurious.

"Yes, is that you, Michael?" Harry asked.

"Yes, how's retirement?" asked Michael.

"It could be better, but I'm enjoying not having to take orders," replied Harry, smiling.

"Well, we need your skills for a mission," Michael said bluntly.

"Why me, and not someone else...?"

"Because I can trust you to get the mission completed without any fallout. Besides, you have the skills necessary for this mission. I can offer you a substantial financial reward, but since you have retired from the organization I can't take you back on as an employee. You would be working solely as a sub-contractor for the CIA," Michael said.

"What's the mission?"

"I can't reveal that on the phone...you need to come in and we will talk then," Michael replied.

"Okay, first, I need to talk it over with my wife before I commit to anything you have to offer. I will let you know what happens," Harry said and hung up the call.

***

The next day, Harry Steel was on a flight from Nebraska to see his former boss, Michael Kurious Director of Counter-Intelligence at the headquarters of the CIA at Langley, Virginia.

"Would you like a drink, sir?" the air stewardess asked.

"Yes, please, another JD and coke," Harry replied.

As Harry Steel's mind drifted back to six weeks before when he took his first job as a security consultant as a private citizen looking after the personal security of a high-value asset, in the shape of, an overweight corporate executive, in the IT business, during a three-day conference in Miami, Florida at the Hilton Hotel along the Miami main drag. It was a task he loathed and not what he wanted to do in his retirement from the CIA. The executive had recently received numerous death threats, but neither the police nor the executive could work out the origin of the death threats. And why the executive would have any enemies, but Harry knew at the time, that the executive may have not told the complete truth about his business dealings. The behavior of the executive alerted Harry to his first suspicions, which suggested he may be guarding a toe rag. To Harry, it was something that cut across the grain and the idea of protecting a potential criminal regardless of the money went straight to his heart as if someone had struck him with a dagger.

The first couple of days of the assignment went off without any incident as he just watched as the executive spent his time entertaining loose women and frequenting the casinos and spending money recklessly. He had been glad he didn't have these vices in his life to contend with. He had been careful with his money and over the years had saved up enough money with his pension from the CIA to live a comfortable life in retirement. He wasn't greedy. He had enough to enjoy his retirement and wished he hadn't accepted the job offer from a friend in the security business to babysit the executive. His grandfather would always say don't get caught out by greed. Then his grandfather would tell stories about some of the people who were caught by greed and what happened to them. His grandfather would say the people who get caught by the demon greed are never happy they continually want more and in the end, it wrecks their lives and they end up poorer than when they started on the never-ending merry-go-round.

His grandfather would also say always do the right thing, that way you don't have to keep looking over your shoulder at whom may be watching you. These wise words and more Harry had always adhered to the moment his grandfather had told him. Since his grandfather's death, he could feel his grandfather's presence while at UCLA University when he studied politics and when he joined the Marines to serve his country in the Second Iraqi War. His grandfather's words were always at the back of his mind even when he joined the CIA nearly twenty years ago. He had seen the consequence of greed among past associates and friends who got caught up with the demon greed. It had seen it wreck lives that had promising careers only to see it fade in the ashes of disappointments.

On the final day of the babysitting assignment, it had begun like the two previous days without incident, until it all went pear-shaped in a moment of madness. Harry and the executive were just leaving the casino in the early morning hours waiting for their car to be brought from the car park by a vale when a person in a balaclava over their head and with a gun approached the executive demanding money. There were many people waiting for cars and so Harry didn't immediately draw his gun, he didn't want to see innocent people get shot by any stray bullets from the assailant. As soon as the assailant turned to leave Harry shouted out for the assailant to stop, but he just started to fire his gun at Harry. Harry returned a single shot, which killed the assailant. Later, when the police unmasked the assailant they found a young African American in his early twenties who had died for a few dollars of madness. In the police investigation, Harry was later told that they had found a sheet of writing paper beside the assailant's bed with the words 'I need to make some money' written in bold letters. The police never found out why the young man needed to make some money, it was just a waste of life, he thought.

Over the following weeks since the shooting, Harry had reflected on the incident and was saddened by the death of the young man. He knew the boy didn't stand a chance against his training and his accurate shooting and had wished he hadn't been present at the incident. It wasn't the type of work he had envisaged in his retirement, he had been too highly trained to consider any further babysitting roles in the future. If he couldn't work advising large corporations on security strategy then he would find something else to do that didn't involve shooting his gun at people. He had enough of killing people throughout his career in the Marines and the CIA to last a lifetime and considered it was time to stop, he said to himself.

Harry became a cynical soul without having too much persuasion from fellow comrades or colleagues during his time in the Marines and the CIA. He didn't need to stand on a soap box and preach his doctrine to the masses and whoever would listen to his spiel. But it takes a special sort of person to legally kill someone and continue with their life as if nothing had happened. He believed he had taken early retirement from the CIA at just about the right time before his cynicism had time to prematurely imbed itself into his job. Now, that Harry had retired, he now had the luxury to have an opinion about the state of the world for the first time in many years.

It wasn't his normal cut-of-the-mill job, his normal missions didn't involve babysitting and he had had already enough of that role and didn't fancy doing it again, he said to himself. Harry's world was changing; it was now in the ether silently causing bedlam to countless individuals and countries. Cybercrime was now the big thing and Harry was old school. The days of espionage were changing to a digital world, where everyone's data is collated and shared across the wires in microseconds. Privacy was a big issue, but that didn't matter, they were shown by Edward Snowden the insider who told the world what was going on and paid the price by escaping to Russia. The world was spending fortunes on cyber security but not a dime on a solution to a comet strike. It didn't make sense, he said to himself. The world was spinning in its relentless drive with new technology without taking care of its risks. And a comet strike was one of them.

Harry wondered what was so important that the CIA now needed his skills. He knew his friend and former boss, Michael Kurious often kept the truth close to his chest, rather than reveal to him the full truth, which was one of the reasons he had decided to take early retirement from the CIA.

***

Arriving at CIA headquarters, Harry made his way to his former boss's office.

"Shut the door and sit down, Harry..."

"How's retirement, Harry?" Michael Kurious asked curiously.

"As I said before, it beats working," Harry replied, smiling.

"I have a mission that needs your skills to handle it. First, I'm glad to see you back here, I always thought you retired too early. That episode about not following procedures was unfortunate. Anyhow, I need you to investigate a group of individuals and ascertain whether they pose a threat to national security. As always you have the authority to use lethal force in any situation. The file is in front of you on the desk, which explains the mission and the individuals involved," Michael Kurious said.

"Why is the government so concerned, that it needs my skills and not someone else at Langley?" Harry asked curiously.

"I brought you in because you have the right skills for the mission. Also, we have a leak, but, we are not sure, at the moment," Michael said.

"I wanted someone I could trust, and that's you, it's as simple as that," Michael said.

"Yes, is that all?"

"It's called national security of important assets, with the new president's strategy on strategic commodities used in the production of green technology, now, a major national asset for the continuation of America," Michael said emphatically.

"Oh, I see…our paradigms have changed, since, the new president was elected," Harry said.

"Yes, they have…the government has completely changed course…and for the good. There is an urgency to secure certain commodities for the security of our country. It's all in the file…you will understand when you have read the file," Michael said.

***

That afternoon, Harry was sat in the corporate jet on a flight to Boston. Harry was looking forward to seeing his sister, Rebecca. On the flight, he relaxed and started to read the file. The government was concerned about the security of America, without access to certain rare earth metals. These metals were very rare on Earth, and now, they had become essential commodities for future technologies. Gram for gram certain rare earth metals were worth more than the current price of gold. The file went on to explain how Lithium, Byzantium, and a few other rare earth metals were now so scarce that future technology could be halted or delayed by the scarcity of these metals. They were important for the progress of billions of dollars in car production every year and greener energy production. Another was the mobile phone market, which was worth billions of dollars in trade. The main problem was the high cost of processing these rare earth metals and the energy costs to recover the metals contained in raw ore.

Harry took note of the individuals involved and read their profiles before he fell asleep with a JD and coke in his hand.

***

On arrival at Boston airport, Harry took the short drive to his sister's home. He was looking forward to seeing his sister.

"Hi, sis, how's it going?"

"Great and it's great to see you. How's married life?" Rebecca asked.

"I'm enjoying it!"

"Good!"

"It's only a flying visit, just to check in and find out how you are," Harry said.

"So, what are you up to?" Rebecca asked.

"Well, I'm back working as a sub-contractor for Langley, at the moment, but I'm still retired and not quite a couch potato, yet. Apart from that, I can't say anymore, you know how it is," Harry said.

"Yes, I understand."

"And you?"

"Much the same, but had another good paranormal experience the other day."

"Oh, yeah, what was that?" Harry asked intently.

"In was in the old port district of Boston, like those two events you attended with me before. Anyhow, the house was built on a former Civil War massacre site. The house was indeed spooked, with ghosts of all sorts haunting the house and its residents. Raymond was impressed, as I was," Rebecca said.

"I bet he was."

"Anyhow, the reason I asked you to stop over, is this problem in Brazil, and if you can sort it out," Rebecca said.

"Right, tell me more."

"Some friends were kidnapped and warned not to say a word about a gold mining operation in Brazil. It turns out, they came across a large deposit of Lithium and not gold…" Rebecca said

"Lithium, you say, hmm."

"Important?"

"It may be, we will see."

"This mining operation may have been illegal, I don't know. Anyhow, they escaped, but they are still worried about a Dr. Leo Schapiro and his daughter who live in Brazil and were also warned not to say a word, otherwise, their lives were at stake. Here are my friend's phone and email details, and Joe will update you on the latest information from Brazil," Rebecca said.

"I will look into it for you, don't worry, sis," Harry said.

"Joe and Isabella are very close friends," Rebecca said. Continuing, she added, "Joe and Isabella said they would cover all your expenses."

"Don't worry about the money it's not as important as people's lives," Harry said. Continuing, he added, "Tell me more about Joe and Isabella."

"We met at Boston University during a conference, where we shared time together discussing a whole range of issues. Over the course of three days, we shared all our meal breaks together. From that moment, we became friends and have had a regular relationship discussing and debating issues as well as the paranormal, since then. I have spent time in their home in Sonora, California nestled below the Sierra Nevada Mountains. Isabella and Joe are a great couple, who first met while at university. Isabella ended up as a biologist and Joe studied as an astrophysicist. Isabella is a lot like me; she likes adventure and is willing to travel the world to find it. And Joe who hasn't popped the question, yet, but is likely to do so, when it suits him, is also an adventurer, although, I would say a lot more street-wise," Rebecca said.

"Why would you say that?" Harry asked.

"What…street wise?"

"Yes…"

"I formed that impression from the time we spent all together at that three-day conference. His answers to questions and issues we were discussing, at the time, seemed to always have a street-wise character to them. They were down-to-earth but smart. He's an intelligent guy," Rebecca said.

"And Isabella …?"

"Yes, as I said before, a bit like me. She's an intelligent girl, who likes adventure. She won't suffer fools gladly. And a very good friend," Rebecca replied.

"Okay, I will contact Joe and Isabella and take it from there," Harry said.

Chapter 9

Meanwhile, Isabella and Joe were standing on the balcony of Joe's apartment overlooking a vista of central Los Angles as the sun was just about to set. A cool breeze gently cooled their skin as they discussed the merits of the mysterious Piri Reis Map.

"I never tire of this view, especially at this time of day, when the day is just about to drift into night," Joe said.

"Yes, the sunset is beautiful," Isabella said meaningfully as she savored another sup of her glass of wine.

"Yes, it is. Luckily where we are…we avoid most of the pollution in the air because of the prevailing wind."

"Hmm…"

"What are your thoughts," Joe asked intently as he took another slurp of wine from his glass.

"I hope you are right, Joe. I need to find out how some of the anomalies have occurred over time. The Piri Reis map is one major mystery where I don't know where to begin. I will need your help with that, for sure. Fancy a trip to Turkey?"

"Oh, hmm…"

"It's probably the best place to start our quest…"

Isabella explained that the Piri Reis map was produced around the sixteenth century but was based most likely on earlier maps, which she said have not survived to the present day. She told Joe that if they could find any earlier references to the Piri Reis map then it may be possible to link the two together. Isabella explained that they could also check ice core samples for climatic changes that occurred around twelve thousand years ago and see if she was right about what may have happened. She told Joe that it could also be something they haven't thought about and they don't know anything in the Cosmos that may have happened such as a nearby exploding star. Isabella explained that an exploding nearby star with its wave of radiation may have been just enough to kill off some of the animals exposed as the earth rotated into its path. The evidence should be out there somewhere, she thought.

"You have to ask, why there are so many anomalies?"

"Well, there's the anomaly of how an ancient map got produced showing the remarkably accurate outline of the Antarctic continent without ice. You, have to ask how this could be…without using sophisticated technology, but clearly not available thousands of years ago. What are your thoughts on the matter?" Isabella asked.

"It's a difficult question to answer," Joe replied.

"Hmm…"

"Perhaps, we should visit Turkey and see the original Piri Reis map, we may find another clue we can't see at the moment. Let's face it, who in their right mind, would travel a great distance without having a map to guide them? It seems obvious that the Piri Reis map is a copy of a much older map, maybe from early Vikings. Who knows, perhaps we will never find out, but it's worth a visit, and now that the university is closed for the summer break we have the time to squander on such a mystery," said Joe carelessly who was relishing his glass of wine as he thought about what to say.

Perhaps, we will find a clue, we were not aware of…it happens like that in life…you end up finding something you were not aware of that sparks further research," Isabella said philosophically as she sat enjoying the early evening on the balcony with Joe.

"Without the evidence your theory …is just that a theory going nowhere. We could be in Turkey tomorrow testing out your theory before someone else beats you to the finish line…wherever that is," said Joe, smiling.

"Who knows how far the Vikings ventured…we know they traded right into the Mediterranean Sea and right across what is now Russian, so it's plausible they could have crossed the oceans all over the world and made maps," said Isabella matter-of-factly.

"Look, a flock of swallows dancing."

"Yes, I often see them resting on that nearby church tower. As soldiers stood to attention they often wait there," Joe said.

"Yes, it's a beautiful display of nature and one that we should always cherish," Isabella said cheerfully.

"Not sure, what to say, but it is clearly a mystery. The only way a map could have been made was if someone had surveyed the continent when it was ice-free. And according to conventional science that was millions of years ago. Modern man according to most scientists started two hundred thousand years ago or thereabout. Clearly, more research is needed on this subject. There is clearly a paradox! I'm not sure what to say," said Joe, who had not thought about the subject that deeply, until Isabella had said she was interested in the Piri Reis map.

***

The following day, Isabella and Joe boarded a flight to Istanbul, Turkey from LAX, and were hoping they would learn more about the mysteries of the Piri Reis map, which was currently on display in the Topkapi Museum in central Istanbul. On the flight, they had time to discuss their plans for their trip to Turkey. They discussed numerous plausible ideas about how the map could have been produced, but none ticked all the boxes except one where for a brief moment in time the continent of Antarctica was ice-free just long enough for someone to sail around the continent and be able to produce a remarkable rendering of the shape of the continent without the ice sheet around its shoreline. This scenario may have lasted only a few short weeks or months before the ice sheet soon covered Antarctica again, Isabella thought.

"How long would it take for someone to sail around Antarctica, Joe?" Isabella asked candidly.

"To be honest, I don't know. But, let's presuppose a year for example, and then I guess it would be enough time to survey and draw a map. But, I'm still baffled how the mountain ranges and rivers were drawn; now that's a complete mystery," Joe replied.

"Yes, that would mean someone surveyed the land when there was hardly any snow and ice," Isabella remarked.

"Would you like another drink madam?" the airline stewardess asked.

"Why not, I don't intend to drive when we land in Istanbul. For me another gin and tonic, please," replied Isabella.

"Yes, for me another rum and coke, please."

"What's that you say?"

"It's like we're chasing the gold at the end of a rainbow," Joe said.

"Well, it's better than sitting on a beach somewhere getting burnt by the sun…at least this is a lot more interesting," Isabella said.

"Now, you put it like that…you're right," Joe said succinctly.

"Anyhow, I've been lucky to fix a meeting with the curator of the Topkapi Museum, who hopefully will be able to shed some light on the subject."

What's his name…the curator?"

"Dr. Joachim Anderson."

The airport was as busy as any other international airport with people coming in and out of Istanbul. Finally, they were able to find a taxi driver who could speak a little English and take them straight to the museum in the capital. After brief introductions with the curator, they were able to explain their reasons for wanting to see the original Piri Reis map. Dr. Anderson explained to Isabella and Joe all he knew about the provenance of the map and how the museum came into possession of the map. It had passed through various hands before the map was bought by the museum. Dr. Anderson explained that Piri Reis was originally a pirate, who then became an admiral in the Turkish navy before becoming an expert cartographer. He told Isabella and Joe that Piri Reis was fastidious in his production of maps and he wanted his maps to be as accurate as possible. Piri Reis used older maps as sources for his maps, but unfortunately, these older maps have not survived to the present time," Dr. Anderson said.

"Not being rude…but how do you know this map is genuine," Isabella asked cheekily.

"It has been checked by expert cartographers and also the gazelle skin parchment that the map was drawn on has been carbon dated…so we have a pretty fair idea when the map was produced. We believe the map dates from fifteen thirteen as signed by Piri Reis. The sources for the map it was said by Piri Reis was made from twenty or so other maps available at that time," Dr. Anderson said.

"So, it's a compilation of maps…"

"Yes, that's correct…a compilation of maps," Dr. Anderson repeated.

"What about Antarctica…it shows the continent ice-free and remarkably accurate rendering of the continent ice-free…how was that possible?" Isabella asked incredulously.

Shrugging his shoulders, Dr. Anderson replied, "Well, that's a question many people ask. We have theories as to how that could have happened, but no proof."

"What theories do you have?" Joe asked intently.

"We believe the Piri Reis map is a copy of a much older map from when the continent was free from the ice sheet when someone must have surveyed the continent. This we believe is the only plausible answer," Dr. Anderson replied.

"That would imply that the whole continent of Antarctica must have been completely ice-free for this to have happened," Joe said sarcastically.

"So, you believe the continent must have been free from the ice sheet at some time in the near past…is that what you are suggesting," Isabella asked incredulously.

"Our studies of the ice sheet suggest that for brief moments…say only weeks or months the ice sheet melts and the outline of the continent can be seen just enough for it to be surveyed and drawn," Dr. Anderson said.

"Do you have the evidence for this assumption?" Isabella asked intently.

"Yes, around twelve thousand years ago a climatic change occurred for this to happen. It was rapid change… one where the climate changed overnight instead of over thousands of years as it is doing now as we speak," Dr. Anderson said emphatically.

"Do you have any evidence though?" Isabella asked again.

"Yes, we believe we do… some ice core samples suggest a radical change occurred in the climate enough to send temperatures soaring and long enough to affect the ice sheet, which normally surrounds the continent. Some scientists believe that it would take only a slight variation in the earth's orbit to cause major disruption to the ice sheet. We believe this may have caused the ice sheet to rapidly melt. This may have caused the earth's axis to wobble enough to help speed this on; our scientists are trying to prove this as we speak. We know the earth's orbit is not perfectly circular around the sun and every so often it gets out of kilter every twenty thousand years but it may also occur on a shorter time frame, it's something we are investigating, at the moment. We know that global temperatures vary a lot over the planet. We know that the Arctic is warming up three times faster than other regions of the earth, so it's possible to have many tens of degrees difference between regions of the earth's surface depending on different factors like wind speeds in the upper atmosphere," Dr. Anderson said.

"Only a slight tilt in the angle of the earth, as it goes around the orbit of the sun, could have dramatic changes on different parts of the earth," said Isabella succinctly.

"When will you be able to know for sure?" Joe asked intently.

"It's like when you spin a top...it wobbles for a bit before it finds its equilibrium. At that time...it may have caused great floods to occur all over the earth. That is why most cultures speak about a great flood. A great flood of warmer water could have helped the ice sheet to melt in record time...who knows, but it's plausible," Dr. Anderson said.

"Yes, but what about the contours of mountain ranges and rivers that are drawn on the map?" Joe asked incredulously.

"We think Piri Reis copied what he saw from a much older map, it's the only plausible answer," Dr. Anderson replied who looked visibly stressed by the intense questioning.

"Hmm, it would seem a paradox to me," Joe said laconically.

"Yes, you're right, Joe there is a paradox. But there must be an answer to this paradox. The answers are there, but sometimes difficult to see, at first, but they are there. We just have to take off the blindfolds we have been subjected to since our early days of education. Not everything is black and white in history or nature," said Isabella philosophically.

"Just suppose a polar shift occurred which lasted only for a few days, maybe only weeks, and in that time frame no significant volcanic activity occurred, well at least no volcanoes, which were actually ejecting any magma. There may have been volcanic activity, but only smoke and not any magma ejection. Where the magma would align with the magnetic poles and the iron contained in the magma would align with the poles as it cooled, therefore leaving a permanent record. That is a possibility and one that the scientific community has failed to address. It could be why many of the animals disappeared around twelve thousand years ago across the American continent. There have been many major extinction events over the existence of Earth's history, but minor extinction events could be quite common and caused by local environmental changes," said Joe.

"I hear what you are saying, Joe. But the world needs to know what we have found out so far. Do you agree?" asked Isabella.

"Yes, I agree with you. But you have to be careful how you present your research because there will be many that view your research as pseudo-science," Joe replied.

"Do you mean the government?"

"Yes, the government," Joe replied. Continuing, he added, "There will be many in the government with a different agenda."

"I plan to contact some scientists who have been researching the minor extinctions that occurred around twelve thousand years ago and hear what they have to say about my theory. It could be there are other minor extinction events all around the world, at this time, but have never been researched. It's now my plan to see if I can corroborate my research with theirs if it exists," Isabella said.

"As you know global temperatures vary a lot over the world, and in some places, these varied local temperatures could affect the local environmental conditions for some of the larger species domiciled in the area. It may take only a few degrees rise or fall in temperature for some species to find it hard to survive, especially, if they have other environmental factors to contend with like the rise of man preying on these larger animals. Everything is a balance and when things get out of balance then the whole ecosystem with the larger animals could deteriorate within a matter of years. If a local ecosystem gets out of helter-skelter then it's usually the more dominant larger species that get affected first before other smaller species get a chance to take their place. That even includes mn. As you know many animals are currently under threat of extinction because of a number of reasons, but mainly due to man's destruction of their ecosystems," Joe said.

"Yes, that's true, but a small group of extinctions taking place in localized areas would indicate a major shift in conditions that helped hasten the extinction of those animals. I understand that a few conditions may have combined to contribute to the demise of some of the larger species in specific areas around the world. Namely, in North America where we see in the fossil record how quickly a number of larger species quickly died out. I'm still shaken from the news about the recent evidence, which as you know I've been searching for years," said Isabella.

"Don't get too far ahead of yourself, it's still early days and you need to pull all your research and evidence into one clearly defined theory and then let the scientific community peer review your work. This will take time. So, you need to iron out the ripples and work on that theory of yours before someone else beats you to the finishing post. Let's hope everything falls into place like it should," said Joe.

"You know there are places in the world where the archaeological evidence doesn't stack up," said Joe.

"What do you mean?"

"Well, in South America there is a place only recently discovered where a whole village of stone statues was found, but archaeologists are clueless as to who produced them. They resemble stone statues in some parts of India related to the Hindu religion. What I find interesting is how they crossed a vast ocean to get there. Did they already have a map, which would have guided their journey? They travelled across a vast ocean knowing what was on the other side. It wasn't a journey of hope; they had a purpose one would assume. If they did have a map then you have to ask who produced that map," said Joe.

"What was the place?" Isabella asked.

"At the moment, the name escapes me, but I will let you know when I find it for you," said Joe.

"Maps seem to be a clue to our quest because like you I just don't see a group of people setting out on a journey into the unknown without something like a map guiding their journey. Would you take a long journey without checking a map before setting out? No, you wouldn't, it seems that simple," Isabella said.

"Another question to ask is why they took the journey, what were the reasons. It's a genuine question that needs an answer," Joe said.

"What do you think?"

"Another question to ask is how they did this. What type of boat did they have? Because mainstream science suggests they didn't have significant migration across oceans because they didn't have the boat-building skills or the seamanship to cross oceans thousands of years ago. Before the Vikings, there isn't any evidence of boats that could have crossed a vast ocean like the Pacific or the Atlantic Ocean. The whole thing is a mystery," said Joe.

"What do you think doctor?" Isabella asked.

"It's obvious to me that the Piri Reis map is a copy of a much older map that hasn't survived into the present day, so we have to make assumptions based on the facts we do know. Whoever drew the map had a good idea that other lands existed across the Atlantic Ocean; you can see that from what is drawn on the map. What do you plan to do now?" Dr. Anderson asked.

"Fly back to the States and collate what we do know and make some decisions on what to do next," Isabella said.

"There's one thing I hadn't realized before is the mosquito problem here in the summer. I think I've been bitten on just about every part of my face since I got here," Joe said, laughing.

"Yeah, at least you've got more than one admirer, I would hate to be the odd one out," Isabella said, laughing.

Chapter 10

Later that week, Isabella and Joe were on a flight to South America and hoping to see the village of statues. They wanted to see the statues in situ before making any conclusions as to their likely artistic influence from a far. Most archaeologists had failed to make any connections with the South East Asia and the Indian Hindu culture. But there was one archaeologist who had published his findings and was also currently studying the village and was willing to meet with Isabella and Joe.

It was a long and trying drive to the village, through dense jungle as there hire car climbed higher and higher into the surrounding slopes beneath the mountain range. Most of the road was just a dirt track, which had been recently cleared of vegetation to allow for a vehicle to pass through the jungle.

After driving for most of the daylight hours they finally reached the distant village and were met by their host, Dr. Pannee Righa, who was glad Isabella and Joe had made it safely to the village. After introductions Dr. Righa showed them his camp and where Isabella and Joe could set up a tent for the night. Apart from Dr. Righa and a couple of assistants the village was empty due to its distance from anywhere nearby. Apart from the few tourists that visited the village during the day the village was deserted most of the time.

"You best set up your tent now…it will be dark within the hour," Dr. Righa said.

"Okay will do," said Joe.

"Come and join us around the camp fire…my assistants have made some food," Dr. Righa said.

"Sounds good to us," Joe said.

"Eat...there will be plenty of time to talk later," Dr.Righa said.

"Look!" Joe pointed to the sky and they could see the stars in all its glory.

"Well, Dr. Garcia and Dr. Goldstein..."

"Please just use our first names it's a lot easier if you don't mind."

"Okay, Isabella and Joe, what made you come all this way to see the village?" Dr. Righa asked.

"We wanted to see the statues in situ and the whole village for ourselves, even though we have read your published work on the village we still wanted to see it for ourselves," replied Isabella.

"Yes, we wanted to understand why people came here thousands of years ago to live and make their homes here," added Joe.

"Well, that question I believe is easy to answer. It was gold that made the first people come here to set up home thousands of years ago. The first archaeologists who excavated the site in the early nineteen hundreds found numerous gold objects. So the assumption is that it was gold that made some people set up home in this desolate place far from any other civilization, at the time. Gold was the driving force, I believe. There are still many years of excavating and digging to be sure, but from earlier digs and my findings it would seem that was the case. Unfortunately, the people who lived here didn't leave any written records just carved statues for us to understand. The people who lived here we call them the Almecs, but we have little information about their culture and what they believed in. That's why I'm here to try and understand how these people lived and died," Dr. Righa said.

"Where did the word Almecs come from?" Isabella asked.

"It was derived from the word used by the Aztecs in the fifteenth century to describe the people who lived in the Gulf lowlands area of Mexico called the 'rubber people' who harvested rubber from the trees in that region," Dr. Righa said.

Dr. Righa continued to explain to Isabella and Joe what he now believed about the mysterious people of the San Augustin village. He explained that the village goes back to around 1500 B.C.E. and that there were over 500 hundred sculptures in the village and they could relate to the Almecs in Mexico. He stressed there must have been a relationship between the two cultures here in Columbia and in Mexico because of the likeness in stone sculptures. He explained that the Almec culture lasted from around 1500 B.C.E to 400 B.C.E. And then they suddenly died out from that period onwards, which he explained was probably due to volcanic eruptions in the area, which may have ruined their food production in the region. He explained that recent evidence suggests this was a leading factor or other environmental factors such as climate change. Dr. Righa said recent evidence suggests they may have had a written language because symbols and glyphs have been found carved into stone and it's believed they were the forerunners of the Maya civilization, which had a written language. He explained that the Almecs were great astronomers because a series of stone statues have been found that were assembled in such a way as to accurately predict the winter and summer solstices and other astronomical events. Dr. Righa stressed that the Almecs used this information for when it was the right time to plant their crops and when it was likely to rain.

"I read your paper on the comparison of the stone statues, which you say resemble Hindu sculptures found in South East Asia and India," Isabella said.

"Well, do you agree with what you have read and seen?" Dr. Righa asked.

"I can only guess because I am not an expert on Hindu culture or indeed the Almecs. I will have to see more evidence before I can make a positive assessment of the situation. But, from an initial perusal of your work it would seem that there is a connection here with the Indian and South East Asia Hindu culture," Isabella replied.

"What about you, Joe do you agree with Isabella's assessment so far?" Dr. Righa asked.

"Not completely, we often disagree. I agree with what Isabella said, but there are a few things I am not sure of. For instance, why come here in the first place. It's difficult to imagine coming all this way just to find gold. That doesn't stack for me, at the moment," Joe replied.

"Oh, I see…"

"I think, Joe is right, it does seem an out of the way place to make home, but I'm still on the fence, so do speak," Isabella remarked.

"Yes of course…"

"Well, over the coming days I will show you," Dr. Righa said.

"We look forward to seeing everything you have to offer us," Isabella remarked.

"Look, shooting stars!" Joe said as he pointed to the stars.

"Listen, did you hear that?"

"What was it?"

"It sounded like a panther's growl somewhere nearby," Dr. Righa remarked.

"Oh, no…"

"It's okay; we are safe here in the camp with the roaring fire. We also have guns for protection if needed," Dr. Righa said.

"Do you have any protection from the ferocious mosquitoes that are a menace?" Joe asked sarcastically.

"Just rub some of this insect repellent around your necks it will keep the little bastards away from your face. It pays to keep most of your skin protected at all times, especially at night when they seem to be more active," Dr. Righa replied.

"Roll on, tomorrow…"

"Yes, tomorrow, I will show you both what I have found and you can judge for yourselves. It is truly a mystery, which I am totally engrossed in. When I first saw the images online I had to get out here and investigate further. I couldn't believe my eyes and the fact that no other archaeologists had made the connection. I guess that's because India is so far away that no other archaeologists could reasonable make the connection. It sounds so outlandish, but you will see what I mean tomorrow," Dr. Righa said.

"I can't wait to see your evidence," Isabella said cheerfully.

"Nor me," Joe remarked.

"I believe that many ancient civilizations were more advanced then we give them credit for. We still don't fully understand how they lived because we don't have written records, but all we have is the few artifacts we find and stone carvings we find. From that we make assumptions, but most likely we are way off the mark, but that's archaeology," Dr. Righa said, smiling.

"What about new technology hasn't that made archaeology a lot easier, in terms of finding sites, deep in jungles and completely covered over," Joe asked.

"Yes, the new Lidar technology – short for light detection and ranging is a tool that can help us see beneath the canopy of a jungle or sand and dirt and reveal previously hidden structures," Dr. Ragha replied.

"Yes, I've heard about that, but not used it before," Isabella said matter-of-factly.

"Yes, by surveying the ground with Lidar from an aeroplane we can make a map of a region covered by the jungle here. It's become a game changer for archaeology," Dr. Ragha said cheerfully.

"Are you using this technology here, at the moment?" Joe asked.

"No, not us, but there are archaeological teams here, at the moment who are conducting surveys in the area and all over Central America and South America," Dr. Ragha said matter-of-factly.

"But, don't you think it would be useful to check if there are any other structures nearby this village?" Isabella asked curiously.

"Hey, put some more wood on the fire its getting cold out here," Dr. Ragha said to one of the assistants. Continuing, he added, "Yes, to answer your question, Isabella. I've asked for the funds to do exactly that, just in case previous archaeological digs have missed something."

***

The following day, after breakfast, Isabella and Joe began their investigation of the village with Dr. Ragha. As they strolled around the village Dr. Ragha showed Isabella and Joe pictures of other sculptures found in South East Asia and India and the correlation between the two cultures and Dr. Ragha was adamant it represented a Hindu influence.

"Yes, I can see what you mean…not an exact correlation, but there is an influence there. Can you see that, Joe?" Isabella asked.

"Yes, if I hadn't seen the pictures of Indian Hindu sculptures and had the expertise of Dr. Ragha to guide me then I would have passed up the connections, for sure," Joe said.

"Have a look over here at these sculptures," Dr. Ragha said. He explained that the middle of the three statues represent a single deity and flanked on each side by a single guard. He showed some more pictures of Hindu sculptures in situ and continued to show the connections between the two. He explained the deity was showing its fangs just as in the Hindu deity in India and flanked by its guards who represented not by people but Nagma, which was clearly defined by the fish scales down its belly carved on both sculptures in the village and the pictures from India and South East Asia.

"I can see the influence...now that you have shown us the pictures from the Hindu culture. But, how could this be in South America...they would have had to cross a vast expanse of ocean to get here? I assume they possibly crossed the Pacific Ocean by means of navigating across the Indonesian Islands by island hoping until they finally reached South America or Central America. It's still a vast ocean to cross in hope of finding land unless they already knew, because they had a map guiding them here. And then they made it home here, because as you say they were looking for gold and found it here in such a remote region far from any other civilization," Isabella said.

"Yes, it would seem so...it wasn't until the Spanish invaded this region in the early sixteenth century that there were any chance of a foreign influence. But the Spanish never found this place. So it is a mystery for sure. Early analysis of this site suggests it's in the region of three thousand years old. During the time of the Almecs of Central America in what is now Mexico. But there is no conclusive proof that this is an Almec establishment other than the remarkable close correlation between the sculptures in this village and what is found in the lowlands in the Gulf of Mexico," Dr. Ragha said.

"What knowledge was lost when they burnt down the great library of Alexandria, we will never know?" asked Joe rhetorically.

"Yeah, even today, we could lose most of our knowledge, which is currently stored digitally with an electromagnetic pulse from the sun," Isabella said.

"Yes, you are right…it wouldn't take many disasters for our civilization to go back to the Stone Age, that's for sure," Dr. Ragha said.

"Many empires come and go and then they are lost to history as if they never existed, that's how precarious our understanding of ancient civilization is and without stone sculptures we would have little chance of understanding their cultures. Without written records we can only make assumptions of how our ancestors lived and died," Joe said authoritatively.

"Let me show you another example of a sculpture which I believe corroborates what I believe to be proof of the Hindu influence here in this village," Dr. Ragha said. Continuing, he added, "Look! Tell me what you see," as the doctor pointed to another series of statues.

"The faces of the statues look South East Asian or from India, you can tell there not the typical face of one of the indigenous Indian tribes from this part of the world. The eyes are more squinted like that of someone from India. And the whole shape of the face is different from someone not from around here, that's for sure," Isabella said strenuously.

"Yes, I can see the same…clearly someone from Asia or India, for sure," Joe agreed.

"And the clothing doesn't match with the indigenous Indians as they have carved these statues. So we must make the correlation with what we see in sculptures carved in South East Asia and the Indian sub-continent. That is the only conclusion to make…it's too close a correlation to ignore," Dr. Ragha stressed.

"From what you have shown us today we would have to believe that is the case, even though the sculptures are not an exact copy of those found in South East Asia and the Indian sub-continent. But, you wouldn't have expected that because these sculptures would have been original created from memory and the information passed down by word of mouth throughout the generations. But there are enough identifying features to make the connections between the two distant parts of the world to say they had been influenced by what they originally saw," Isabella said.

"Dr. Ragha have you had any other experts on the Hindu culture to back up your findings?" Joe asked.

"No, not up to now, but I hope to invite some fellow experts in the field to visit this place as soon as possible," Dr. Ragha replied.

"It's starting to rain heavily, we need to get under cover," Isabella said.

"Yes, quick over there under that canopy."

As they all stood under the canvas canopy protecting a large stone sculpture they could see they were directly in line with a mountain in the distance. In a recent storm, a series of trees had been blown over on the gentle hill that rose from the bottom of the slope where the statue had been placed, revealing the sight. They all wondered if this was deliberate on the part of the people who had erected the statue and if had any astronomical significance.

"Can you see what I see there looks to be a reason why they placed this statue here…and until now I believe never understood," Dr. Ragha said.

"We are above the equator here…so the summer solstice is only a few days away, we will have to stay a few extra days and see if that stone statue was put here for that reason, we shall see if that is case," Joe suggested.

"Yeah, that would be an interesting observation to witness," Isabella said.

"When it stops raining we'll head back to camp and have some lunch and then later continue our tour of the village. There's a lot more to see," Dr. Ragha said cheerfully.

Over the next few days, Dr. Ragha continued to show Isabella and Joe many more stone sculptures and the comparison with Hindu sculptures found in South East Asia and the India sub-continent. As the evidence became more convincing Isabella and Joe could not ignore the cultural connections, which Dr. Ragha was suggesting. Finally, the day had arrived when it was time for the arrival of the summer solstice and as all three of them gathered at the bottom of the hill by the stone statue they waited for the sun to rise early that day. They watched as the sun rose above the mountain peaks and centered between two mountain peaks as the light shown down upon the stone statue as they had anticipated.

"Wow! That is truly amazing," Isabella exclaimed.

"Yes, what a beautiful sight," Joe said excitedly.

"These people who built this place were true astronomers and new what they were doing," Dr. Ragha suggested.

"If they did originally come from South East Asia and India then it's a mystery how they got here three and a half thousand years ago," Joe said.

"Having thought about the problem I have changed my mind on which way they travelled. It makes sense to me that they crossed the Pacific Ocean rather than the Atlantic Ocean," Isabella said.

"So you agree with my assertions that what we see here is from people who originally came from a Hindu culture?" Dr. Ragha asked.

"Yes, from what we have seen here in this village the evidence would seem to be overwhelming even though the scientific community considers this site to be of unknown origin. You have shown us too many comparisons and similarities that you can't dismiss. And I have done some research, which suggests that this site is unique in Columbia and you have to ask the question why, that is the case. And the only reasonable assumption to make is that the people that built this place were not indigenous to this area they came from another land far from here," Isabella said.

"Yes, I agree with Isabella's assessment. There is too much evidence pointing in that direction. It may be many years before the scientific community all agree on your theory, Dr. Ragha. But the question that puzzles me is why, they came here. What was the reason they would have made such a long journey from their home to come here. I agree, the likely route was across the Indian Ocean onto the Indonesian Islands and across the Pacific Ocean to South

America. It still is a very long way to get here three and a half thousand years ago. So it begs the question, why?" Joe asked.

"It's a difficult question to answer, but it could have been many reasons such as climate change where they were living at the time forced these people to migrate. Perhaps, we will never know. But once they arrived in South America they chose this place because they found gold and an available supply of fresh water and a temperate climate to grow crops in the valleys between mountains. They probably chose this place because it's high in the mountains and difficult to get to so they felt safe from the indigenous tribes around at that time. Perhaps, over time we will find the answers to some of these questions you ask, Joe," Dr. Ragha said.

"In the meantime, we will continue to do our research and perhaps we will find the missing piece of the puzzle," said Isabella optimistically.

Chapter 11

Meanwhile, deep in the Amazon jungle, a former supply barge was now slowly heading up the Amazon River carrying a group of scientists and crew that were heading for the last known village on the river. The small village, on the river, was populated by an indigenous Indian tribe called the 'Wnaggee' and had lived in the Amazon jungle for thousands of years before the first white explorers in the early eighteen hundreds discovered them. Since then, the tribe had had little contact with the outside world. They traded with other tribes down stream, but that was as far as they ventured.

The source of the mighty Amazon River had already been charted and discovered earlier in the nineteenth century and much was known about the indigenous tribes that lived along its shores, but beyond only a few feet from the river bank much was unknown and it was still a virgin jungle and also a mystery.

As the barge tugged up the river the smoke from its single stack blew aimlessly away into the sticky and humid evening air. The cumulative heat and humidity of the day made the scientists on the barge feel ready to jump into the river just to cool down; such was the sweat pouring out wherever it could. But, that would be far too dangerous, with crocodiles in the water. They could see the crocodiles sunbathing along the river's edge on sandy banks as the barge slowly passed by. The group of scientists was anxious to meet the Indian tribe before they continued farther up the river. The scientists also wanted a blessing from the tribe's shaman. It would be early the next morning before they reached the village.

Apart from the stories the scientists had heard from the locals and crew who had heard tales and folklore from illegal logging crews who had ventured deep into the jungle searching for mature hardwood trees to fell, the jungle still kept its mystery locked inside its green and virgin canopy for those to seek. Its size was immense and once inside difficult to comprehend. It was never silent even in the darkness when the birds and monkey calls had stopped there were the sounds of millions of insects of all shapes and sizes making their noise. A relentless buzzing in the background like a constant ringing in your ears you can't stop.

The stories of mystical lost cities of gold kept many adventurers searching deep into the jungle and never appearing again. These stories circulated like a plague among would-be adventurers. Over the years, countless people had entered the Amazon and were never seen again nor any sign that they had even existed. The huge size of the Amazon was equivalent to the size of America and a barrier for any would-be explorer, not least, a forest full of killers in the shape of the numerous predatory animals such as panthers, wild hogs, venomous snakes, and other organisms that could strike a lethal blow at any time. It wasn't a place for the foolhardy or for those ill-advised and not well-equipped for the perilous journey into a deadly jungle.

The prospect of surviving without medical attention was limited when the nearest hospital would be weeks away without immediate air evacuation if available. It was almost a suicide mission for any explorers venturing into the heart of the jungle and they knew the risks. For some people, just the mention of gold was enough for them to give up their present preoccupation and venture into the unknown. Whether they believed the legends and folklore or the tales

140

the loggers told is unknown but the lure of the prospect of gold and adventure was enough for many to travel halfway around the world just to journey into the jungle of possibilities.

For one young scientist and his girlfriend, the opportunity of a lifetime had come his way and there was no way he and his girlfriend were going to pass up the chance to explore the Amazon River and the surrounding jungle and there was a lot of it to explore, he said to himself.

Dr. Benjamin Denarii and his girlfriend Dr. Shelia Attworth are both geologists with four other scientists with various roles and are employed by their oil company to chart and survey oil and gas deposits in the Amazon basin. Stood, on the barge's bridge with the Brazilian captain, Ben and Shelia viewed the ship's progress, as it slowly made its way around another meandering bend in the river. The two members of the crew were busily keeping the old vessel going. One was in the engine room and the other sat on the bow watching for obstacles the captain couldn't see from his position in the bridge.

Thirst overrides the fear; the necessity to keep well hydrated under relentless heat quickly depletes the amount of fresh water available among the explorers. One of the scientists spent his time boiling river water to purify it, as their stocks of fresh water had been running out faster than they could replace it; such was the demands on the water supply by the explorers and the crew.

"When do we see the village?" Ben asked.

"Tomorrow morning," the captain replied.

The barge was heading for the northern part of the river where the barge was unable to travel any farther on the Amazon River, where the party of scientists would then disembark and then venture into the jungle and walk for several days before reaching an area of the jungle previously unexplored by the oil company and other scientific missions, except possibly by gold prospectors and illegal loggers.

It was felt that the area was too deep into the jungle for loggers to have reached. From Google Maps and satellite images of the area which the scientists had studied it was just a sea of green like a carpet without any clearings or hills to break the view. From above the scientists could see only a green carpet that stretched for miles in every direction without a mountain or hills to break the flat surface of the jungle. Only the brown color of the Amazon River broke the green canopy of the jungle on either side of the river.

The party made camp on the river shoreline and hoped to make their way on foot into the jungle the following morning.

"Look, at the stars…it's a clear night…the Milky Way in all its glory," Ben said.

"Yes, truly an amazing sight out here," Shelia replied.

"Tomorrow, we start our trek into the jungle," Ben said.

"Are you threatened by the jungle?" Shelia asked.

"Yes, it scares me!" Ben replied.

"Why?"

"What may be lurking in the shadows waiting for us to pass by? A ready meal for a lurking predator to strike us without warning, you know, anything is possible. It reminds me of what Enzio said the other day…when he told us a story about a gold prospector who had been beaten by the lure of gold, which ultimately secured his death," Ben replied.

"Oh, what was that?" Shelia asked.

"Weren't you listening?"

"No, probably not, thinking about other things, at the time."

"Oh, I see…"

"You know me…a complex girl…with many things on her mind," Shelia said, smiling.

Ben went on to retell Enzio's story about the gold prospector to Shelia while the other scientists listened on under the shade of the canopy at the stern of the barge. Ben explained that it started with a rumor that had been circulating around the many bars in the port district of Manaus for some time concerning an apparent gold deposit in an area of the Amazon that not many people had ventured into. It was understood to have been a rumor started by illegal loggers who spread the rumor around the port. Anyhow, one night, this gold prospector heard the rumor and decided he would venture into the jungle to find the gold deposit for himself. Ben explained that the following day the gold prospector hired a fishing boat to take him up the Amazon River as far as it could go. The gold prospector told the fishermen not to wait and that he would find his way back via the local Indian tribes and there he would wait for a supply barge to arrive before returning to Manaus.

"Did he return with the gold?" Shelia asked.

"Wait there is more to the story," Ben replied.

Anyhow, several months went by, and Ben explained that no one had seen or heard from the gold prospector. Until, one day when a group of local Indians found the gold prospector's camp, no sign of the man was found. Eventually, the local Indians told the Manaus authorities, and a search was made of the area. Ben explained that search parties were sent out in all directions, but they didn't find any sign of the man except for his camp where they did find a small quantity of gold. Ben told Shelia that since that time around five years ago, no one has seen the gold prospector. It was a mystery to this day what may have happened to the man, but it's a warning to others not to go into the Amazon jungle alone.

"It was foolish to go into the jungle alone, but I guess that is the lure of gold. It makes people do strange things when greed takes over," Shelia said.

"We are just the same…oil and minerals…"

"Yes, I guess so…"

"Don't blame the oil companies…you should blame the customers who are thirsty for the stuff," said Henry.

"Anyhow, I have a story to tell from the Australian outback," Shelia said.

"Please tell, Shelia…"

"Look, a family of otters playing on that shoreline," Ben said as he pointed to the spot on the river bank.

"Yeah, they're so happy," Shelia remarked.

Shelia explained that two brothers who were middle-aged and overweight and not in the best of health went into the outback looking for gold. They traveled to an area known for finding gold on the surface of the ground, especially after floods, which leave the gold and wash away the dirt. Anyhow, after some recent storms in the area, the brothers decided to make their way into the outback hoping to strike it rich. The brothers packed their metal detectors into their old pickup truck and by all accounts very little else of essential supplies. Shelia explained that the first mistake the brothers made was underestimating the quantity of diesel that would be needed for the return journey, especially if they needed to return in a hurry. When they got into the outback, it was blistering hot, and very little breeze, and the brothers started to use up their meager water supplies at a very fast rate. They hadn't anticipated how much water they would need and so they started to dehydrate at an alarming rate it is thought. Shelia explained that the brothers must have decided too late to return because their bodies were found almost together along a dirt track some miles from their vehicle, which was found empty of diesel.

"A sad story and a warning to others," Ben remarked.

"What happened next?"

"A local aborigine found the bodies and alerted the authorities in a nearby town, which happened to be only a few miles away from where they found the brothers," Shelia replied.

"It goes to show you should always have more than you need," Charlie said.

"And planning is essential," Henry said.

"No shit…"

"It's easy to make mistakes a lot harder to correct them," Ben said.

"A sad and important lesson to us all how not to fuck up," Charlie remarked.

"That's right, boss," Slim said.

"Every step you make to some extent depends on fate. If fate decides it's your turn then there isn't much we can do about it," Charlie said philosophically.

"You believe in fate then, boss?" Slim asked candidly.

"Yep, it's that unseen force that governs all our lives whether we like it or not," Charlie replied. Continuing, he added, "I'm not the boss, our boss is most likely sitting on his fat ass in his luxury leather office chair dwindling his pen in San Paulo. That's the local headquarters of the oil company."

"Yeah, we're just the grunts who do all the heavy work," Henry stated.

"Anyone else got a story they wish to tell about why we wait for this old crate to get us to our destination," Charlie asked.

"Let's have those binoculars, Charlie, I want to see if we are near the last village on the river," Henry asked.

"I have a story to tell, but it's for the benefit of our new recruits. I have told the story many times before," Slim said.

"If you must…"

"I was in the Congo in Africa working for an oil company. It happened to be my first experience working in the jungle. I was with a group of explorers surveying the land looking for oil deposits. We had been hacking our way through the jungle with machetes for several days when one of the guys got bitten by a snake. By the time, I had found the snake antidote and administered it to the guy he had died. I blamed myself for not being prepared sufficiently for such an emergency. It took too long for me to find the snake antidote and administered it, so these days, I carry some snake antidote, right here in my pocket ready, for such an occasion," Slim said pointing to his canvas trouser pockets.

"No shit…"

"Yeah, all ready to go," Slim said.

"Well, I'm glad you're thinking about us," Ben remarked.

"My pleasure…"

"No worries, glad someone is on the ball," Shelia stated.

"Anyone else got a story to tell?" Charlie asked.

"It sounds like we're slowing down," Tex said.

"This barge can't go any slower it's slow enough," Henry said.

"It's the village…we've made it at last," Charlie said excitedly.

"Great, I can stretch my legs," Slim remarked.

"Make the most of it because we won't be here long," Charlie stated.

"I need to do the same," Ben said.

"Me too…"

"Tex, you best stay behind and watch the cargo," Charlie said.

As the barge pulled up against the wooden jetty and anchored from the bow and stern the barge was also tied to the jetty and wooden planks were also fixed to allow access to the jetty from the barge. The scientists could see the crowd of Indians watching the scene and waiting for their supplies to be unloaded. Charlie was the first to leave the barge with one of the Indians he had hired for the expedition and greet the village leader, while the crew and some Indians began to unload the supplies for the village. Charlie explained through the Indian interpreter that his party was traveling farther up the Amazon River and wished for the village shaman to bless his party's mission into the jungle. One by one, the other scientists followed Charlie and the Indian leader to the center of the village surrounded by a crowd of Indians. The village leader spoke with the shaman who began to dance around the scientists and chanted and blew smoke from a wooden pipe. This ritual lasted for almost an hour before the shaman had finished and he had blessed the scientists on their trek into the jungle. Finally, Charlie gave the village leader a gift of bottles of liquor and thanked him for his help before making their way back to the barge.

"That took some time," Tex remarked.

"Yeah, but it's essential to keep the local Indians on our side," Charlie stated.

"Yep, especially, out here," Henry said.

"It looks like the captain is ready to leave," Slim said.

"Good, we can get on our way. Tex, did you watch what cargo was unloaded carefully?" Charlie asked.

"Yes, of course. Everything went as normal, I checked everything off the barge and made sure the Indians didn't take any of our supplies by mistake," Tex replied, with a wry smile.

"Slim tell the captain that we're ready to leave," Charlie stated.

As the crew raised the anchors and untied the barge from the jetty the scientists watched from the stern under the canopy the crowd of Indians that had gathered on the shoreline as the barge slowly made its way farther up the river again. Black clouds could be seen and before long it started to rain heavily as the scientists sheltered under the canopy and watched the rain almost block out their view of the river.

"That's strange…"

"What's strange?"

"The rain…it's meant to be the dry season. This time of the year it never usually rains, but then again climate change is happening all over the world," Charlie said.

"You said that the other day…"

149

"Yeah, I know, but it's raining again very unusual," Charlie said.

"Will it hamper our trek into the jungle?" Ben asked.

"At least, it will be cooler for a while, until all that water starts to evaporate and it gets hot and sticky again," Tex said.

"No shit…"

"Eh, no, it won't affect us too much…by the time we reach our destination most of the water will be gone, but our feet are likely to get wet in parts of the jungle where it pools, then it's a problem for Slim," Charlie remarked.

"Yeah, that's right. Soggy feet end up getting infected and that's a problem to watch for," Slim said.

"I have a story to tell," Tex said.

"Not that same story again," Slim said.

"Yeah, but it's not for your benefit it's for Ben and Shelia's benefit," Tex remarked.

"Okay, go on…"

"It goes back to my early days as a wildcatter in Texas."

Tex explained that he had joined a group of wildcatters sinking wells in an oil-rich region of Texas flat lands when on his first day he almost died. He told the scientists that a part of the rig collapsed and just missed hitting him by inches. The reason he explained it was due because one of the crew had forgotten to tighter the fixing bolts to a part of the gantry above the oil well. The person responsible for not securing the bolts he found out was himself. He explained that the crew had stopped for a break and after he forgot to secure the bolts and tighten the nuts. Tex explained that once the rig started drilling for oil the vibration forced the bolts free and the steel brace came tumbling down and nearly killing him. It was only the quick action of a fellow crew member who pushed me out of the way.

"So, you nearly killed yourself…on your first day," Ben said.

"Yes, so the moral of the story is not to forget your job or you or someone else could end up paying the piper," Tex said, smiling.

"No worries, I'll keep my mind on the job," said Shelia.

"Yep, you best do that…and not on his nuts," Slim said, laughing.

"It's serious stuff…anything can happen, especially, out here," Tex stated.

"Calm down, calm down…we don't want any arguments, today," Charlie said.

"Listen!"

"Monkey and bird calls are busy this afternoon," said Henry.

"We can hear the jungle because the diesel engine on this barge has stopped working," Tex remarked.

"Slim; go ask the captain what is happening?" Charlie asked.

"Okay, boss, will do…"

Chapter 12

After many days of traveling up the Amazon River, the barge could not go any farther because of a series of shallow rapids, which blocked the way forward. The captain had the barge anchored at the bow and stern and as close to the river's shoreline as he could safely go. The group of scientists and their two Indian helpers made their camp on the river's shoreline for the first time. The captain and his crew of two stayed on the barge just in case they had to make a quick escape from the area. There was a fear that illegal loggers, gold prospectors, or rogue Indians could target the vessel for what they could plunder, the captain thought. And so did Charlie who gave explicit instructions to the captain not to leave the barge unguarded because they were in a region of the Amazon, which was virtually uncharted. Except for the occasional army helicopter they had seen pass overhead, which used the river to navigate its way to its destination, they were now in no man's land.

"Listen!"

"Shush, listen to the jungle…the sounds of the birds and the monkeys and all the other animals. I always think it has a reassuring feeling. Nature at its best," Henry said.

"Now, you're starting to get philosophical," Tex remarked.

"Ben, Shelia can you help Henry and Tex put up the tents," Charlie stated. Continuing, he added, "Make sure they're high enough above the water line. We don't want to sink before we can swim."

"That's calling the kettle black…"

"Yeah, like you can't run before you can walk, so to speak," Shelia stated.

"Of course…"

"Well, you know what I mean. It could rain again and the river will flood, anything is possible," Charlie remarked.

"Yeah, especially, these days when climate change has altered the ball game. Weather patterns are not as predictable as they used to be," Tex said.

"Yeah, you're right on the money, Tex. We've had rain this week when it's meant to be the dry season. And with the black clouds, I see in the sky, it doesn't look good," Henry said.

"Yeah, you're right, it doesn't look good for tomorrow," Ben said.

"Make a fire, it will soon be dark," Charlie said.

"No shit, we will have to watch for the predators lurking in the shadows. We don't what to end up on their dinner plate," Tex said, laughing.

***

"Slim get the fishing gear, I plan to fish for supper," Charlie stated.

"Right, boss…"

"What about the mules?" Tex asked.

"Leave them on the barge, until we're ready to break camp," Charlie replied.

"Okay, will do…"

***

The first night, camping along the shoreline was a welcome experience for the group of scientists. It was the first time they had space to stretch their legs after the long journey in the barge.

"The barge cannot go any farther up the Amazon River due to rapids and large rocks and boulders in the way," the captain said.

"Well, at least the barge got us this far," Tex remarked.

"Yeah, the old crate did well, I thought," Charlie said.

"It smells good that fish you got cooking," said the captain.

"Where are the Indians?" Henry asked.

"I sent them into the jungle to look for bush meat," Charlie replied.

"Did you hear that…gunshot?"

"Yes, it sounds like they have found some bush meat to add to our fish meal, tonight," Charlie remarked. Continuing, he added, "They should be back any minute, now."

"You sent those Indians in with guns…"

"Yes, how else would they find some bush meat," Charlie muttered.

"Aren't you worried they would run off with the guns?" Ben asked.

"Oh, no…they live in Manaus…they have families to care for. I hired them to interpret with the local Indians and mainly to cut our way through the jungle with machetes. It will sap the strength swinging a machete all day long and they are used to hard graft," Charlie said.

"I'm glad you did because I don't fancy swinging a machete all day…it just takes all your energy and you need plenty of water just to keep going," Henry remarked.

"Yeah, we have to watch our water supplies carefully, otherwise, we could be in serious trouble," Slim said.

"Don't worry we have plenty of supplies…I had Henry boil more water from the river just in case. In the meantime, Tex gets some more dry wood to burn…we need to keep that fire burning all night. And keep the wood dry because I don't like the look of the clouds. It looks like it could rain again, tonight," Charlie said.

"Shit, the fish is starting to burn," Tex said.

"Get it off the fire and tuck it in…I've cooked up some rice to go with it. We will wait to see if the Indian s bring back any bush meat to cook," Henry said.

The captain and the crew sat with the group of scientists around the campfire and ate their fish and rice meal while they all waited for the two Indians to return to camp. It was over an hour before the Indians arrived back at camp carrying a dead wild hog. The Indians had already disemboweled the animal before trekking back to the camp. Thereupon, Henry and Tex made a spite to roast the hog above the fire and waited with the rest of the group while the hog cooked on the fire. In the meantime, Charlie discussed with the group the following day's endeavor.

"It looks like it could rain, tomorrow. So we may have to stay here another day before we trek into the jungle. It will be hard enough work without the rain hampering our progress through the jungle. So it's best if we avoid trying to cut our way through the jungle with the rain pouring down our necks," Charlie said.

"Is that really an issue?" Shelia asked.

"It is out here the rain just makes it harder to deal with. That's why we chose the dry season to come here. Normally, this time of year we don't experience any rainfall," Charlie replied.

"Tex, Henry, turn that hog over..."

"Well, at least, we know what we have to eat...there's plenty to go around," the captain said.

"Why would the rain hamper our progress?" Ben asked.

"Simple, son, it's harder to cut through the vegetation when it's wet...the machete slides off the vegetation like water off a window," Tex replied.

"Don't you mean water off a duck's back?" Shelia asked.

"Yeah, that as well," Tex replied, laughing.

"Don't worry, Shelia, he often comes out with his own way with words," Charlie remarked.

"No worries, I was just making an observation of sorts," Shelia said.

"No shit so was I," Tex said.

"Now, now boys and girls let's keep it friendly," Charlie stated.

"Listen!"

"What?"

"You hear a different sort of noise from the jungle at night compared to the day. It's just that constant buzzing sound of the crickets, frogs, and insects that is just relentless," Henry said.

"Yeah, after a while you just get used to it…until you need to sleep then it can be an annoying sound that keeps you awake," Slim remarked.

"Just be thankful it's not the growl of a panther coming at you," Tex said.

"Or a hog that's charging at you…"

"That reminds me…that hog should be cooked by now," Charlie said.

"I'll do the honors and cut it up and share it out," Tex said.

"Leave enough for tomorrow," Charlie stated.

"There's plenty to go around and enough for tomorrow," Tex remarked.

"It's the lesser of two evils," Tex said.

"What's that?"

"The lesser of two evils. My vices for example; I like a drink, but I have also rules, I don't drink on the job. But out here at night when all you here sometimes is the constant croaking of frogs and toads. But, whatever it is, you need a drink just so I can sleep.

"You said two evils…so what's the other one?"

"I didn't say there had to be…"

"I'm thinking about my daughter and her fella. I guess anyone really. We could all have something hidden in the closet. Just the vices we all have. I was considering the possible vices one can have. And the one I consider to be the most destructive."

"Come on, Tex that's have your view?" Charlie asked.

"Well, you never stop thinking about your family when I'm away from home, and that's Texas," Tex replied. Continuing, he added, "The rest is private."

"Oh, come on, Tex…"

"You probably already know…figure it out for yourselves," Tex said.

"Is this a sermon?"

"No, it's not…"

"Everyone has a brother or sister or indeed themselves who has a problem with a vice that destroys their lives," Tex remarked.

"The smell is good!"

"It tastes really good this meat…"

"Yeah, it has a certain flavor when it's cooked this way," Tex said.

"Yes, I agree with that…"

"There's plenty of people in Manaus who prefer bush meat…it's cheaper than buying home-produced beef and pork," Slim said.

"Yeah, no doubt…"

It's not just that, but the taste is totally different…there's a flavor to the meat. I guess it all comes down to what the animal is feeding on," Henry said.

"Listen!"

"Did you hear that…the sound of a distant gunshot…someone else is close by and hunting for bush meat," Tex said.

"Yeah, you're right…"

"It could be…"

"Anyhow, it's time to settle down for the night with a good story," Charlie said.

"Have you got one, boss," Slim asked.

"Yeah, a black hole story… and it's not about the notorious prison in India called the Black Hole. Although, I've had the pleasure of many experiences in similar environments, which I may discuss on another night. No, tonight, I have a story of the paranormal," Charlie said.

"Oh, a ghost story…just what we need out here. We don't need to be spooked when just about everything at night in the jungle spooks me when you know that's the time when the predators tend to go hunting for their meal.

"Perhaps, you'll be next…but I doubt it…you're as thin as a rake, Slim. I don't know if a panther would want such a skinny subject," Tex said.

"You joke, but it's a real threat out here," Slim replied.

"This story goes back to my youth…so about twenty-five years ago off the coast of Africa. Not far from Muanda, Congo.

"Is that when you had hair, boss?" Slim asked, smiling.

"Yeah, you're right…"

"Go on," Slim remarked.

"I was on an oil company supply ship, we were doing early oil exploration when several days after a recent storm, we came across a large oil tanker adrift in the ocean. Initially, we thought the vessel just needed repairs and that was presently happening. Our captain decided to send a number of people over to the tanker to help. On board the ship, we went high and low through every bulkhead and throughout living quarters and on the bridge, but we found no one on board. We made a thorough search of everywhere on the ship. The strange thing was we found the canteen had hot food out as if people had been eating only minutes before we arrived," Charlie said.

"What happened?"

"We did another search of the ship but again found no one," Charlie said.

"Why was it drifting in the ocean?" Tex asked.

"We found the navigation wasn't in sync, but there were no other problems that we could find. Eventually, authorities sent a salvage crew to get the vessel and its cargo to the nearest port for a full inspection. What happened to the crew of the tanker is still a mystery, today," Charlie said.

"Was the crew ever found?" Ben asked.

"No, not a sight or sound of the crew was ever found on land or sea. But, the strangest thing was the tanker's lifeboat was never launched, so how the crew disappeared is a complete mystery to this day," Charlie said.

"That is really spooky," Tex said.

"Yeah, as if everyone on board jumped ship from a perfectly sound ship, which doesn't make sense," Charlie said.

"What's your view, Charlie?" Henry asked.

"I don't have one; it's a complete mystery what happened. Even, today, I don't have an answer to give you."

"Well, that's that…does anyone else have a spooky story to tell?" Tex asked.

"Yes, I have one," Henry replied.

"Go on, Henry let's hear it," Tex said.

"Wait!"

"Did you hear that?"

"Yeah, what was it?"

"It sounded like the growl of a panther on the prowl," Slim replied.

"No shit…"

"Keep that fire burning…put some more wood on the fire, we need to keep whatever it was away from here and keep your wits about you," Charlie stated.

"Anyhow, the story goes back to when I was studying to be a geologist about twenty years ago and sharing digs with some other students in an old house in Clifton, New Jersey that had an attic and a basement. The house had been a two-family home at one time but had been converted to house students on both floors and the attic. The basement contained the heating boiler and a pool table and not much else, but the students would spend much of their time in the basement hanging about playing pool, and partying. The house was probably at least one hundred years old maybe more and was built mainly of wood and hadn't been painted in a while so it would creak a lot, especially, when a storm hit the area," Henry said who paused briefly to lite a cigarette.

Henry explained that one night during a winter storm all the students had gathered on the second floor in the living room watching the TV when the TV suddenly cut out and all the electrical power to the house also cut out. Henry explained that they had no candles, so they were in complete darkness for several hours before the power was eventually restored to the property. Henry explained that all he and his fellow students could do was sit and wait for the power to come back. At first, all they could hear was the house creaking as the storm raged outside. But, after about an hour they suddenly heard footsteps coming down the stairs from the attic and no other students were there. At first, we played no attention to the noise. We figured it was just the house creaking from the storm somehow. Henry explained that one of the students checked the attic stairs and no one was there. After about thirty minutes it happened again, we could hear a series of footsteps loud and clear coming from the attic. But, this time the stray cat that we looked after darted under the sofa and made a loud scowling sound as if it had seen something that frightened it. Henry explained that he and all the other students experienced the room suddenly get cold as if someone had opened the door to the outside.

Anyhow, Henry explained that some weeks later a student had done some research about the house and found out that a grisly murder had taken place in the property where a family man had murdered his wife in the attic. Henry told the group that all the time they rented the property they would often hear weird noises, which would often scare the cat and the students.

"Yeah, that is spooky…but that's the paranormal hard to unravel," Tex remarked.

"Is the house still there?"

"No, shortly after we finished renting the property the house was sold and pulled down to make way for a car park for the local Bell exchange," Henry replied.

"Well, it's time we all got some sleep…we have a big day tomorrow. We should be able to break camp and continue with our expedition…weather permitting," Charlie said.

"You say weather permitting…"

"Yes, if it's pissing down with rain then it's best if we stay here until the weather permits us to trek. It's hard enough trekking into the jungle without the rain hampering our efforts. Besides, we are in no hurry. We have plenty of supplies to last for weeks just in case things go pear-shaped," Charlie said.

"I hope you're right, boss," Slim said.

"Tex, you've got the first watch…wake me and I'll take the second watch for tonight," Charlie said.

"No problem, Charlie…I'm wide awake, at the moment," Tex said.

The scientists' mission was to explore an area of jungle previously unexplored by the oil company. They would be looking for oil deposits and minerals that could be exploited by their company.

***

The following morning, light rain and mist hid the morning sun around the camp. The talk among the scientists was about the weather and whether it was a good idea to begin their trek due to the weather conditions. It was mid-summer and the dry season for the Amazon delta but it could all change in an instant that is how the climate was changing around the world. Weather records were being beaten every year somewhere on the earth. Although the rain wasn't heavy it was enough to make conditions even harder getting through the thick vegetation on the jungle floor with a machete.

It didn't rain for long before the scientists decided to start their trek into the jungle. It would be several days before they reached the region they wanted to explore. At first, they had the energy to cut their way through the thick jungle with machetes, but they soon realized the amount of water needed to exert the energy was far above what they had originally counted on. They had to conserve enough to return back to the barge on the river. During the day little sunlight reached the jungle floor, but it was enough to see where they were heading, without being able to see a mountain in the distance for guidance.

"When you have a five hundred-pound hog staring down your nostrils, you get concerned because those pigs are just as likely to kill you and eat you as any other large predator out here in the Amazon," Tex said.

"It's an important animal for the ecosystem in the Amazon jungle, where they act as nature's garbage cleaners. In the process of the hogs using their snouts to move leaf litter they expose the topsoil to the sun and elements and allow new seedlings to grow." Henry said authoritatively.

Chapter 13

Ben had many reasons to be on the expedition, he wanted to explore different parts of the world before much of the world was known. He had thought about teaching, but that was when his days of exploring were over when he was nearing retirement, but not now when he was single and in his youth. There was plenty of time, later, for teaching, Ben said to himself. The other scientists had different reasons to be on the expedition, for some, it was purely the money it was just a job to them. Some had no choice it was all they knew. Although Charlie the boss had the most experience, especially in the Amazon jungle, he thought. Slim the doctor had had his experience of jungles, but they had all been in Africa, by all accounts the Amazon was a completely different scenario, Ben said to himself. Henry the group's tactician of understanding graphs and a knowledge of geology was unsurpassed within the group, he thought. And Tex the Texan was an old-school wildcatter who had an uncanny intuition when it came to finding oil. And finally, Shelia from Australia jumped at the chance of an adventure for her first job as a qualified geologist straight from university, Ben thought. The same as for Shelia, Ben also jumped at the chance of adventure, he said to himself.

"Can you smell that?" Charlie asked.

"What Charlie?"

"Can you smell it?"

"What…?"

"The smell of the jungle…it has its own unique smell. I've had to put up with the smell of diesel all the way here, but now, I can appreciate the freshness of the Amazon there's nothing like it anywhere in the world," Charlie said.

"Oh, I see…"

"Do you see…it's like the smell of freshly cut lawn grass, but sweeter with a taste of the wild animals mixed in as we cut our way through with machetes it releases the essence of the plants added to the lingering scent of the many animals that mingle with the vegetation here," Charlie said.

"Whatever you say, Charlie," Tex said.

"I know what he means…it's like when you catch the first whiff of meadow Lavender in a forest…and you almost forget you have senses," Shelia said. Continuing, she added, "You try and hold on to the smell as if you want to capture it forever."

"That's right, Shelia," Charlie said. Continuing, he added, "Exactly right!"

"No worries, there Charlie, we're on the same wavelength."

"I'm glad someone is for a minute I thought I'd missed the boat," Tex said, laughing.

"I have a taste for honey and its smell," Slim said.

"Oh, yeah…"

"No shit…"

"Did you know the ancient Egyptians used honey for thousands of years in their medicine? They used the honey to stop infections and it worked because they saved many soldiers who would have most likely died or had to have their arms and limbs amputated. In the West, we lost all this information and in wars like the American Civil War it could have saved countless needless deaths. It would have also made a huge difference during the World Wars in Europe, but for some unknown reason...scholars chose to discount the knowledge and not to pass it on to the right people, it got lost to history. We had to relearn it again, "Slim said.

The first day they turned northeast leaving the relative safety of the river's shoreline the conditions changed completely. Now, they were trekking into the Amazon where, at times, they only saw shadows in daylight as most of the daylight never reached the ground. The humidity struck as if hitting a brick wall. It suffocated your very existence. Sweat would pour from every part of your body. Yet, the hired help, the two Indians who did most of the machete work, never seemed to sweat and drank less water than anyone else. The local Indians were a different species, they were used to the conditions and their bodies had adapted to the environment, whereas the white man had not, Ben said to himself.

Tex always wore his baseball cap, which he said helped to keep him cool. Charlie's bald head always seemed to be perspiring as if a river of motion. There was now no breeze from the river to keep them cool. Henry and Slim wore their Panama hats which they said helped to keep them cool. Ben and Shelia both wore their straw hats hastily purchased in Manaus.

That was the first day on the trek into the Amazon jungle proper, Ben said to himself. It was difficult to see your bearing as everything looked the same. It was just a thick mass of vegetation and trees in every direction. There was no mountain or hilltop to focus on in the distance as the explorers ventured deeper and deeper into the jungle.

After reaching the survey area they soon found a deep depression in the lay of the land, which had lain hidden for thousands of years.

"Climate change has certainly changed the ball game."

"Its changing all around the world," Charlie said.

"Yeah, you're right, Charlie," said Shelia.

Sunsets were redder and pinky orange more often in our skies, the world was changing fast without little regard to the hidden dangers that could send mankind back to the Stone Age faster than a speeding bullet, Shelia said to herself. Living on a takeaway and watching streaming movies was the norm now the world consumers' traits had changed overnight. People's habits had changed on a massive scale since the Covid-19 pandemic forced millions of people to change to a different way of living, she thought.

The scientists soon realize from the graphs that they are sitting in a large depression.

"Is it an asteroid strike?" one of the scientists said.

"It could be," another scientist replied.

"In the meantime, let's get the detectors out and search for any meteorites; it all depends on whether part of the basin gets regularly flooded. Then it's doubtful any evidence of meteorites would be present to this day. But, we will check, just the same," Ben said.

"That's near impossible, with so much thick vegetation to cut away just to clear an area to detect," Shelia replied.

"Carry on."

"Okay will do."

"I've got a strong signal. I've found what looks like a meteorite. It's not like any other rocks found in the area that I have seen. Yes, it's definitely a meteorite. So, this place did get hit. So all we have to know is when that happened," Shelia said excitably.

Dr. Benjamin Denarii heard another bird call then a monkey call and in the background, the constant buzzing sound of millions of insects and grasshoppers communicating. Stretching to look at the meteorite at first glance it was perfectly smooth like someone had polished the surface. It had an irregular form and the tell–tale concave shape and its color was almost deep reddish brown and had been an immediate giveaway to its origin. The meteorite had come from the orb cloud far out near Neptune. Its elliptical orbit had been on millions of miles on a journey before the day the earth and the asteroid collided for the first time in its life span, he said to himself.

***

"Ecclesiastes said all is meaningless."

"You're not getting religious are you, Henry?" Tex asked.

"No, not me, I was just thinking about what Ecclesiastes says in the Bible, he points out that everything is pointless, and that in time all man's efforts will be forgotten," Henry said philosophically.

"Yeah, but some last the test of time...like Achilles's heel, which has lasted for thousands of years and will no doubt continue on through time.

"Indeed some legends live on through the ages."

"Name another..."

"That's easy...the wisdom of King Solomon," Henry replied.

"What about Moses?"

"Yes, but just a handful...most are forgotten in time," Henry said.

"Yeah, you're right...it's only pointless if you want it to be. Ecclesiastes was right and wrong, I believe at the same time. Perhaps, say thousands of years before our

171

present civilization there existed another civilization that had its heroes and legends that their memory lasted over generations and thousands of years. But, in a cataclysmic moment in time, all evidence of their existence got washed away such as the Great Flood in the Bible," Ben said.

"No, you're right, Ben," Shelia said.

"Yes, in time everything will be forgotten, so in a sense, it is pointless, if you choose to agree with Ecclesiastes, otherwise, who fucking knows what is real or not," Tex said.

"Slim, you have something to say."

"Yeah, I agree with Ben, but Ecclesiastes was also right. If that makes any sense," Slim said.

"Boss…what's your thoughts…?"

"Well, time marches on and waits for no one, but unless we get up tomorrow and trek on we won't reach our destination," Charlie replied, smiling.

"I've got a mortgage to pay…"

"And so do I…"

"We all have…a stake in finding oil or whatever…it pays the bills whatever way you shake it. I'd hate to be a ghost and forever wander without rest. When my time comes, well, there's not a lot I can do about it, but I hope I have a few more years, yet," Henry said.

"Well, you never know what's in store, because fate has its own direction," Ben said.

"I didn't know you believed in fate, Ben?" Shelia asked, smiling.

"Yes, it's there in the background even if we are not aware of it. At some point, things tend to meet. Chance or whatever you want to call it takes over and the strangest things happen, which you would have not expected to happen. But, I believe on a much bigger scale fate is controlling everything that happens."

"That pretty theoretical philosophy you have there," Shelia said.

"I've always wondered why we apparently only use ten percent of our brains capacity, yet we have evolved with a large brain, yet have we lost in the echoes of time the ability to use our brains full capacity?" Ben asked.

"I see what you are saying, Ben."

"This is a question that has puzzled my brain for some time," Ben said.

"Perhaps, you need something to loosen the brain cells a little...like a drop of this rum," Tex offered.

"Yeah, you're right, Tex...but no thanks, I'll keep to water," Ben stated.

"Argh..."

"That fucking bastard..."

"It fucking bit me...that fucking snake..."

"Slim, get the needle in him quick..."

"Someone, get a machete and cut that snake's head off..."

"Before it bites someone else..."

"The caretaker that's what we called him, but his real job was as an engineer in the oil supply industry. It was a cold and windy night, late in the summer, but cold in the evenings. It had rained, earlier that day when the caretaker walked into my office, which was located at the north end of the port district of Manaus, I was in shock momentarily," Charlie said.

"If I had hair on my head, then it would have stood up because for some reason it spooked me. And I don't often get spooked. The sight of the caretaker and a storm brewing outside made me feel spooked. No one had seen the man for months when he just appeared in my office looking all disheveled. His clothes looked like rags, worn out with large holes everywhere you looked. He was a mess. He was as thin as Slim is now just like a rake.

Anyhow, I was in a state of shock, we all thought the man had died, months ago, that was all everyone said. The truth was really unknown. Rumors abounded, everyone had one, some creditable and others completely off the wall.

"Millions would have been spent looking for the guy. The local authorities sent out helicopters that spent days searching the area. That's not cheap. And the land and river search was extensive with a small army of paid employees of the state. And there is the insurance company, which spent a small fortune on finding the man before they would pay out on a multi-million dollar claim by the family. And here he was standing with the biggest grin you could imagine across his face as if to say I'm back. It was like seeing a ghost because everyone had accepted the guy had died somewhere out in the Amazon jungle."

"Why do they call him the caretaker?" Ben asked.

"He was a problem solver...a fixer of problems within the oil industry, and well known throughout this part of the world. You could rely on the caretaker to get things done. His real name was Frank Harland, most people who didn't know him called him the caretaker. But, his friends and family called him Frankie, which he preferred."

"What did you do?" Shelia asked.

"Yeah, what did you do?"

"Yeah, what happened?"

"It was during the rampant inflation Brazil suffered during the communist rule, which overshadowed our oil industry in the country. Here's a guy that cost the debt-ridden country a fortune. I sat the man down while I phoned the hospital and local police. After all, the insurance may have paid out on his life insurance, I don't know. In the minutes that followed, he told me his story. He told me he was the only survivor from the plane crash, which he said was easily covered by the surrounding trees and vegetation. He said he was dazed from the crash and wandered the forest going in no particular direction, where he came upon a small pool of water that he had found by accident," Charlie said succinctly.

"By the time, he said, he came to his senses he was already lost and never saw the plane wreckage again. Then and there he realized he had to survive by living off what the jungle could offer. He could hear the sound of aircraft in the distance but had no means to alert the authorities. He tried to make a fire but by the time he had a decent fire going he heard no aircraft in the vicinity. He said at times it was difficult to keep or start a fire at the beginning of the rainy season. He said he hadn't been trained to survive in the jungle, he wasn't a soldier. He said he caught a fever and it caused him to have hallucinations he felt he went in the wrong direction, and until after the fever had passed did he realize he was heading in the wrong direction. He said he had decided to head for the river and west of the rising sun. This was his path."

"Only some days did he have the strength to walk through the thick jungle without the aid of a machete. Most days, he said he would slept up a tree, which offered protection from any predators. He said a panther strolled by one night and paid no attention to him up in the tree, even though it could have easily climbed up the tree and attacked him."

"What happened next, Charlie?"

"The caretaker said he eventually reached the Amazon River and proceeded to follow the river shoreline down to Manaus. He said it was many days and weeks before he came upon the first Indian village, where he rested up for several more weeks always hoping a supply barge would come by, but it never did. He said he needed to rest and find treatment for the tick bites he had all over his body, and many were infected. The local witch doctor in the village treated the bites with their own medicines derived from local plants found in the jungle. He said without the treatment by the Indian witch doctor he would not have made it back to Manaus. I told him that everyone in Manaus thought he had died somewhere in the Amazon and it would come as a surprise to a lot of people that he was alive."

"Eventually, the police and the ambulance arrived and I haven't seen him since, but a heard he filed for a divorce and is now living with another woman in Manaus somewhere near the port district of town. He certainly upset a lot of people's plans when he suddenly turned up from the dead. It was almost as if some people would have preferred him dead, he was worth a lot more money dead than alive. But, I was glad to see him, we had many a night together playing poker at the back of the local bar down near the port, before he disappeared," Charlie said.

"The reason I brought up the story is the caretaker that is Frankie revealed to me back then that he believed that he was in a gigantic depression in the Amazon basin, the very area we are about to survey. I took no notice, at the time, about what Frankie was trying to say. I was more concerned with his well-being. He said it was a miracle he found the depression because it saved his life with the water that had pooled at the bottom of the depression and was enough to save his life."

"We are about to survey the very area where he said his plane went down, so if it is true then we should find the major depression and confirm his findings."

"Do you believe he was telling the truth?" Tex asked.

"I don't see why not," Charlie replied.

"After several more days trekking through the jungle and with water supplies becoming lesser by the day, they started to feel they were walking inside a large depression on the ground."

"I can feel we are in a crater of some sort," Henry remarked.

"Yeah, you can sense it without it being obvious," Slim said.

"We can make a quick check with our survey equipment, which should give us a rough idea," Charlie stated.

"It looks promising!"

"Get the survey theodolite out, Tex and we will take some readings and test the lay of the land."

"The rest can get the camp setup and make a fire...it'll be dark within the hour," Charlie said.

"Tomorrow, we'll do a proper search of the area and see if we can find any pools of water...we need all the water we can find," Charlie said.

"What's cooking tonight," Tex asked.

"I sent the Indians out to find some more bush meat, so I hope they return with some or we will have to have what we have in supplies...and that is just cans of corn beef, and rice."

***

The following day, their search of the area revealed a large pool of water at the bottom of the depression, which hadn't had time to evaporate or drain away. That night, the group of scientists discussed the depression and how it may have been made around the campfire, while they ate their bush meat of monkey and rice.

"It's most likely an asteroid strike that has been previously undiscovered and has been gradually filling up every time the area gets flooded by the Amazon River," Tex said.

"Yeah, it looks that way," Henry remarked.

"Tomorrow, Ben and Shelia can get the metal detector out and check for any more meteorites, that should tell something about the area," Charlie said.

"From the initial size of the depression it looks to have been a substantial object that had hit this region sometime time in the recent past," Henry said.

"Do you have any idea when that happened?" Ben asked.

"No, not yet."

"Did you hear that...monkey calls...warning a predator is on the prowl," Tex said.

"Yeah, it was loud enough to warn just about everything in the jungle," Slim said.

"It must be an asteroid strike to make such a deep depression in the lay of the land," Henry said.

"I agree..."

"So, do I..."

"Tomorrow, we will know for sure with our seismic survey...the graphs will tell us what happened here," Henry said.

"And any more meteorites found will add to the story," Tex said.

"If we confirm it was a meteorite strike or asteroid then I'll get on the satellite phone and inform the company what we have found. They'll want to know, so they can inform the authorities in Manaus," Charlie said.

"I don't care what they say this monkey meat tastes good…you can see why it's so popular in Manaus and not because it's cheap to buy," Tex said.

"Yeah, the Indians did us proud by acquiring the bush meat so easily. They are used to hunting for bush meat, so it's not a problem for them in the jungle.' Charlie said.

"It takes a special person to survive out here when all you can see is just a green carpet of vegetation and trees and nothing else," Slim said.

"You're right about the bush meat it tastes so good…more like kangaroo meat we eat a lot of in Australia, where if we didn't then the whole country would be overrun with kangaroos," Shelia said, laughing.

"I heard that kangaroo meat was very popular in Australia…more popular than beef and pork. Is that true, Shelia?" Tex asked.

"Yeah, you're right. Again it all comes down to price. But, a lot of people just like it… it's good-tasting meat."

"And why not, it's free to hunt and catch just like what we are doing eating monkey meat, which other monkeys will prey on just like we do," Charlie said.

"It may feel like we're eating our cousins, but we're not the same species. We have just as much DNA that matches in cattle and we like the beef in our beef burgers, don't we?" Shelia asked.

"Yes, you're right, Shelia," Charlie said.

"If you were starving then most people would eat just about anything after a while including resorting to cannibalism," Shelia said robustly.

"You don't intend to start cooking one of us, do you Shelia?" Charlie asked, laughing.

"No worries, on that score, I think I would find plenty to eat out here before I started on the likes of you," Shelia said, laughing.

Chapter 14

The area the scientists wanted to survey would take several days perhaps weeks to get to such was the distance from the river. There were no roads or tracks they could use they would have to cut their way through the jungle vegetation with machetes. The task was made harder because of the heat and humidity and every foot forward drained the strength of everyone in the party, including the hired help used to ferry their supplies and cut their way through the jungle. Dehydration became an issue because of the lack of sufficient water and predators also became an issue, especially at night.

Finally, after many days of hacking their way through the jungle, they had arrived at their designation. They could begin their survey for oil deposits. They soon realized there was a large depression in the ground.

"All indications suggest an area around two hundred meters in diameter," Ben said.

"You can see from the radio graphs the shape of the depression...like the formation of a crater. Could it be an asteroid strike?" Shelia asked.

"We'll have to see what the other scientists think," Ben replied.

The following day, Ben and Shelia began their search for meteorites around the perimeter of the depression. It was hard work using the metal detector, in the dense vegetation because there was limited space to swing the metal detector over and around the mass of vegetation.

***

"Look."

"It's a clear night…I can see the Orion constellation."

"It's a beautiful sight."

"Yes, it is."

"It was the ancient Babylonians who invented the zodiac."

"Why did they invent the zodiac?"

"It was invented to give hope to the population at that time. It was a kind of fortune teller. People could see if the gods would favor them. I also think it was invented to tell what time of the year it was."

"Out here we can see what they saw in the night sky…the glory of the Milky Way."

"It was also a means to navigate oceans at night."

"They were great astrologers and astronomers and could accurately predict the motion of the planets."

"With limited technology, you have to wonder how they managed to accurately plot the movement of the planets so successfully," Shelia said.

"It's one of the mysteries of our ancient ancestors…they were smarter than we are led to believe," Charlie said.

"What's on the menu, tonight?" Tex asked.

"We have some monkey meat and rice to fill your bellies," Charlie replied.

"What are your plans for, tomorrow, Charlie?" Tex asked.

"Get out the seismic charges and get some data, while Ben and Shelia continue to look for meteorites. We have a large area to cover, which will take several days to complete. And then we move camp and continue with our survey of the region. Don't forget we're here to find oil deposits and minerals, so we have a lot of work to do. When we are sure this depression was caused by an asteroid then I will contact base and inform them of what we have found. The company will then need to inform the local authorities in Manaus," Charlie replied.

"I guess, they will send out someone to investigate the depression at some stage, but by then we will have moved on to another area of the jungle," Henry said.

"Yeah, most likely," Charlie muttered.

"Did you hear that…gunshot," Tex said.

"Yeah, unmistakable…there must be local Indians in the area searching for bush meat. It sounded like it was many miles away and shouldn't bother us here," Charlie said.

"Is that meat cooked, yet?"

"Not long to go…should be ready in a few minutes," Tex replied.

"Hey, Charlie you never said what happened to the caretaker when he turned up in Manaus?" Slim asked.

"I thought, I did," Charlie replied.

"No, you said he mentioned the pool of water in the depression, but you never followed it up, is that right?" Slim asked.

"Yeah, you're right, I never did...I must have forgotten. Well, I made a mistake and at the time was busy with other things, so the information from the caretaker got lost in the moment. And to be honest, I didn't believe everything the man was telling me. So I made no further enquiring on the matter, which was my mistake. And I wasn't sure where the caretaker had been in the jungle, so it was easy to forget," Charlie replied.

"I dare say they will send out Dr. Leo Schapiro if this depression turns out to be an asteroid strike," Henry said.

"Yes, you're probably right. The man is a legend in these parts," Charlie said.

"What makes him a legend?" Tex asked.

"Well, it's a long story," Charlie replied.

"Go on...let's hear the story," Tex said.

"Huh, I don't know...let's eat first," Charlie said.

"You did well cooking this food, tonight," Tex said gulping down large mouthfuls of meat.

"Yeah, it tastes good."

"I agree with that."

"It was many years ago, now, when Dr. Leo Schapiro first arrived in Manaus. It wasn't long after he took his post at the local oil and mineral authority in the city because he wanted a quiet life after a divorce from his wife that he chose to take up a low-ranking position in the government with a significant drop in salary. Anyhow, only a few weeks into his new position early one morning, while crossing the city from his current home to his place of work during the early morning rush hour when he was shot at," Charlie said.

"Yeah, I remember the big news it made in the local papers," Slim said.

"You were working in Manaus back then?" Tex asked.

"Yeah, for my sins," Slim replied, smiling.

"What happened next?"

"There was what I describe as a gun battle in the middle of the rush hour traffic with people darting in every direction to avoid the bullets. Dr. Schapiro was carrying a gun because he had been warned by the police that a contract had been put on his head by a local gangster in San Paulo who was involved in a relationship with the doctor's wife. Apparently, Dr. Schapiro's ex-wife knew nothing about the contract her lover had put on her former husband," Charlie said.

"No shit..."

"Anyhow, bullets were flying in every direction in the middle of the city square near the port area. Luckily, Dr. Schapiro had done his national service and so was able to use his gun in an effective manner because he was against two armed assassins, who cared little for the public safety in the vicinity. Because the gun battle was during the early morning rush hour traffic...and you know what it's like on the roads at that hour every road was blocked leading to this city square and so the police couldn't get to the gun battle," Charlie said.

"What happened then?"

"Dr. Schapiro had killed one of the assassins and wounded the other before police arrived on the scene on foot and they continued the gun battle with the wounded assassin, who refused to surrender for nearly an hour before he was killed by the police. Dr. Schapiro was hailed a hero by the public nationwide and locally was seen as the same but also became something of a legend because of the many stories true or false that people told around Manaus," Charlie said.

"Yeah, the stories…the gossip flamed his legend status," Slim said.

"When the trial came to court more details of Dr. Schapiro's life came to light and the legend grew from there," Charlie said.

"You know the man well, is that true," Tex asked.

"Yes, I have known Leo since he moved to the area and I found him an unassuming man and of impeccable quality. He's the sort of man you would trust your life with and not prone to corruption, which as you know is rife in Brazil," Charlie said.

"Listen!"

"Did you hear that?"

"I think we all heard that…it's just some monkeys alerting the jungle that a predator is on the prowl. It's probably a panther nearby on the hunt," Henry said with a quirky smile.

"Just make sure we keep the fire burning all night to keep the panther away," Charlie said.

"Changing the subject, boss, what are our plans for, tomorrow?" Slim asked.

"As I said earlier, we have a lot of work to do, tomorrow. Before, we move out of the area and deeper into the jungle. We need to finalize our survey of this depression and interpret the results and then inform the company of what we have found. And it's essential that we take enough water with us, so that means boiling and storing sufficient water for our plans to succeed from the pool at the bottom of the depression," Charlie replied.

"Yeah, you're right, we need more water than we first anticipated," Slim said.

"Talking about, tomorrow…how do you feel Ben and Shelia with your first taste of the jungle?" Tex asked.

"So far so good," Ben replied.

"And you, Shelia?"

"Well, it's been an eye-opener, but I have enjoyed the experience so far. And now that we have found this depression, which could have been caused by an asteroid strike just adds to the excitement. Tomorrow, we could find the evidence that proves the depression was caused by an asteroid strike, which will make history around the world," Shelia replied.

"Yeah, it's not every day that you find an asteroid crater on land…if it turns out to be the case. If it wasn't for us surveying this region then the possible asteroid strike could have lay hidden for who knows how long if ever. We have the asteroid to thank for that pool of water, which we can exploit," Henry said.

"Hold on, we don't know if it was an asteroid strike that caused the depression, for sure. But we are lucky that pool of water exists, otherwise, we would be in deep shit," Slim said.

"How did we miss calculate the water supplies?" Henry asked.

"I don't know, but we did and we just have to deal with it," Charlie replied.

"If you are not acclimatized to the jungle conditions you can drink a lot more water than allowed for, but it's not their fault it's just the way things have panned out," Tex said.

"Are you referring to Shelia and me?" Ben asked.

"Yes, I am, but it's not your fault...it's just the way things are," Tex replied.

"Yes, don't blame them; you should blame me for not getting the correct water supplies needed for this expedition. I may be the boss, but even these days I make mistakes. But it's how you overcome mistakes that make the difference between success and failure. And I am determined to make this expedition a success and lead us all back to the safety of Manaus if it's the last thing I do. So, that means Tex for you to keep off the rum because we have a lot work to do, tomorrow," Charlie said.

"Will do, boss," Tex said.

***

The following morning, Ben and Shelia took to the arduous task of finding any more meteorites surrounding the depression. It was felt that any more meteorites would be buried too deep in the depression to be found because over thousands of years, the crater had the time to fill up with silt from yearly flooding of the area.

"I got a signal…a very strong signal," Shelia said.

"Good, let me start to dig and see what it reveals," Ben said.

"It's definitely metal because that's what the detector is showing, but I do not know what metal it is? It feels about a couple of grams or more in weight and as black as tar, but apart from that we will have to see what the other guys think, later," Ben said. Continuing, he added, "Let's continue our search, we have to find more to make our case for an asteroid strike."

"You believe it was an asteroid strike?" Shelia asked.

"I'm pretty certain it was an asteroid strike, but as scientists we need the proof, otherwise, we're just making assumptions," Ben replied, smiling.

"Yeah, you're right."

"It definitely looks like a meteorite, but I'm not an expert on meteorites. But, Charlie or someone else will know, for sure," Ben said.

"Did you hear that?"

"Yeah, it's probably just some birds or other creatures squawking as they do," Ben replied.

"I hope you're right."

"Don't worry, Shelia, I've got my gun handy. Do you have yours?" Ben asked.

"No, I forgot to bring it this morning it just slipped my mind."

"Well, that wasn't the best move you've made, especially, out here anything could happen, and the more guns the merrier," Ben said.

"Huh, yes I know."

"Good!"

"Don't say anything to Charlie or anyone else. Charlie would probably go ballistic about it, especially when he took the time to instruct us on what we should be doing in the jungle."

"I won't if you don't," Shelia said, smiling.

"The monkeys are making a lot of noise…there must be a predator on the prowl," Ben said. Continuing, he added, "Make sure you stay close to me."

"No shit, I will."

"Grab a large stick you can use just in case something comes close," Ben said.

"Anyhow, I'll clear some more ground and you can scan the area, we have a lot of work to do," Ben said.

"No worries."

***

Later that day, after several more hours of hard work they were able to find a couple more meteorites to show to the other scientists.

"It's hard to say what metal these meteorites are but it looks like Lithium from what I have seen in the past," Henry said. Continuing, he added, "But whatever they are it does prove an asteroid did make this depression."

"You really think so…"

"Yeah, it looks that way," Henry said.

"Let me see…"

"I think, Henry is right…they look like meteorites and it would be unusual to find this many meteorites in such a small area. And I am sure if you continued your search of the area you would find more," Charlie said.

"That's great and so exciting…"

"What does our seismic survey of the depression reveal, Henry?" Charlie asked.

"I've not finished analyzing the data, but early indications suggest a large rock sits at the bottom of the crater around one hundred and fifty feet below ground. I need to spend some time to figure out how big the rock is and if it's metal," Henry replied.

"If it is Lithium then it's like finding gold because that metal has become sort after since the popularity and advent of electric cars," Charlie said.

"Yeah, gram for gram it's on par with the price of gold," Tex said.

"If that rock below ground is pure Lithium then it could be worth a fortune, but we're here to find oil and gas deposits for our company not chase a possible rainbow," Charlie said.

"Changing the subject…what's on the menu, tonight?" Tex asked.

"Corn beef and rice…"

"I'm starving…let's eat," Tex said.

"Tomorrow, we need to finalize our survey of this area and then move deeper into the jungle the following day and continue our survey of the region," Charlie said.

"The mosquitoes are biting, tonight," Henry said.

"Here rub some of this cream around your neck it will keep the little bastards away," Slim said.

***

The following day, they finalized the survey around the depression and made ready to break camp the following morning and go deeper into the Amazon jungle. That evening, they discussed their plans for the trek deeper into the jungle.

"Another few more weeks of this and we will have done our job," Charlie said.

"We still have a sizable area of this region to survey," Henry said.

"We now have plenty of water supplies thanks to the efforts of Henry," Charlie said.

"Are you sure about the water supply?" Tex asked.

"Yes, we now have sufficient to see us through and back again to the river," Charlie said.

"What's on the menu, tonight?"

"I've sent out the Indians to hunt for some bush meat," Charlie said.

"Good, I'm starving," Tex exclaimed.

"You're always hungry, Tex…"

"Yeah, I know…I'm used to a good steak most nights back home in Texas…you can't beat it."

"You should try kangaroo steaks…it's one of the best steaks you'll experience," Shelia said.

"The trouble is it's so far away from Australia that it's a mission just to get there," Tex said, smiling.

"You should try and visit someday," Shelia said.

"Perhaps, one day I will," Tex said.

"They don't export Kangaroo meat then?" Slim asked.

"No, it's mainly for domestic consumption. I think people would find it strange to be eating Kangaroo meat in another country, such as our different cultures around the world," Shelia replied.

"They certainly wouldn't go for monkey meat anywhere else in the civilized world," Ben said. Continuing, he added, "Especially, in Britain they would be horrified at the prospect of eating monkey or even kangaroo meat."

"When you're hungry then you'll eat anything to stay alive and that includes cannibalism," Tex said.

"Yes, you're right, Tex…just about anything…"

"Tomorrow, I'll inform the company what we have found so far and make a claim with the authorities just in case this rock at the bottom of the crater is worth the hassle," Charlie said.

"If that is Lithium then it could be worth a lot of money in the current headlong rush for electric cars," Tex said.

"Especially, if it's mostly metal and not just rock then it would be worth mining," Henry said.

"That's hope someone else hasn't already made a claim. We heard those gunshots, which seem not too far away the other day," Tex said.

"Who do you think it was?"

"It could have been some local Indians in the area hunting for bush meat," Charlie said.

"Or illegal gold prospectors…"

"Whatever it was, we will soon find out," Charlie said.

"How's that…?"

"Well, the company should be able to tell me if someone else has made a claim or not," Charlie said.

"It could have been local Indians hunting for bush meat," Tex said.

"Yeah, that's a possibility, but normally the Indians won't travel this far away from their village to hunt," Charlie said.

"Talk of the devil…our Indians are back without any bush meat it seems…so its corn beef and rice again, tonight," Tex said.

"Someone put some more wood on the fire… it's cold, tonight," Charlie said.

"Yeah, no clouds, tonight…"

"Look!"

"The Milky Way in all its glory to see," Ben said.

"Let's eat…"

"That reminds me of the time I went hunting with two of my friends in Washington State last summer. It was cold that night and a clear sky. The three of us watched the Milky Way around our campfire and all of us started to wonder about what was out there. It was then that we all heard the sound of knocking…it wasn't the normal sounds you hear in the forest. It sounded as if someone was knocking on a wooden door. Then came the smell, it would be best described as the smell of shit, but an overpowering stench. Shortly after this smell came the roar of something I had never heard before in the forest or indeed my friends felt the same. It wasn't the sound of a bear, it was like a human roar than any animal I had heard before in the forest. It made us all stand up in shock at what was out there close to our camp. Then moments later, a rock the size of a baseball comes

196

flying across our camp at us. We fired several gunshots into the air and heard in the distance the sound of something moving fast through the forest. The following morning, we all had a good look around our camp around the forest and found foot marks on the ground and they were huge compared to ours. We took photos on our phones and saw no sight of the creature, but I always felt we were being watched some days on our hunt." Tex said.

"It was a Bigfoot then…"

"Yes, the Sasquatch as it is called in Washington State," Tex said.

Chapter 15

Leo Schapiro had lived all his life in Brazil and was born in São Paulo and studied at the prestigious university in the capital Brasília before moving to the backwater city of Manaus on the outskirts of the Amazon jungle. He had decided to take the job of working for the local government oil and resources department authority in Manaus after spending much of his career working for the São Paulo Department of Oil and Resources Authority as a leading geologist, but after a failed marriage which led to a near-death assault by an unknown assailant which had left him with a permanent scar on the right side of his face. With a bald head and a Roman nose, he looked younger than he was, but he suffered from back problems that restricted his mobility, although he could still do his job satisfactorily. The house he had bought was right on the perimeter of the city almost at the edge of the jungle, which he liked because it was quiet and secluded from the daily throng of traffic in the center of the jungle city.

Leo was now nearing retirement and had decided he would spend the rest of his days living in Manaus. With his small pension and the money he had saved over the years he knew he could live a comfortable life in Manaus where the cost of living was cheap compared to other parts of Brazil. He had decided he would pursue his love of fishing on the Negros River and Amazon River when he retired and let the world go by.

Sat in his office in downtown Manaus, he was reading the latest reports that were filtering through to his department at the oil and resources authority. He was excited at the news that a large depression had been found in the jungle and that he would have to investigate for the local government using the latest Lidar equipment. Lidar stood for 'Light Detection and Ranging' using laser pulses that reflect the light of an object or area to determine its shape and size by measuring the reflected beam of light and was used by the government to discover ground disturbance over a given region and likely geology. Any excuse to get out of the office and a chance to explore the jungle would be a good day, he said to himself.

"Hello, Enrique it's me Leo…get the Cessna ready we're taking a trip into the jungle. And have the Lidar onboard ready to use," Leo said.

"When are you planning to leave?" Enrique asked. Continuing, he added, "Oh, and where are we going?"

"Around two hundred kilometers up the river," Leo said.

"Okay, will do," Enrique said.

"As soon as possible…so make sure it's fully fueled with supplies. I will give you the exact coordinates when I see you later," Leo said.

"You will have to leave a flight path with the tower," Enrique said.

"No problem…will do when I arrive. Just make sure the airplane is all clear for takeoff. Expect me there within the hour. Is that understood?" Leo asked.

It was only a short drive across the city to the airport as Leo was able to avoid most of the traffic by using the back roads across the city. He knew the city like the back of his hand and enjoyed using his knowledge of the city's roads to avoid many of the daily traffic jams in the city. He had a ready 'go bag' in the office with binoculars and a chart of the Amazon jungle and other essential items just in case they crashed in the jungle.

"Okay, Enrique let's go," Leo said as the plane slowly taxied to the runway and began its takeoff from the airport.

"Why in so much of a hurry?" Enrique asked as the Cessna climbed to a cruising altitude of around 1000 feet and both men relaxed into their journey.

Laughing, Leo shouted, "I'm in no hurry."

"No hurry, just thought conditions are good…with blue skies in all directions. And I needed to get out of the office. You should know by now, any excuse to get out of the office and into the field and it's a good day for me," Leo replied.

"Yeah, that's okay with me," Enrique shouted out over the noise of the Cessna's engine, which was roaring away and a constant reminder of how difficult it was to have a conversation in the cockpit. Enrique worked for the local government serving several departments when they needed aerial support for surveying and wildfire control.

"How long before we get there?"

"About two hours…we will follow the river and then bear right nearer the target region."

"Hmm, yeah…"

"What are we looking for?" Enrique asked.

"An area in the jungle with a large depression…we will not be able to see much without the Lidar to find it," Leo replied. Continuing, he added, "A group of oil explorers found the depression and I need to know how big it is. The Lidar may reveal a lot more…we will see," Leo replied.

"What caused the depression?" Enrique asked.

"Asteroid…"

"Really…"

"Most likely an asteroid strike…but until I get the data from the Lidar survey I won't know for sure," Leo replied. Continuing, he added, "The oil explorers seemed to think so…they found a meteorite in the area, but I still need to know for sure, there could be a deposit of rare metals from the asteroid."

"Do you mean gold?" Enrique asked in excitement.

"Yes, that's possible, but I think more likely something like Lithium, for example," Leo replied.

"Oh, I see."

"Hopefully, some rare earth metals would be a good result, but whatever I need to know for the government," Leo said.

"I hope it's gold!"

"I hope not, because as soon as you mention gold everyone and their granny will be out here looking for it and we'll get no peace," Leo said.

As the Cessna banked right from the Amazon River and dropped to around 500 feet above the jungle canopy. Soon Enrique and Leo were over the selected area guided by the coordinates provided by the oil explorers.

"We are over the area from the coordinates you gave me," Enrique said.

"Start circling the area and let the Lidar do its job," Leo said.

"I don't see any depression from up here."

"You won't…"

"Okay…"

"Just keep circling the area…over a wide area," Leo said

"Okay, will do."

"As I said before, you won't see anything from up here; it's only the Lidar that will be able to scan for depression. When I get the data back to my office I will then be able to check the information," Leo said.

"How many circles of the area do you want?" Enrique asked.

"Go around another time just to make sure we have covered the region for sure," Leo said. Continuing, he added, "Sweep lower, and bank right, I want to see if I can get a picture of the forest distribution, to see if I can see the formation of the forest canopy. I want to take some photos of the area," Leo replied.

"Okay, will do."

"Now, take this bird home," Leo said.

"How long will it take before you know for sure there is a depression?" Enrique asked.

"Later today, I will be able to scan the Lidar data and access the information," Leo replied. Continuing, he added, "Why do you ask?"

"Oh, just interested, that's all," Enrique said.

"Well, don't be…just keep your mind on flying this bird home," Leo said.

"Yes, boss."

"Keep what you have learned to yourself, otherwise, you risk losing your job," Leo said intently.

"I was just making conversation, that's all," Enrique said.

"Yes, yes…but you got excited when I mentioned gold deposits, which may not be true," Leo said intently.

"Oh, no…just interested, that's all," Enrique said.

"Well, don't be…because you could start rumors and make it dangerous for the scientists who are working in the area. We don't want a gold rush to take hold, which could threaten your life and mine," Leo said intently.

"Really! I don't believe…"

"I remember, hearing about a gold prospector who went missing around two years ago now in these parts. His name was Charlie Watkins a middle-aged man and was well known around Manaus for his exploits into the Amazon jungle searching for gold."

"What happened to him?" Enrique asked intensely.

"We're not sure, that is the local authorities are not sure."

"Oh, I see…"

"Charlie Watkins was a man well experienced in surviving in the jungle, so it was no surprise the man went into the jungle near the region we have been in today in the search for gold all alone," Leo said.

"I think, I have heard of the man. Didn't he live somewhere near the port area in Manaus," Enrique said. Continuing, he added, "Why are you telling me this?"

"Because when people talk about gold they get caught in the lure of gold and end up pursuing it until it consumes them or they find gold. But, most of the time people never find gold and end up losing everything they possess and their lives. It's like cancer that eats away and can take over a person and all common sense in some people. It's greed that some will stop at nothing to possess it. It's a curse of the treasure seeker who then gives up everything in pursuit of finding riches beyond their wildest dreams. I'm telling you this story because some people are just greedy and they are never satisfied with what they already have. This happens every day to some people who are just dreamers and never achieve anything and so look for the quick fix of finding treasure like gold," Leo said philosophically.

"Yes, I know this."

"Anyhow, Charlie Watkins had been told or had heard a story about a small stream that fed into the Amazon River and that there was gold to be found nearby. Who had told Charlie this story I don't know, but whoever it was probably caused the man to lose his life. It was in the same area we have been surveying earlier today," Leo said.

"What happened?"

"He was never seen again," Leo said shrugging his shoulders.

"Why what happened to him?" Enrique asked.

"As I said, he was never seen again. Sometime later, some indigenous Indians found his camp and belongings in the jungle near a stream and reported it to the authorities in Manaus, then a search was conducted in the area for the man, but he wasn't found. They searched for days for the man, but never found a trace of the man or any signs of gold. And to this day not a sight of this man has ever been reported. He completely vanished. No bones or clothing was ever found, so the authorities eventually gave up and police decided to declare the man as a missing person and that was how it was dealt with." Leo said.

"Okay, boss!"

"Yes, yes…just keep your mouth shut, otherwise, you risk lives…and I will know where the information came from," Leo said. Continuing, he added, "And stop…asking so many questions!"

"Of course, I will."

"Follow the river back home…it's the easiest course back to Manaus," Leo said.

"I was just about to bank left…and follow the river."

"Good, and keep your mind on flying and not on gold."

"It will take another hour before we see the city," Enrique said intently.

"It will be early evening before we arrive back," Leo said.

"Tomorrow, I'm working for the fire department looking for wildfires, so I will be busy with that for the day," Enrique said.

"Good, keep busy and forget about what I said about possible rare metals being found, and don't mention to anyone about gold," Leo said.

"Yes, boss will do."

***

Later that day, Leo began the task of downloading the data from the removable hard drive from the Lidar equipment back at his office in Manaus. As Leo started to analyze the data on his computer system he soon saw the outline of the depression found in the jungle. The shape of the depression was like that of an egg, which had all hallmarks of an asteroid strike, it was about two hundred feet in length and around one hundred and fifty feet across at its widest point. The depth of the crater was around thirty feet at its lowest point, but Leo recognized its depth would have been a lot deeper, but over the thousands of years since it struck earth the crater would have been filled up due to floods. He recognized that it would take the skills of an astrophysics scientist to work out the size of the asteroid strike and the angle it hit Earth and when that may have happened. For now, he was only concerned with making a report on his findings so that further investigations could be done at a later date if necessary. He decided he would keep the possibility of rare earth metals deposits being found secret until he had further proof. He didn't want a stampede of treasure seekers racing to the region, just in case there was gold to be found in the area. He realized the local indigenous tribes would not be pleased to see hordes of prospectors overrunning the region and it may end in conflict between the two groups. He didn't want to see any loss of life on his account because of some careless words by him about rare earth minerals in his report. He thought about Enrique and hoped he could keep his mouth shut, he said to himself. Just then, his phone was ringing, which was odd because it was after office hours and he had been working late and not expecting any calls, he said to himself.

"Hello."

"Hello, is that Leo?"

"Yes, who is it calling?"

"It's Benny from the Manaus Daily."

"I understand, that you found an asteroid crater out in the jungle, is that correct?" Benny asked.

"Yes, who told you?" Leo asked.

"The oil company…they said that you had been surveying the area, today," Benny replied.

"Oh, I see…what do you want from me?"

"A story…is it an asteroid strike and when did it hit?" Benny asked.

"Yes, early indications suggest an asteroid hit the region many thousands of years ago. When it hit earth will need further investigation to determine the exact timing and that's not my job that will be someone else who decides that," Leo stressed.

"How big is the crater?" Benny asked.

"It's around one hundred and fifty feet in diameter and around thirty feet deep," Leo replied.

"Not very deep for an asteroid strike, is it?" Benny asked.

"No, you're right but don't forget it's had thousands of years to fill up from floods, so what you see now is the last remnants of the strike," Leo replied.

"I understand, that a Lithium meteorite was found in the area of the crater, is that right?" Benny asked.

"Yes, who told you that?" Leo asked.

"Again the oil company, I have a person on the inside feeding me information. Have you found out anything else, today?" Benny asked.

"Well, it looks like you don't need my assistance you have plenty of sources for your newspaper story," Leo replied.

"Did you find out anything else?" Benny asked again.

"No, that's it…it will take an astrophysics scientist to work out the ins and outs of how big the asteroid was and when it happened," Leo replied.

"Oh, okay Leo thanks for your help," Benny said and hung up the call.

***

The following morning, Leo was in his office reading the story in the newspaper Benny had written about the asteroid strike. He had also heard the news broadcast on the local radio about the asteroid strike and wondered how far the story would travel. He wasn't expecting any further calls about the matter when his phone started to ring.

***

Meanwhile, Dr. Isabella Garcia and Dr. Joseph Goldstein were at Home in Sonora, California listening to the TV news broadcast about a possible asteroid strike, which they were told occurred in the recent past.

"A group of scientists has found a large depression on the surface in the Amazon jungle. They were using Lidar technology data that suggested an unnatural depression on the ground in the jungle. The size is huge, with a diameter of around two hundred meters. It's a crater from an asteroid strike," Dr. Joseph Goldstein said.

"When did it happen?" asked Dr. Isabella Garcia.

"That's currently being assessed, but early indications suggest around twelve thousand years ago," said Joe emphatically.

The meteorite had been on a collision course for Earth the day it was flung out from the orb cloud and on its orbit to the sun. It was only a matter of time before the two would collide, and was it twelve thousand years ago? That was the question Dr. Isabella Garcia would ask herself. Could it be the evidence she had been searching for?

Most of the evidence of meteorite strikes were in the sea and had washed away with sea currents and the scientific community had previously had the wrong idea on the number of substantial collisions that had occurred in the past. New evidence using Lidar-type equipment and other techniques that a pattern of strikes could be mapped out and a predictive frequency generated based on this new information. The data showed that Earth had been hit more often than previously thought, in fact, a lot more often and this caused alarm bells to ring in her ears. The thought of the earth having only a few months to do something about a collision was deeply disturbing to her. But, the scientists hadn't explained to the general public their misgivings because they had only considered an asteroid before and not a comet from the orb cloud and potentially a lot more difficult to deal with. What would the world do to avoid such a catastrophe, she said to herself? If there were only four months we were doomed as a species. The world would go back to the Stone Age. But, mankind was riding strange horses that were close to the wind of destruction at the time.

"Wow! That is amazing." Isabella said excitedly.

"Yes, it is. And another thing the location is an ideal spot to cause the possibility of a polar shift. It would all depend on the angle of the path of the Asteroid. At the right angle, it could tilt the earth and make it wobble enough to cause major land masses to go up and down like a sea wave.

210

It's happened before, but whether this strike caused a polar shift around twelve thousand years ago, is up for further study and debate. Your idea that a polar shift may have occurred sometime around twelve thousand years ago could be plausible now that they have found the first evidence to support your theory," Joe said succinctly.

"It's only a theory. I haven't proved anything yet. But, you are right. This is the first piece of evidence that I have been searching for," Isabella said, excitedly.

The area the scientists wanted to survey would take several days perhaps weeks to get to such was the distance from the river. There were no roads or tracks they could use they would have to cut their way through the jungle vegetation with machetes. The task was made harder because of the heat and humidity and every foot forward drained the strength of everyone in the party, including the hired help used to ferry their supplies and cut their way through the jungle.

Dehydration became an issue because of the lack of sufficient water and predators also became an issue, especially at night.

***

Finally, after many days of hacking their way through the jungle, they arrived at their designation. They could begin their survey for oil deposits. They soon realized there was a large depression in the ground.

"All indications suggest an area around two hundred meters in diameter," Ben said.

"You can see from the radiographs the shape of the depression…like the formation of a crater. Could it be an asteroid strike?" Shelia asked.

"We'll have to see what the other scientists think," Ben replied.

The following day, Ben and Shelia began their search for meteorites around the perimeter of the depression. It was hard work using the metal detector, in the dense vegetation because there was limited space to swing the metal detector over and around the mass of vegetation.

"Look."

"It's a clear night…I can see the Orion constellation."

"It's a beautiful sight."

"Yes, it is."

"It was the ancient Babylonians who invented the zodiac."

"Why did they invent the zodiac?"

"It was invented to give hope to the population at that time. It was a kind of fortune teller. People could see if the gods would favor them. I also think it was invented to tell what time of the year it was."

"Out here we can see what they saw in the night sky…the glory of the Milky Way."

"It was also a means to navigate oceans at night."

"They were great astrologers and astronomers and could accurately predict the motion of the planets."

"With limited technology, you have to wonder how they managed to accurately plot the movement of the planets so successfully," Shelia said.

"It's one of the mysteries of our ancient ancestors…they were smarter than we are led to believe," Charlie said.

"What's on the menu, tonight?" Tex asked.

"We have some monkey meat and rice to fill your bellies," Charlie replied.

"What are your plans for, tomorrow, Charlie?" Tex asked.

"Get out the seismic charges and get some data, while Ben and Shelia continue to look for meteorites. We have a large area to cover, which will take several days to complete. And then we move camp and continue with our survey of the region. Don't forget we're here to find oil deposits and minerals, so we have a lot of work to do. When we are sure this depression was caused by an asteroid then I will contact base and inform them of what we have found. The company will then need to inform the local authorities in Manaus," Charlie replied.

"I guess, they will send out someone to investigate the depression at some stage, but by then we will have moved on to another area of the jungle," Henry said.

"Yeah, most likely," Charlie muttered.

"Did you hear that...gunshot," Tex said.

"Yeah, unmistakable...there must be local Indians in the area searching for bush meat. It sounded like it was many miles away and shouldn't bother us here," Charlie said.

"Is that meat cooked, yet?"

"Not long to go...should be ready in a few minutes," Tex replied.

"Hey, Charlie you never said what happened to the caretaker when he turned up in Manaus?" Slim asked.

"I thought, I did," Charlie replied.

"No, you said he mentioned the pool of water in the depression, but you never followed it up, is that right?" Slim asked.

"Yeah, you're right, I never did...I must have forgotten. Well, I made a mistake and at the time was busy with other things, so the information from the caretaker got lost in the moment. And to be honest, I didn't believe everything the man was telling me. So I made no further enquiring on the matter, which was my mistake. And I wasn't sure where the caretaker had been in the jungle, so it was easy to forget," Charlie replied.

"I dare say they will send out Dr. Leo Schapiro if this depression turns out to be an asteroid strike," Henry said.

"Yes, you're probably right. The man is a legend in these parts," Charlie said.

"What makes him a legend?" Tex asked.

"Well, it's a long story," Charlie replied.

"Go on…let's hear the story," Tex said.

"Huh, I don't know…let's eat first," Charlie said.

"You did well cooking this food, tonight," Tex said gulping down large mouthfuls of meat.

"Yeah, it tastes good."

"I agree with that."

"It was many years ago, now, when Dr. Leo Schapiro first arrived in Manaus. It wasn't long after he took his post at the local oil and mineral authority in the city because he wanted a quiet life after a divorce from his wife that he chose to take up a low-ranking position in the government with a significant drop in salary. Anyhow, only a few weeks into his new position early one morning, while crossing the city from his current home to his place of work during the early morning rush hour when he was shot at," Charlie said.

"Yeah, I remember the big news it made in the local papers," Slim said.

"You were working in Manaus back then?" Tex asked.

"Yeah, for my sins," Slim replied, smiling.

"What happened next?"

"There was what I describe as a gun battle in the middle of the rush hour traffic with people darting in every direction to avoid the bullets. Dr. Schapiro was carrying a gun because he had been warned by the police that a contract had been put on his head by a local gangster in San Paulo who was involved in a relationship with the doctor's wife. Apparently, Dr. Schapiro's ex-wife knew nothing about the contract her lover had put on her former husband," Charlie said.

"No shit…"

"Anyhow, bullets were flying in every direction in the middle of the city square near the port area. Luckily, Dr. Schapiro had done his national service and so was able to use his gun in an effective manner because he was against two armed assassins, who cared little for the public safety in the vicinity. Because the gun battle was during the early morning rush hour traffic…and you know what it's like on the roads at that hour every road was blocked leading to this city square and so the police couldn't get to the gun battle," Charlie said.

"What happened then?"

"Dr. Schapiro had killed one of the assassins and wounded the other before police arrived on the scene on foot and they continued the gun battle with the wounded assassin, who refused to surrender for nearly an hour before he was killed by the police. Dr. Schapiro was hailed a hero by the public nationwide and locally was seen as the same but also became something of a legend because of the many stories true or false that people told around Manaus," Charlie said.

"Yeah, the stories…the gossip flamed his legend status," Slim said.

"When the trial came to court more details of Dr. Schapiro's life came to light and the legend grew from there," Charlie said.

"You know the man well, is that true," Tex asked.

"Yes, I have known Leo since he moved to the area and I found him an unassuming man and of impeccable quality. He's the sort of man you would trust your life with and not prone to corruption, which as you know is rife in Brazil," Charlie said.

"Listen!"

"Did you hear that?"

"I think we all heard that…it's just some monkeys alerting the jungle that a predator is on the prowl. It's probably a panther nearby on the hunt," Henry said with a quirky smile.

"Just make sure we keep the fire burning all night to keep the panther away," Charlie said.

"Changing the subject, boss, what are our plans for, tomorrow?" Slim asked.

"As I said earlier, we have a lot of work to do, tomorrow. Before, we move out of the area and deeper into the jungle. We need to finalize our survey of this depression and interpret the results and then inform the company of what we have found. And it's essential that we take enough water with us, so that means boiling and storing sufficient water for our plans to succeed from the pool at the bottom of the depression," Charlie replied.

"Yeah, you're right, we need more water than we first anticipated," Slim said.

"Talking about, tomorrow…how do you feel Ben and Shelia with your first taste of the jungle?" Tex asked.

"So far so good," Ben replied.

"And you, Shelia?"

"Well, it's been an eye-opener, but I have enjoyed the experience so far. And now that we have found this depression, which could have been caused by an asteroid strike just adds to the excitement. Tomorrow, we could find the evidence that proves the depression was caused by an asteroid strike, which will make history around the world," Shelia replied.

"Yeah, it's not every day that you find an asteroid crater on land…if it turns out to be the case. If it wasn't for us surveying this region then the possible asteroid strike could have lay hidden for who knows how long if ever. We have the asteroid to thank for that pool of water, which we can exploit," Henry said.

"Hold on, we don't know if it was an asteroid strike that caused the depression, for sure. But we are lucky that pool of water exists, otherwise, we would be in deep shit," Slim said.

"How did we miss calculate the water supplies?" Henry asked.

"I don't know, but we did and we just have to deal with it," Charlie replied.

"If you are not acclimatized to the jungle conditions you can drink a lot more water than allowed for, but it's not their fault it's just the way things have panned out," Tex said.

"Are you referring to Shelia and me?" Ben asked.

"Yes, I am, but it's not your fault...it's just the way things are," Tex replied.

"Yes, don't blame them; you should blame me for not getting the correct water supplies needed for this expedition. I may be the boss, but even these days I make mistakes. But it's how you overcome mistakes that make the difference between success and failure. And I am determined to make this expedition a success and lead us all back to the safety of Manaus if it's the last thing I do. So, that means Tex for you to keep off the rum because we have a lot work to do, tomorrow," Charlie said.

"Will do, boss," Tex said.

***

The following morning, Ben and Shelia took to the arduous task of finding any more meteorites surrounding the depression. It was felt that any meteorites would be buried too deep in the depression to be found because, over thousands of years, the crater has had the time to fill up with silt from flooding in the area.

"I got a signal...a very strong signal," Shelia said.

"Good, let me start to dig and see what it reveals," Ben said.

"It's definitely metal because that's what the detector is showing, but I do not know what metal it is? It feels about a couple of grams or more in weight and as black as tar, but apart from that we will have to see what the other guys think, later," Ben said. Continuing, he added, "Let's continue our search, we have to find more to make our case for an asteroid strike."

"You believe it was an asteroid strike?" Shelia asked.

"I'm pretty certain it was an asteroid strike, but as scientists we need the proof, otherwise, we're just making assumptions," Ben replied, smiling.

"Yeah, you're right."

"It definitely looks like a meteorite, but I'm not an expert on meteorites. But, Charlie or someone else will know, for sure," Ben said.

"Did you hear that?"

"Yeah, it's probably just some birds or other creatures squawking as they do," Ben replied.

"I hope you're right."

"Don't worry, Shelia, I've got my gun handy. Do you have yours?" Ben asked.

"No, I forgot to bring it this morning it just slipped my mind."

"Well, that wasn't the best move you've made, especially, out here anything could happen, and the more guns the merrier," Ben said.

"Huh, yes I know."

"Good!"

"Don't say anything to Charlie or anyone else. Charlie would probably go ballistic about it, especially when he took the time to instruct us on what we should be doing in the jungle.

"I won't if you don't," Shelia said, smiling.

"The monkeys are making a lot of noise…there must be a predator on the prowl," Ben said. Continuing, he added, "Make sure you stay close to me."

"No shit, I will."

"Grab a large stick you can use just in case something comes close," Ben said.

"Anyhow, I'll clear some more ground and you can scan the area, we have a lot of work to do," Ben said.

"No worries."

***

Later that day, after several more hours of hard work they were unable to find any more meteorites to show to the other scientists.

"It's hard to say what metal these meteorites are but it looks like Lithium from what I have seen in the past," Henry said. Continuing, he added, "But whatever they are it does prove an asteroid did make this depression."

"You really think so…"

"Yeah, it looks that way," Henry said.

"Let me see…"

"I think, Henry is right…they look like meteorites and it would be unusual to find these two meteorites in such a small area. And I am sure if you continued your search of the area you would find maybe more," Charlie said.

"That's great and so exciting…"

"What does our seismic survey of the depression reveal, Henry?" Charlie asked.

"I've not finished analyzing the data, but early indications suggest a large rock sits at the bottom of the crater around one hundred and fifty feet below ground. I need to spend some time to figure out how big the rock is and if it's metal," Henry replied.

"If it is Lithium then it's like finding gold because that metal has become sort after since the popularity and advent of electric cars," Charlie said.

"Yeah, gram for gram it's on par with the price of gold," Tex said.

"If that rock below ground is pure Lithium then it could be worth a fortune, but we're here to find oil and gas deposits for our company not chase a possible rainbow," Charlie said.

"Changing the subject…what's on the menu, tonight?" Tex asked.

"Corn beef and rice…"

"I'm starving…let's eat," Tex said.

"Tomorrow, we need to finalize our survey of this area and then move deeper into the jungle the following day and continue our survey of the region," Charlie said.

"The mosquitoes are biting, tonight," Henry said.

"Here rub some of this cream around your neck it will keep the little bastards away," Slim said.

***

The following day, they finalized the survey around the depression and made ready to break camp the following morning and go deeper into the Amazon jungle. That evening, they discussed their plans for the trek deeper into the jungle.

"Another few more weeks of this and we will have done our job," Charlie said.

"We still have a sizable area of this region to survey," Henry said.

"We now have plenty of water supplies thanks to the efforts of Henry," Charlie said.

"Are you sure about the water supply?" Tex asked.

"Yes, we now have sufficient to see us through and back again to the river," Charlie said.

"What's on the menu, tonight?"

"I've sent out the Indians to hunt for some bush meat," Charlie said.

"Good, I'm starving," Tex exclaimed.

"You're always hungry, Tex…"

"Yeah, I know…I'm used to a good steak most nights back home in Texas…you can't beat it," Tex said.

"You should try kangaroo steaks…it's one of the best steaks you'll experience," Shelia said.

"The trouble is it's so far away from Australia that it's a mission just to get there," Tex said, smiling.

"You should try and visit someday," Shelia said.

"Perhaps, one day I will," Tex said.

"They don't export Kangaroo meat then?" Slim asked.

"No, it's mainly for domestic consumption. I think people would find it strange to be eating Kangaroo meat in another country, such as our different cultures around the world," Shelia replied.

"They certainly wouldn't go for monkey meat anywhere else in the civilized world," Ben said. Continuing, he added, "Especially, in Britain they would be horrified at the prospect of eating monkey or even kangaroo meat."

"When you're hungry then you'll eat anything to stay alive and that includes cannibalism," Tex said.

"Yes, you're right, Tex…just about anything…"

"Tomorrow, I'll inform the company what we have found so far and make a claim with the authorities just in case this rock at the bottom of the crater is worth the hassle," Charlie said.

"If that is Lithium then it could be worth a lot of money in the current headlong rush for electric cars," Tex said.

"Especially, if it's mostly metal and not just rock then it would be worth mining," Henry said.

"That's hope someone else hasn't already made a claim. We heard those gunshots, which seem not too far away the other day," Tex said.

"Who do you think it was?"

"It could have been some local Indians in the area hunting for bush meat," Charlie said.

"Or illegal gold prospectors…"

"Whatever it was, we will soon find out," Charlie said.

"How's that…?"

"Well, the company should be able to tell me if someone else has made a claim or not," Charlie said.

"It could have been local Indians hunting for bush meat," Tex said.

"Yeah, that's a possibility, but normally the Indians won't travel this far away from their village to hunt," Charlie said.

"Talk of the devil…our Indians are back without any bush meat it seems…so its corn beef and rice again, tonight," Tex said.

"Someone put some more wood on the fire… it's cold, tonight," Charlie said.

"Yeah, no clouds, tonight…"

"Look!"

"The Milky Way in all its glory to see," Ben said.

"Let's eat…"

"That reminds me of the time I went hunting with two of my friends in Washington State last summer. It was cold that night and a clear sky. The three of us watched the Milky Way around our campfire and all of us started to wonder about what was out there. It was then that we all heard the sound of knocking…it wasn't the normal sounds you hear in the forest. It sounded as if someone was knocking on a wooden door. Then came the smell, it would be best described as the smell of shit, but an overpowering stench. Shortly after this smell came the roar of something I had never heard before in the forest or indeed my friends felt the same. It wasn't the sound of a bear, it was like a human roar than any animal I had heard before in the forest. It made us all stand up in shock at what was out there close to our camp. Then moments later, a rock the size of a baseball comes flying across our camp at us. We fired several gunshots into the air and heard in the distance the sound of something moving fast through the forest. The following morning, we all had a good look around our camp around the forest and found footmarks on the ground and they were huge compared to ours. We took photos on our phones and saw no sight of the creature, but I always felt we were being watched some days on our hunt." Tex said.

"It was a Bigfoot then…"

"Yes, the Sasquatch as it is called in Washington State," Tex said.

***

"You need to get out there…and have a look for yourself, Isabella," said Joe.

"Nah, no, no! I'll wait for the data to be published before I step into a mosquito-infested jungle. And God knows what else," said Isabella, smiling.

"What other news do you have?

"Are they sure it isn't a man-made depression…such as an ancient open mine?" Isabella asked curiously.

"No, it was a direct hit made by an asteroid…they found a couple of meteorites as proof of an asteroid strike. That's for sure. That strike could have caused the flood talked about in the Bible. And that has many scholars say it occurred around twelve thousand years ago. The two events could now be tied together like a knot. But not only, the

'Great Flood', but the possibility of a polar shift, as well. You were right about your theory, perhaps!" said Joe.

"Well, I'm not sure about that…it was only a few anomalies that didn't stack up. And the mainstream consensus had refused to accept these anomalies had even happened. Such were the blindfolds being used. So it became an interesting scientific endeavor…and one I fully accepted as an approach worth the time involved," said Isabella, who was happy the evidence had started to surface for the public to be aware of.

Her mind had drifted back to her time at university arguing with students and sometimes teachers concerning Darwin's theory of evolution. She remembered her debates concerning her concerns about childbirth and why so many women would die from this basic evolutionary necessity. It didn't stack up in her view why so many women would die in the course of giving birth. Wouldn't evolution have found a way to remedy this problem, she had said to herself? And of course, was one of the anomalies in Darwin's theory of evolution. Natural selection would have found a way over the eons of time. If you observe other animals on the Savannah they don't have the same problem, she said to herself. We evolved at the same time as other animals. Now, why is this? These and other anomalies were often discussed in her days at university, she said to herself.

"What do you plan to do, now that you have the proof you were looking for?" Joe asked.

"I haven't got that far. I'm accessing the information. I still need to do some more research. Perhaps find more proof. I'm not sure…it's a lot to take in…in. But I'm on top of the world with this new information…evidence." Isabella replied emphatically.

"What research?"

"There's plenty to find…I've started to construct a timeline of events and the evidence…hopefully, I will have a clearer picture of what may have happened in the recent past. If I can prove a polar shift did happen then I would have proved the theory," Isabella said emphatically.

***

"Hello."

"Is that Dr. Leonardo Schapiro?"

"Yes, who's calling?"

"My name is Joseph Goldstein. I would like to talk to you about the asteroid strike," Joe said.

"Where are you from?" Leo asked.

"Sorry, I should have explained. I'm from here in the United States California. My girlfriend and I are very interested in the crater that you found in the jungle," Joe said.

"What do you want to know…all the information is already in the newspaper and by all accounts around the world?"

"Yes, it's a big story around the world…it's not every day you find a previously undiscovered asteroid crater on Earth's surface," Joe replied. Continuing, he added, "My girlfriend and I would like to come and see the crater and analyze your data…we would pay all your expenses. Would that be okay with you?" Joe asked.

"Oh, I'm not sure, I'm very busy at the moment," Leo stressed.

"I'm an astrophysicist and would like to work out when the asteroid hit and how big it was and at what angle it hit Earth. We could be there within the next few days, is that okay?" Joe asked.

"Oh, I'm not sure," Leo replied.

"Please, Dr. Schapiro it would mean so much to us."

"Yes, okay…but I must ask that you keep what you find out private until an official investigation is conducted by our local government department, is that okay with you?" Leo asked.

"Yes, that's fine with us. When would a local government investigation take place?"

"I don't know, probably not for some time if ever that's how things are done here. I could do with new computer systems, but that was two years ago when I first put in a request. So you see how it is here," Leo replied.

"Yes, I see what you mean. Well, we will see you in a few days' time and we will look forward to meeting with you, bye for now. Oh, and thank you so much," Joe said and hung up the call.

***

Later that day, in Los Angles, Californian at Isabella's home, Isabella and Joe were discussing Joe's conversation with Dr. Leo Schapiro. Joe explained to Isabella how reluctant the doctor was initially with their request to visit the site of the asteroid crater. Joe explained to Isabella that they would pay for all the expenses incurred by their visit to the crater and this seemed to have swayed the doctor in letting them visit.

"Will you have to let the FBI know you are leaving the country?" Isabella asked.

Shrugging his shoulders, Joe said, "They didn't say I couldn't leave the States," Joe replied.

"Perhaps, you should tell them before we leave," Isabella said.

"Nada, I don't plan to do so, because I haven't done anything wrong, so why should I have to tell them what I'm up to."

"Are you sure?"

"Besides, we will only be gone a few days at most," Joe said dismissively.

"Oh, okay it's up to you."

"I will work out our flights to Brazil and get them booked for tomorrow or the day after. Then it's just the connecting flight to Manaus we have to schedule in," Joe said.

"Manaus, where is that?" Isabella asked.

"It's right on the east coast of Brazil in the heart of the Amazon jungle on the Amazon River delta," Joe replied.

"Is that where Dr. Schapiro lives?" Isabella asked.

"Yes, where he lives and works, but the asteroid crater is miles away up the Amazon River and deep in the jungle," Joe replied.

"It says on the Internet that the crater was found using Lidar technology…will we be able to use the doctor's data to figure out when it hit the earth or will you need to gather other information?" Isabella asked.

"I will be able to figure out the size of the asteroid and at what angle it hit Earth most likely from Dr. Schapiro's Lidar data, but when it hit Earth is another matter," Joe replied.

"Does that mean a trek into the jungle at some point?" Isabella asked.

"Yeah, you know it goes, how else, can I tell when the asteroid hit the Earth? So be prepared for a trip into the jungle when we get there and take plenty of insect repellant," Joe replied, smiling.

"I hate the thought of getting attacked by mosquitoes and other nasty insects," Isabella said.

"That's not all you have to worry about in the jungle... there are all the other predators to worry about. But don't worry, we'll take precautions out there," Joe said.

"Oh, okay."

"We won't be going into the jungle alone, we will take a guide who knows what they are doing, which will keep us safe," Joe said.

"I hope you're right."

"Dr. Schapiro will know the right people to advise us, so don't worry, we will enjoy the adventure. How often do you get a chance to see a previously undiscovered asteroid crater?" Joe asked.

Chapter 16

Two days later, Isabella and Joe were on a flight from LAX, California to São Paulo, Brazil and then on a connecting flight to Manaus in the heart of the Amazon jungle. During their flight, they discussed what they hoped to achieve in Brazil. Manaus was situated 900 miles west of the Atlantic Ocean, along the northern bank of the Negro River, which flows into the Amazon River. Manaus lies 200 miles south of the equator in the southern hemisphere. They were both excited about the adventure they were about to start. As their airplane began its descent below the clouds they could see the green carpet of jungle forest, which was in view to the horizon.

"If this asteroid strike was big enough, then it could help validate my theory," Isabella said.

"Yes, it's in the right place near the equator to have been pivotal to your theory. It all depends on the size of the asteroid and the angle it hit the Earth. I will have to determine if that was the case, either way, we will have an adventure and find out for sure," Joe said.

"Did you let Dr. Schapiro know when to expect us?" Isabella asked.

"Would you like a drink?" the air stewardess asked.

"Yes, a glass of orange juice, please," Isabella replied.

"And would you like a drink, sir?"

"Yes, please rum and coke cola," Joe replied.

As the airplane landed in Manaus airport and Isabella and Joe disembarked and went through customs they soon felt the heat of the midday sun as they waited outside the terminal building for a taxi to take them to their hotel. On the short journey to the airport hotel inside the old Ford sedan taxi, they felt the sweat on their bodies in the humid air as they tried to adjust to the hot and sticky climate. After settling into their hotel room on the fourth floor they decided to change and take a shower before their meeting with Dr. Schapiro at his office.

***

"Hi, Dr. Schapiro this is my girlfriend, Dr. Isabella Garcia," Joe said.

"Glad to meet you both, did you have a pleasant journey here?" Dr. Schapiro asked.

"Yes, it's a tiresome journey, but it was okay," Joe replied.

"Yes, fine, do you mind if we use first names?" Isabella asked.

"Yes, that's fine, I was going to suggest that myself, it saves a lot of fuss," Leo replied. Continuing, he added, "Where are you staying?"

"At the airport hotel, it has a nice view of the city."

"It's about the only high-rise building in the city; most of the buildings in the city go back to the colonial days like this one when the Portuguese ran the place. Beautiful architecture with its arched windows, doorways, and cornices like this one, but many need restoration," Leo said.

"Well, let's get down to business and analyze the Lidar data, I've been itching to see the data since I first read about your find. I've also brought my laptop with some sophisticated software that can refine what you have," Joe said.

"He has been like a little boy in a sweet shop eager to examine what you have and so excited since he heard about the news of the find," Isabella remarked.

"Isabella is right about that, how often do you get the chance to find an undiscovered asteroid crater on land when most have vanished due to Earth's tectonic plate displacement and erosion," Joe said.

"To be honest, I've been the same, but for different reasons, which I will explain later," Isabella said.

"As you can see the Lidar data clearly shows the shape of the crater with its perimeter marked by the low points on the screen. The graphical representation shows it to be about two hundred meters in length and about one hundred and fifty meters across its widest point. And the Lidar data shows it to be around thirty meters at its deepest point. Not that deep for an asteroid crater, but then over time and the constant floods in the area the crater would have filled in," Leo said.

"Yes, clearly an asteroid crater, have you been able to work out when it hit the earth?" Joe asked.

"No, I was hoping that information could be ascertained from the scientists who are currently in the area searching for oil deposits, but I haven't heard anything back from the oil company. Apparently, they found a meteorite, which they think was part of the asteroid, which should tell us when it struck the earth," Leo replied.

"Let me run the Lidar data through my software it should tell us at what angle the asteroid hit the earth," Joe said.

"Okay, it's all on this thumb drive."

"You can see the software is processing the Lidar data and working out the most likely angle compared with the earth's axis during either a winter or a summer rotation of the earth. We are around two hundred miles south of the equator so this would have a bearing on the results the software will allow for this," Joe said succinctly.

"It is indeed sophisticated software; can you let me have a copy of the software before you leave?" Leo asked.

"Yes, no problem, I will install a copy on your computer system in a minute," Joe replied.

"Good, thanks for that," Leo said.

"Now, that we have the angle of the asteroid strike we will be able to work out the size of the asteroid from any meteorites found in the area. We will also be able to have a good idea when it likely hit the earth," Joe said.

"Now, that's what I'm interested in when the asteroid struck the earth," Isabella remarked.

"Why is that so important?" Leo asked.

"Well, as I said earlier, I would tell you why. It's part or could be part of my pet theory about the possibility of a polar shift due to such an event as an asteroid strike hitting the earth at just the right spot to cause a polar shift," Isabella said.

"Yes, that's Isabella's theory, which she has been gathering data on for some time, but there's still a lot more evidence to find before we can be sure if her theory is right or not," Joe remarked.

"Oh, I see…on a quest to find the answers," Leo said.

"Yeah, it's been a quest for some time, but one I've enjoyed, and hopefully Joe has as well," Isabella said.

"Oh, almost forgot…I took some aerial photos of the area of the depression. Take a look at these pictures. You can't see much, but a sea of forest canopy, but you can just make out the shape of the depression from the height of the trees in the depression," Leo said.

"Yes, it's visible enough from the angle you took the pictures," Joe remarked.

"Yes, I can see it also," Isabella said.

"I would like to invite you both for dinner tonight, say around eight, would that be okay?" Leo asked.

"Yes, that would be great," Isabella replied.

"Here is my address…it's on the outskirts of the city, but the taxi driver will be able to find my place easy enough," Leo said.

"Great, see you later…and thanks again for your time," Joe said.

"Yes, thanks again…and we will look forward to dining with you this evening," Isabella said.

***

Later that day, in the evening, Isabella and Joe took a taxi to Dr. Schapiro's home. Isabella and Joe noticed how remote Dr. Schapiro's house was at the edge of the city bordering the jungle. The house had beautiful arched windows and doorways with ornate cornices painted white supporting the roof fascia with plastered walls a magnolia color and stood detached from the nearest building on the dirt road almost a mile away. Dr. Schapiro had told them that the house had been built back in the colonial days for a local Portuguese government official and that he had been gradually restoring the building to its former glory since moving to Manaus from São Paulo ten years ago.

"Good evening, you had no trouble finding the place then?" Leo asked.

"No, the taxi driver seemed to know without any trouble," Isabella replied.

"Yeah, no trouble at all," Joe reiterated.

"Good, that's have a drink before we sit down and eat, I've cooked a paella, I hope you will like it," Leo said.

"Sounds great!"

"Yeah!"

"Let's take a walk into the garden we can sit on the terrace and feel the cool breeze, which always seems to be available there," Leo said.

"Great idea, yes, I can feel the cool breeze on my skin," Isabella said.

"There's something I have to tell you, I hope you can oblige?" Leo asked politely.

"Yes, what's that…we are at your mercy," Joe said cheerfully.

"Well, I guess you'll want to visit the site of the depression. You'll want to hire our pilot to fly you out there. It's likely he'll want to ask you a thousand questions of why you're here and what you hope to find. Whatever you do don't mention anything about finding rare earth metals or gold, especially gold," Leo stressed.

"Why's that?" Isabella asked.

Well, just the mention of gold will likely spark a stampede of prospectors into the region and upset the delicate balance of peace between the local Indians in the jungle and the people of Manaus. The other day, while I was using the Lidar, Enrique our pilot didn't stop asking questions when I mentioned the possibility of finding gold in the area. I could have kicked myself for mentioning the word gold. I had to warn him of the repercussions if he started to spread rumors of gold. Enrique is in his mid-thirties with a young family to support and I guess he started to dream about finding riches in the jungle. He probably doesn't earn that much working for the local government authority, which is par for the course in this part of Brazil. I know I don't but then again I moved here to get away from the rat race and money doesn't interest me," Leo said.

"Hey, no problem, on that score, Leo," Joe said.

"Yeah, no problem, we'll watch what we say in front of him," Isabella confirmed.

"Good, because a couple of years ago there was a rumor of gold being found in the very area where the depression exists. Apparently, a well-known gold prospector in Manaus got wind of the rumor and went into the jungle alone and was never seen again. Some local Indians found his camp, but no sight of the prospector they informed some local Manaus traders who work along the river and they eventually informed the government authority. A search was conducted in the area for the man, but they didn't find anything, not a single bone or human remains were ever found. It was assumed the man had fallen prey to maybe a panther or had died from a snake bite and been eaten by other predators. Anyhow, the man was never seen again and his home in Manaus still lies empty. This didn't stop many treasure seekers from visiting the area and clashes with the indigenous tribes ensued and several Indians died as well as prospectors before the government put a ban on any further prospecting. So, careless words could spark another gold rush and before we know it we have people dying unnecessarily. I care more about keeping the peace and allowing the local Indians space to live their lives the way they have for thousands of years than the white man's greed," Leo said.

"Huh, that's a sad story, for sure," Joe said thoughtfully.

"That's the trouble with greed, once it bites you...it then is difficult to let go. Rich or poor greed has no favorite, but itself and is one of the seven deadly sins in life," Isabella said philosophically.

"Yes, you're right, Isabella," Leo said calmly.

"I'm always reminded of the story about one of the family of the Rothschild banking dynasty. It was said that one day a newspaper reporter asked one of the Rothschilds about how he made his fortune. He said that he always sold his stakes in the stock market too early, but was able to always bank a profit from his dealings. He, therefore, avoided the pitfalls of being greedy by cashing out not at the top of the market, but before the market went south. This he said was the strategy of success," Joe said.

"I will have to remember that should I ever tip my toes into the stock market," Leo said, laughing. Continuing, he added, "But money doesn't interest me, I have enough to live on and prefer the quiet life out here in the heart of the jungle away from the daily grind of wanting more than you really need."

"Yeah, I agree. My grandfather used to say that the stock market was just a rich man's casino and should always be avoided," Isabella said philosophically while looking straight at Joe with a cheeky smile, which Leo noticed.

"Very true," Joe said laconically.

"Hmm, have I missed something?" Leo asked patiently.

"Go on tell him Joe about your recent brush with the law," Isabella said, smiling.

"Okay, I will. A few days ago, while we were driving back from LAX airport, we were being followed by a black sedan vehicle. It turns out the FBI had followed us all the way from the airport to our home, which was scary at first until I recognized the car had government license plates. Anyhow, the FBI wanted to ask me about my purchase of some stock in a computer company, which I had purchased some weeks back and had sold only a few days before the

FBI were asking questions. They told me they were conducting an investigation for possible wire fraud in the computer company. They asked me many questions and I told them exactly what I had done. I had bought some shares in the cloud computing company because I figured at some point the company may get bought by another cloud computing company or companies wanting to get into the space. Anyhow, I figured it was a good risk, so I bought in and, sold out when there were rumors of a possible takeover of the company, making a handsome profit. The FBI wanted to know if I had inside knowledge of the company. I told them, that I sold out soon after buying the shares, but it was still several weeks before I sold my shares because I needed the money. I told them, that I had no dealings with anyone involved with the company and had no knowledge of insider trading. I had bought the shares on a hunch and sold them when I needed the funds. As simple as that," Joe explained.

"What happened next," Leo asked interestingly.

"Hmm, well, not much, they said that I would have to come in for questioning at a later date and provide all email, contacts that sort of stuff, and advised me to get a lawyer, which I thought was presumptuous on their part. But, I will see a lawyer. I innocently bought and sold the shares without any inside information from anyone and if any fraud has been taking place then I'm not involved, I'm totally innocent and I don't have anything to hide," Joe replied.

"Let's go inside, and we can talk more later I would like to hear more about your pet theory, Isabella," Leo said.

"This fish is great! And the spices really make your taste buds soar," Joe said.

"Yes, I agree…the fish is supreme!" Isabella remarked.

"Leo, what's the name of the fish?" Joe asked inquisitively.

"It's called Arapaima and is caught locally in the Negro and Amazon Rivers. It pays to support the community. The local fishermen rely heavily on what their sell locally. But in the paella there are several other fish called Tambaqui and Triportheus, which give its taste and flavor," Leo said.

"Even though Brazil is the capital of the world's beef production it's a lot more expensive to buy compared with locally caught fish," Leo said.

"Tell me more about your pet theory?" Leo asked kindly.

"Well, it's not just my theory, but a theory supported by many scientists you would call not in the mainstream of views about the possibility of a polar shift caused by an asteroid strike, which like that one that killed off the dinosaurs sixty-five million years ago may have coincided with the Great Flood that's talked about in the Bible when Noah is told to build a boat and house two of every animal. There's a lot of good evidence to suggest that flood may have happened and was caused by an asteroid strike like this one in the Amazon jungle," Isabella replied.

"What evidence do you have?" Leo asked.

"There are many streams of evidence, but it all needs to be collated together and a date arrived at that can be verified with other bits of evidence, without me suggesting a convenient date that fits my theory. I'm not interested in just being the first person to prove this theory I am more interested in getting the science correct and the adventure it allows. Tying the Great Flood in the Bible to a specific time frame would in itself achieve for me more purpose. Joe sometimes will like to kid me on and say that I'm just like a treasure seeker, but I'm not I'm just interested in the science and of the adventure along the way," Isabella said.

"Oh, come on Isabella …I was just joking around with you. I know you are really just interested in the science," Joe said, laughing. Continuing, he added, "It was just a bit of fun, what I call intellectual foreplay."

"But what is the evidence?" Leo asked patiently.

"There are many flaws in our current method of dating organic matter using carbon dating, recent tests have shown this. There are many eminent scientists who will say that a constant decay of the carbon isotope can't be relied on because of the number of atomic tests that have been performed in the atmosphere over the last fifty years, which will greatly affect the efficacy of carbon testing technology. Depending on how close an artifact is to the surface and how close to an atomic bomb explosion and weather conditions in different parts of the earth's surface would have varying carbon dating variations, which may mean the difference between a hundred years and many thousands of years. So that's just one inherent problem and there's more like the Piri Reis Map, which shows Antarctica ice-free. And the continent of Antarctica hasn't been ice-free so we're told for millions of years. There are many bits and pieces that are not direct evidence, but help to support other primary evidence. But, there are many anomalies, which I will try to solve in my adventure," Isabella replied.

"Isabella's right, there are many anomalies that don't stack up in a scientific way," Joe said thoughtfully.

"Interesting subject matter at least for those who cannot get to sleep at night. Just need to start thinking about your anomalies, that should send you to sleep," Leo said, laughing.

"Hey, you're spot on, Leo," said Isabella, laughing.

"Hmm, I have the same problem," Joe remarked cheekily.

"Well, I've booked the trip on the airplane with Enrique for tomorrow at ten in the morning. We should avoid any cloudy and misty conditions in the region, so you should be able to see the depression from the air as I showed you in those pictures of the area earlier, today," Leo said.

"Great, thanks for that, Leo," Isabella said.

"Yes, thanks again for your help, Leo," said Joe.

"Just remember what I said about not saying anything about rare earth metals or gold deposits to Enrique because he's likely to try and ask you many questions," Leo stated.

***

The following morning, Isabella, Joe, Leo, and Enrique were in the Cessna airplane flying up the Amazon River to the region of the depression in the jungle. As the airplane banked right over the depression, Leo pointed out the area of the depression. They could see faintly the shape of the depression from the height of the forest canopy as they flew over the area.

"Not easy to see, unless you were looking for it," Leo remarked.

"That's for sure," Isabella said laconically.

"Yeah, you're right, Leo but still worth the visit to get an aerial view of the region. It's a fair way into the jungle from the river though and I see what you meant about not seeing any identifying features like hills or mountains to get a perspective of the area. I can see why satellite cameras haven't picked up the presence of a crater before, there's just a sea of jungle from all directions as far as the eyes can see," said Joe.

"Yes, it's an amazing place!" Leo remarked.

"I would like to visit the area on foot and make an assessment of the crater. We will have to take a trip up the river and journey into the jungle to investigate further," Joe said intently.

Chapter 17

In the evening, Isabella, Joe, and Leo discussed over drinks at Leo's home the prospect of hiring a boat to go up the Amazon River.

"Yes, no problem there are plenty of barges that trade on the river that will take us there," Leo said.

"We will take your advice as to whom to employ for the boat trip up the river. Is it possible to arrange it in the next few days?" Joe asked.

"Yes, no problem...I will guide you there. We will have to arrange for sufficient supplies for our trek into the jungle. It will take several days going up the river until we reach the spot where we will have to make our way into the jungle, which will take several more days before we reach the crater," Leo stated.

"Are you sure about guiding us there, we could always employ someone else?" Joe asked.

"I would've made a trip at some point to investigate the depression for the local government authority, so it makes sense to guide you there and kill two birds with one stone as it were," Leo replied.

"Are you sure, Leo?" Isabella asked intently.

"Yes, I'm sure...I like to get out of the office as much as I can," Leo replied, smiling.

"That's settled then...as soon as you can arrange a boat and supplies then we will be ready," Isabella said, smiling.

"I like this wine we are drinking…what is it?" Joe asked.

"It's called Tannat and it's brewed from grapes grown in the southern part of Brazil. It's mostly sold just in Brazil, I don't think they export much of what they produce, though," Leo said.

"Eh, keep the best stuff for the Brazilians…I like it," Joe said happily.

***

Two days later, Isabella, Joe, and Leo were on their way up the Amazon River in the old rusty barge with hired help and two donkeys, which would carry their supplies into the jungle for them. They had plenty of fresh water and food for the expected four-day journey into the jungle with metal detecting equipment that Joe had hired to search for any meteorites in the area of the depression. The barge normally ferried people and supplies up and down the Amazon River and had enough spare cabins to accommodate Isabella and Joe in one cabin and Leo in another with the captain of the barge in one cabin and the crew and the hired help sleeping in one cabin, which had several bunk beds. The two donkeys were stabled in the barge's hold with the other supplies.

On the stern of the barge's deck, Isabella, Joe, and Leo sat on wooden crates under a canvas canopy which provided protection from the elements. They watched the crocodiles on the river's shoreline suddenly move as the barge disturbed their sunbathing slumber as the boat slowly crept up the Amazon River. Above the sound of the diesel engine chugging away, they could hear the varied sounds coming from the surrounding jungle from birds squawking and monkeys calling their mates. They couldn't see more than a few feet into the jungle on either side of the river just a dark blanket of the unknown such as the density of vegetation and forest trees.

"I feel safe on this barge, like a tourist viewing the scene from a point of safety, but out there in that jungle…it scares me…," Isabella said.

"We can always turn back or you could stay on the boat, while Joe and I investigate the crater. It's up to you," Leo said.

"To be honest, it scares me also, but I'm not turning back unless Isabella wants to," Joe stated.

"Hey, just talking out loud making my feelings known, you know how I am, Joe," Isabella remarked.

"I've got a gun…just in case. I wouldn't go into the jungle without one there is too many predators out here not to be cautious," said Leo intently.

"Eh, a gun…shit do I need one, just in case?" Isabella asked.

"Actually, two, one a rifle and the other a handgun for protection," Leo replied. Continuing, he added, "You can have the handgun if you think it will make you feel safer, Isabella," Leo said intently.

"She's an excellent shot; we both go to the local gun range back in Los Angles on a regular basis. Most people in America own guns because they can and it makes them feel safer, but whether that's truly the case, is open to debate," Joe said matter-of-factly.

"That's the world we live in, it's the same here. People who can afford a gun own a gun. Especially, out here if they want to venture into the jungle. You'd be a fool to enter into the Amazon without a gun for protection against hungry predators," Leo said.

"What was that?" Isabella cried out.

"It was only the howling sound from the brown howler monkeys; they make that sound when they are calling their mates. We do the same, but we use words and not so loud, normally," Leo replied, smiling.

As the barge headed for the last Indian village situated along the Amazon River, it slowly made its way to the makeshift wooden pier. Isabella, Joe, and Leo watched as the barge docked to unload some goods for the tribe. It was a chance for Isabella, Joe, and Leo to stretch their legs, while the crew unloaded the supplies for the Indians.

"We should be there by tomorrow morning...hopefully the weather holds," Leo said. Continuing, he added, "We anchor there and then trek into the jungle."

"I cannot wait...although I'm not looking forward to the mosquitoes and the other insects," Isabella said raucously.

Shrugging his shoulders, Joe calmly smiled and said, "Perhaps, but who cares the world will continue spinning regardless of man's mistakes. It could wreck the world and make it unlivable, but it doesn't matter, the earth will, in time, restore its health whatever we do to it. It just depends on whether we want to keep using our oceans as a toilet," Joe said philosophically.

They heard the cacophony of millions of insects and crickets providing the background buzz of the jungle as they watched the crew and hired help trade goods with the Indians. Soon they were off again as the barge slowly made its way up the middle of the river. They watched as a jaguar paid no attention to the noise of the barge passing by as it lay resting on a low tree branch that stretched over the river's shoreline.

"Look! A jaguar," Isabella shouted.

"Yes, I can see it…a beautiful animal and king of the jungle," Joe remarked.

"Majestic in the animal kingdom…a family of capybara on the shore is observed but the jaguar waits until it's hungry and then it will try its luck on a kill. In the meantime, the capybara family play and eat in the river nearby and pay no attention to the jaguar," Leo said.

As the barge slowly negotiated the large elbow in the river, Isabella, Joe, and Leo stood beneath the makeshift canopy, which covered the stern of the boat and it provided much-needed protection from the summer sun and when it rained. Suddenly, it was raining heavily as the barge continued its journey up the river. On the bow, a crew member watched for any fallen trees and guided the captain's path through the storm. Later, in the darkness of the early evening, the captain decided to stop and anchor the barge for the night behind a small bend in the river close to the shore for protection against any debris flowing down the river in the dark.

"Why have we stopped?" Isabella asked.

"It's too dangerous, in the storm and the darkness, to travel up the river from debris that could hole the barge such as fallen trees," Leo replied.

"Will we lose much time?" Joe asked.

"Not much...and the captain is being careful, he knows the river and what it's like in a storm," Leo said. Continuing, he added, "We'll get going again at first light. It's best to get some sleep... we've got a hard day ahead of us trekking through a trenched jungle. Let's hope the rain stops for us, tomorrow," said Leo.

***

The following mourning, Isabella, Joe, and Leo awoke from their sleep with the sound of gunfire and the barge chugging along up the river again. When they appeared on deck they noticed the dead monkey being made ready for cooking by one of the crew.

"You don't expect me to eat that do you?" Isabella said to the crewman who was preparing the monkey meat for cooking.

Shrugging his shoulders, the crewman said, "It's good...you will like it."

Isabella winced at the thought of eating monkey meat, regardless of whether it tasted good or not, and stared straight at Leo and Joe for support.

Joe wasn't so squeamish and was willing to try the monkey meat when it was cooked. Leo nodded his head and said, "The local tribes live on bush meat and it is sold in the markets in Manaus and is fairly cheap compared with home-produced beef, so many people buy it."

"It's better you eat well before we dock and begin our trek into the jungle. You will need all your strength to get through the jungle. Our food rations are needed for our hike into and out of the jungle," Leo stated.

"Okay, if you insist!"

"Look Isabella, Leo's right we need to conserve our food supplies because we are limited to what the donkeys can carry for us. We need enough water and food to get there and back," Joe said.

It was still raining heavily as they sat under the canopy at the stern of the barge and ate their breakfast of monkey meat and bread as they discussed the trip so far. Leo wanted to know more about Isabella's pet theory.

"Tell me more about your pet theory and why it means so much to you, Isabella?" Leo asked.

"Well, as I said before it's not just my theory, but many other scientists support the theory, although none, as far as I know, have followed the evidence like I have endeavored to do. I first became interested while at university studying to be a biologist. When I read about the extinction of many of the larger animals across the American continent, which occurred around twelve thousand years ago, I wanted to know why? There were many theories why this may have occurred such as predation by man and climate change, but all this was just conjecture and not supported by any real evidence. So, I was determined to find the evidence if I could," Isabella said.

"It's where we first met at a symposium in Salt Lake City, and Isabella then told me about her pet theory ," Joe said.

"Yes, that's right, but that's another story for another day," Isabella said.

"Go on…I want to hear the full story."

"There were lots of pieces of evidence just about everywhere I looked, but none of it collated and put together to form a coherent theory. It was all very messy and I like to put things in an orderly manner, otherwise, my brain doesn't function like it should. If you look at a graph showing average temperatures over the past twenty thousand years you will see that large increases and falls in a short period of time have occurred in the average temperatures within this time frame. There has been as much as ten to fifteen degrees difference in average temperatures in a matter of a few years. Many scientists have called this a polar shift as if the poles have changed locations and caused these anomalies in average temperatures. But, I'm not so sure, and prefer to argue that a slight variation in the earth's angle of rotation, essentially, its wobble would be enough to cause these anomalies in average temperatures, perhaps, only a fraction of a degree," Isabella said.

"What do you base your hypothesis on?" Leo asked intently.

"At the moment, all I have is a series of anomalies and a gut instinct."

"Isabella and I both teach at the university and have the time because of the term holiday break to conduct our investigation without compromising our employment," Joe said.

"So this is not a government or university-funded research project it's purely a privately funded adventure quest. Like searching for the elusive Philosopher's Stone the magical element needed by alchemists to turn any substance into gold," Leo said lightheartedly.

"No, just us on an adventure quest while we can," Joe replied briskly. Continuing, he added, "Before we get too old and adventure becomes a thing of our past."

"Don't speak for me, I don't plan to give up just yet," Isabella said, laughing.

"Have you heard about Schrodinger's paradox?" Leo asked.

"No, go ahead."

"What was that howling sound, just then?" Isabella asked.

"Sounded like the mating call of the large otter that frequents these waters, at least, I think so," Leo said. Continuing, he added, "We should be near our designation soon."

"Anyhow, the Schrodinger theory of reality is about his cat. He puts his cat into a box with a tiny bit of radioactive substance, which will trigger a Geiger counter, and then asks the question of whether the cat is alive or not. He proposes that two alternate realities are mathematically sound as to whether the cat is alive or not. We cannot see the cat until one opens the box, therefore two realities exist, but the problem or should I say dilemma is which is true because one can only be true at any one time. But in reality, we know this cannot be true. If we apply the logic to your theory, which some have called 'Polar Shift' we have the same type of logical problem," Leo said.

"Yeah, go on."

"You have to determine whether a mass extinction of around seventy percent of the animals who went extinct around twelve thousand years ago is due to a whole series of factors such as man, climate change, and genetic bottlenecks in a very localized area such as North America or was it caused by a small change in the earth's rotation – its wobble – less than a degree that lasted for a brief time in terms of geological time, tens of years or less and not millions of years. That is the essence of the problem, is it not?" Leo asked.

"Yes, more or less."

"Well, you can't have both, either one is the only true answer. But have you considered that the forces that changed the history of Earth could have been outside this solar system? A rogue star could have passed through our solar system and caused havoc to the orbit and rotation of Earth enough to have caused those mass extinctions you talk about. It would be difficult to prove it happened that way, but it's certainly possible, it's a chaotic universe out there. Far from the predictable and safe solar system, we were taught at school to believe," Leo said emphatically.

"Look! There's the other boat," Isabella said.

As their barge drew closer to the oil exploration tug boat they saw no one on the boat or around its moorings. They checked for life in the shoreline camp and again no one was found. No sight or sound of anyone and the camp looked neat and tidy, as if recently used.

"Perhaps, they had an emergency and joined the scientists in the jungle. I see no signs of a struggle. So, it's possible whoever was guarding this tug boat is with the scientists," the captain said to Leo.

Joe had a cursory look around the camp and saw it was in a clean and tidy state without anything amiss. Isabella couldn't see anything out of place either. The camp looked as though people were living there only moments before they landed that afternoon. The campfire had been a roaring fire the day before, the rain had washed away some of the ashes, but they could see the remains of charred and burnt logs.

"We should camp here for the night and start the trek into the jungle first light, tomorrow," Leo suggested.

"Yes, just in case they come back," Isabella said.

"Yeah, I agree, wait until, tomorrow," Joe agreed.

***

The following morning, at first light, Isabella, Joe, and Leo with their two donkeys and with their hired help the two local Indians could cut a pathway with machetes through the thick dense vegetation. The rain had eased off and now it was just a light drizzle, which helped to cool the air with the light breeze that was blowing as they set forth into the jungle. Progress was slow until they found the pathway cut by the scientists, which had been cut a week before. Using his GPS locator on his satellite mobile phone Leo made sure they were heading in the right direction. They soon came upon the camp area the previous scientists had used and settled down for the night. Around the campfire they discussed the recent events.

"That was strange not finding anyone guarding their boat," Isabella said.

"Uh, well, I don't know what to say," Joe said. Continuing, he said, "All I can hear, at the moment, is the incessant background buzzing sound from millions of insects and the occasional howl from maybe a monkey, broken by the rattle of tree branches swaying in the jungle around us from the prevailing wind."

"What's on your mind, Leo?" Isabella asked.

"Hmm. You're right, Isabella, it was strange for a captain to leave his boat unattended. I didn't what to say much in front of our captain and his crew, in case, I scared them off and they disappeared without us on board. But, something isn't quite right and we need to take care and keep our eyes open out here…," Leo said.

"For what?" Joe asked.

"For predators and foes," Leo said laconically.

"Who are the foes?" Isabella asked.

"I don't know, but maybe local Indians. Perhaps they have upset the delicate peace somehow," Leo replied.

"But, we had their blessing…" Isabella said.

"Yes, but perhaps they haven't. I don't know. Make sure you have your guns ready to use at any time," Leo said. Continuing, he added, "You know what oil companies are like they tend to think they own the land when all there are doing is exploring for resources. The Indians have lived on this land for thousands of years and they respect the jungle they live in. They don't treat it like a toilet like we do with our oceans," Leo said.

"Perhaps, we'll bump into the scientists, tomorrow," Isabella said.

"I doubt it. They'll have moved into a different area, by now, it's been several days, since I received word from their oil company about a possible crater," Leo said.

***

After several days of trekking through the jungle, Leo stood on the rim of a crater; it didn't have the tell-tale crust uplifted by the force of an asteroid strike but did have the feel for one. Over time, floods had washed that evidence away and smoothed the rim of the crater. Leo's experience had taught him when to recognize an asteroid strike. You knew even before he slowly descended into the very bottom of the crater that apart from the trees and jungle around him he sensed the gradient of the depression in the area. From the Lidar data, he already had the exact dimensions and shape of the depression, but he still liked to enjoy the feeling of being in an asteroid's crater.

"Listen! The sound of squawking birds awaits our arrival like a warning call to other animals," Joe said.

"Just as we suspected…a swampy location, the recent rain adding more water and just what we need," Isabella said.

"Yeah, we can boil it and cool it overnight before we drink it," Joe said.

"Well, at least, we can replenish our supplies, I didn't realize how much water you need to keep hydrated in this heat," Joe said.

"The Indians are used to it and we are not. We need a lot more water to survive out here trekking through this heat and humidity than they do. It sticks to you like glue," Leo said.

"Yeah, I'll second that."

"I'm drenched in sweat," Isabella said.

***

Later, as they camped and made a fire and sat talking about the day's events, they all wondered how they had not seen nor heard from anyone in the other exploration party.

"Tomorrow, we'll start checking for meteorites. Before we leave this place with the evidence we need to help prove an asteroid hit this area," Joe said.

"What evidence is that?" Leo asked.

"A meteorite that proves when it hit the earth will do. I will then undertake isotope analysis and other methods to iron down a time frame. From the field samples we take back, in a laboratory, I can then estimate when the asteroid hit the earth. It may suit Isabella's pet theory or not we will see," Joe said emphatically.

"Look, tonight, you can see the Milky Way in all its glory, the sky's night is clear from clouds…it's beautiful as it was born yesterday as if we're seeing it for the first time at the dawn of humanity," Isabella said as she gently raised her arm and pointed to the stars.

Chapter 18

The following day, using their metal detector they were finding traces of rare earth metals. Later that day, Joe set off some survey explosives to chart the formation of the crater. From the seismic graphs of the area, he would be able to tell if anything of the asteroid was still intact below ground. From the data gathered Joe would be able to work out the size of the asteroid that hit the earth thousands of years ago combined with the data from the meteorites found in the area. Later that day, while conducting their survey of the crater, Joe, Isabella, and Leo with their hired help were seized upon by a group of gold prospectors who stumbled upon their whereabouts.

"Shut it!" one of the gold prospectors shouted.

"This leaves us in a sticky situation," Jack Milo said.

"For us or for you," Leo asked.

"You now know where our gold deposits are that's a problem for us," Jack Milo said.

"We won't talk," Leo said.

"Someone always talks it's just a matter of time before someone opens their mouth and spills the beans. It's human nature to tell stories and gold stories are always popular and people will listen and tell more people and before long the whole town knows the story," the gold prospector said.

"Feed them to the crocodiles!" one of the gold prospectors said.

"Hmm, good idea...they have a habit of leaving no leftovers," Jack Milo said, smiling, but it was a wicked grin that was twisted all over his face into the many wrinkles he had from working outside in the sun most of his life.

"First, I have to speak to the boss and see what his instructions are," Jack Milo said.

"Your boss...,"

"In the meantime, tie them up and make sure they can't escape," Jack Milo said.

"Have you found gold?" Leo asked.

No, we haven't found any, yet, but we're still looking..." Jack Milo said.

"You want us to believe that or had you fallen for that old tale about a rich vein of gold to be found in these parts? Which is it, the tale or there's no gold here? It was mined out long ago by the Maya civilization in this region of Brazil, yes?" Leo asked.

"It's none of your business," another gold prospector replied.

"I can't be dealing with all this shit. What's going on here?" Isabella asked.

"Can't you see, Isabella...we've stepped into a hornet's nest of trouble," Joe replied.

"These gold prospectors have found gold deposits and a rich vein of it, by the look on your face. You'd be no good at poker as soon as you had a good hand you'd give it away with your face, it's gone bright red," Leo said.

"You believe what you want...I don't give a flying fuck..." the gold prospector said.

"I'm right then," Leo said briskly.

"Yeah, you're right I'm no good at poker and besides I don't gamble I leave that vice to other mugs," the gold prospector said.

"What are you going to do with us?" Leo asked.

"Tie these guys around that tree there," the gold prospector said.

***

262

"What the fuck…were you doing last night…fucking asleep I bet, the boss won't be pleased, that's for sure," Jack Milo said.

They're heading for the river," one of the gold prospectors said.

"Hopefully we can catch them there, I got an idea!" Jack Milo said.

"What's that?"

"You wait and see," Jack Milo said, smiling.

Jack Milo had worked all over the world in wild and desolate places, but mostly jungles. He carried snake anecdotes where ever he went, since the day, he saw his best friend die of a snake bite in the Congo.

Suddenly, a wild hog walked by, ignoring them as it scurried across the ground in a relentless quest to eat. South America was like the Wild West in North America in the nineteen century, it was lawless, in many parts difficult to control, with illegal logging rife and gold and diamond mining in many parts unregulated. The South American continent was being stripped of its resources with and or without their countries' populations' consent. From the local people tapping into oil companies' pipelines and refining them into their energy source for their cars, mopeds, and scooters. Also, there was illegal open-air diamond mining which was rife in some parts of Brazil with most of the local communities involved in some part of the process.

***

"Hello!"

"It's me, boss," Jack Milo said, as he spoke on his satellite phone to his boss in Manaus.

"We have three scientists who stumbled on our operation here. What do you want me to do with them?

"Fuck, you fucked up big time! Let them go, why did you hold them?" the boss said.

"Paulo found them and held them. It was too late then, he had already overstepped the mark. The stupid fat turd has no brains," Jack said.

"I told you…to expect visitors as they found an asteroid crater in the area and not to get involved…just keep out of the way," the boss said.

***

Meanwhile, Isabella, Joe, and Leo had made their escape and were heading west in search of the river. From the river, they would be able to find their boat, up or down the river.

Meanwhile, Isabella, Joe, and Leo had no idea where they were in relation to their camp on the river, where the barge had been moored. Leo worked out which direction to head to from the direction of the sun.

Look! Over there…someone's made a shelter…"

"Just, what we need for the night," Joe said.

"It is as obvious as chalk on a blackboard; it's the first place they'll look, even if they've already seen it before. Find a tree you can climb into for the night, it will be safer off the ground than on the ground with snakes and other creatures crawling and walking around," Leo said.

"By making a guess, were not that far from the river, when we get there we will be able to follow the river upstream to the boat," Leo said. Continuing, he added, "Good thing, we had a full moon last night so we had plenty of light to see where we were heading. We most likely have only three hours to start on them. They will head for the boat as we are."

Finally, they saw the river and headed upstream figuring they were close to the barge. Within an hour, they saw the captain and his crew on the deck of the barge and realized it was safe they headed towards the barge.

"Get the boat ready to go!" Leo shouted out to the captain on the deck.

"What's happened?" the captain shouted back.

"No time to explain just gets us out of here, now," Leo cried out.

"We think they're out to kill us," Isabella shouted out.

"Yeah, so put your foot on the gas," Joe yelled out.

As the barge steamed down the river and out of view of the other boat moored they felt safe for the first time in days.

"What's all the fuss about?" the captain asked.

"They want us dead, so we don't reveal the location of their gold deposit," Leo replied.

***

As the gold prospectors reached the moorings of the barge they soon realized the scientists had made their escape.

"What do we do now, Jack?" the gold prospector asked.

"They won't go far, we'll catch up with them in Manaus," said Jack Milo.

"Get that barge ready to move, we have to stop them from revealing our location to the world, otherwise, we risk losing all we have achieved going up in smoke," Jack said.

***

"Hello, boss, it's me!" Jack was quick to inform his boss by satellite phone in Manaus what was going on.

"What progress do you have?"

"They escaped last night and…"

"Shit! Fucking hell…you'd better get a handle on this and silence those motherfuckers before they tell the world what they have seen. We don't want an audience watching what we're doing in the jungle," the boss said.

"Yes, boss."

"Do you understand? Otherwise, it's your head that will be for the chop," the boss said.

"I understand."

"Let me know as soon as you have the situation under control. And don't fuck up this time around," the boss said and hung up the call.

***

"Can't this barge go any faster," Jack Milo shouted out

As evening fell, neither boat stopped for the night and they just continued down the river in the light of the full moon, hoping to avoid any dangerous debris floating in the river.

***

"Its best if you go straight to the airport and get the hell out of here," Leo said.

"What about you?" Isabella asked.

"I'll be alright, they won't want to have my demise on their heads," Leo replied.

"We have to go first to the hotel because our passports are there," Joe said.

"Okay, but don't dally around, they'll be after you if they have followed us back here," Leo said.

"Do you think so?" Isabella asked.

"Yeah, they won't want their secret to come out, is my guess," Leo replied.

"What about the samples?"

"Take them with you, it's safer with you than me," Leo replied.

"Okay, will do and thanks again for your help and please be careful," Joe said.

Yeah, thanks again for your help, Leo," Isabella said.

***

"Where are they, doctor?" Jack asked as he slowly tightened the knot around Leo's neck as he began his interrogation.

"I don't know," Leo said gasping for air.

266

"Come now, doctor tell me where they are?" Jack asked for the second time.

"The airport," Leo said choking on breath.

"That wasn't that difficult now was it?" Jack said as he released the knot around Leo's neck.

"What are you gonna do now?" Leo asked.

"Release you, because you won't talk unless you want to finish up as food for the crocodiles. Now, will you?" Jack asked.

"You expect me to believe you, after all this effort to find me," Leo said.

"We have an Ace in the hand namely your daughter Maria who works as a school teacher in San Paulo. Now, you wouldn't want her to have an accident. Because we can arrange that," Jack said calmly.

"You wouldn't dare."

"Huh, do you want to find out?"

"What guarantees do I have that you won't harm her," Leo asked sheepishly.

"You have to make sure your American friends don't breathe a word about our activities in the jungle. Is that understood, you know what it will mean for you and your daughter. Just make sure the American gringos don't say a word about our gold deposits or else.

"We should have fed him to the crocodiles," one of the gold prospectors said.

"No, not for now, we may need his help at a future date," Jack said.

"No, because you have a choice keep your mouth shut or we will find you again and permanently shut it for you," Jack said, laughing.

"You can start now, by phoning them and telling them the situation," Jack said sternly.

"Hello, is that Joe?"

"It's Leo here, I have Jack Milo the gold prospector here, he wants a word," Leo said.

"Listen! Your friend Leo and his daughter will see an unfortunate accident if you open your mouth to the world about our gold operation. Is that understood, because it's their lives you risk if you do, is that understood?" Jack Milo asked firmly.

"Yeah, I'm listening."

"After that, we may then come looking for you, now do I make myself clear?" Jack asked sternly.

"Don't harm Leo or his daughter; we won't say a word about your gold operation in the jungle. Just don't harm them," Joe pleaded with Jack.

"Okay will do."

"Would you like another drink," the air stewardess asked.

"Yes, please."

"That was Leo, those men found him and have threatened his life and his daughter's if we say anything about what we saw in the jungle," Joe said quietly to Isabella.

"Shush!"

"I'll say more when we get back in private, in the meantime, don't say a word to anyone about what we saw in the jungle. Shit...I knew this could happen. Anyhow, I'll write down what Leo said, in a moment," Joe said.

"I hope he's alright..."

"Shush!"

"We" know more when we hear from Leo, later. Those other scientists are they okay and what happened to the captain and the crew of the other boat? No one leaves a valuable boat untended and a camp so well ordered and tidy, something occurred, were not aware of. What that is, I'm not sure of," Joe said.

"I worried about, Leo, is he alright?" Isabella asked.

"Yes, if we keep our mouths shut!"

***

On arrival back in the States at LAX airport, Isabella and Joe talked about what happened in the jungle and Leo's plight back in Brazil. Joe explained that they were not to mention to anyone what happened to them with the gold prospectors and that we were not to mention gold deposits to anyone.

"I plan to focus my effort on analyzing the samples we have. Those meteorites we found should give a clear indication of the makeup of the asteroid and when it hit the earth," Joe said on the drive back through the desert to their home in Sonora.

"Great, but what about Leo and his daughter," Isabella said.

"We can't do anything until it's safe to do so," Joe said.

"Oh, okay…"

"Now, remember don't mention gold to anyone," Joe said.

***

Later, the following morning, in his university laboratory, Joe started the analysis of the samples he brought back from Brazil. He was shocked to find the meteorites contained a high content of a very rare earth element, such as its rarity that was on par with the price of gold and much needed in the current boom in electric cars. Lithium was necessary in greater quantities for the batteries in electric vehicles. Large lumps of it were unknown, at least, until this asteroid turned up, Joe thought.

Large lumps of virtually pure Lithium would avoid all that costly processing of the metal contained in the ore. It would be like finding a gold mine, Joe said to himself.

"No wonder, they wanted to keep us quiet..." Joe said out loud alone in the laboratory on the UCLA campus.

Gram for gram, Lithium had gone past the gold price and its rise predicted would only be higher in the future analysts had said. And it was rarer than gold on the earth and expensive to process and mine.

This information was explosive, if it ever got out in the world's press, he said to himself. From the seismic readings on his screen, he could see the anomalies approximately one hundred fifty feet below the surface and could estimate their size from the data. It would make someone a lot of money, he thought.

***

"What about Leo and his daughter?" Isabella asked.

270

I can't do anything for Leo if I don't know the truth," Joe replied.

"We should have informed the police."

"I have been working towards helping Leo. I have to know the truth."

"I hope you're right, Joe," Isabella said.

"Do you want me to apologize, I get it?" Joe asked. Continuing, he added, "I contacted Leo earlier, and he says don't worry he is fine…and please follow what they want."

***

"When do we plan to return to Mexico?" Isabella asked.

"Whenever it suits you…we can also get some sightseeing while we're there," Joe replied.

"I need to find out the reason why they had to leave San Agustín and move to Mexico. What were the reasons?" Isabella asked intently.

"You mean the Almecs?" Joe asked.

"Yes, of course…who else…"

"None, just clarifying, who we are talking about, one minute we were talking about Leo in Brazil, and the next minute the Almecs in Columbia and then Mexico. Sometimes, you rush ahead of me, and I wonder where we are in our conversation," Joe said, smiling.

"Sorry!"

"Oh, I should have mentioned earlier, I found out what those prospectors in Brazil are so eager to protect. It's not gold but Lithium and is far more precious than gold at today's prices. But, it's a necessity in the making of long-lasting batteries needed for electric cars. At the center of that crater at around one hundred fifty feet below the surface is a giant lump the size of the Eiffel Tower just waiting to be mined. And in the process make someone very rich or poor?

"What do you mean poor?" Isabella asked.

"A quantity of that size suddenly available to the market could substantially affect its commodity price. So certain players in the stock markets would want the availability of the metal prolonged as long as possible. Similar to how they control the availability of diamonds in any one year thereby controlling the price of diamonds rather than a rush of diamonds available which pushes down prices. They essentially have control of the tap and can turn it off and on when they like. They are Masters of the Universe in one respect," Joe said.

"Hmm, I see what you are saying…"

"It's as simple as that…they would want to control availability as much as possible," Joe remarked.

"What are you going to do?"

"I'm not going to do anything, which would jeopardize Leo and his daughter. I'm not going to say a word about this to anyone…it stays between us. You understand?" Joe asked intently.

"Yes, completely…"

"Good, then we're on the same page."

Polar Shift

***

The following day, Harry Steel was on a flight to Los Angles, California to see Joe and Isabella at their home in Sonora. Harry wanted to hear first-hand what Isabella and Joe experienced on their recent visit to Brazil. He wanted to know all the facts about the case before he ventured into the Brazilian jungle.

"Hi, my name is Harry Steel, we spoke on the phone," Harry Steel said.

"Glad you could come here, my name is Joe and this is my girlfriend, Isabella," Joe said.

"Nice place you got here," Harry remarked.

"Yes, it suits us."

"Right, tell me from the beginning about what happened in Brazil," Harry said.

"Let's sit on the balcony and watch the sunset, it's cooler out there," Isabella said.

"We first heard about a possible asteroid crater in the Amazon jungle on the news and we were both excited about seeing it or ourselves. You see…Isabella has a pet theory about a polar shift occurring around twelve thousand years ago…"

"A polar shift…what's that?" Harry asked.

"A polar shift is the movement of the naturally occurring magnetic north and south poles. This can occur when the earth's rotation wobbles in space and the poles are realigned to a different position than previously observed," Isabella said emphatically.

"This has happened many times in Earth's history," Joe remarked.

"Continue."

"We needed to see the crater and gather evidence to support Isabella's theory. So, I contacted the geologist who found the crater ... Dr. Leo Schapiro about viewing the crater. After his initial reluctance, Dr. Schapiro agreed for us to come and view the crater. When we arrived in Manaus, Brazil, we hired a small airplane to view the depression, but couldn't see much, so we hired a boat and ventured up the Amazon River and eventually moored the boat and continued into the jungle on foot. After an arduous trek through the jungle, we arrived at the spot of the crater and began our survey of the area..." Joe said.

"That's not quite correct...a group of oil explorers first found the depression and reported it back to their company. And it was Dr. Schapiro who later confirmed it as a crater through using Lidar technology for the local government authority," Isabella remarked.

"What is Lidar technology?" Harry asked.

"The ability to see through the jungle at the underlying ground formations using a form of ground penetrating radar is the nuts and bolts of the technology," Joe replied.

"Yes, that's correct."

Anyhow, after the second day, at the site, we were surrounded by a group of men and taken away to their camp.

We understood the men to be illegal gold prospectors. We were tied up and they told us not to say a word about what we found at the crater. A man called Jack Milo threatened our lives and the lives of Dr. Schapiro and his daughter should we say anything about what we found out," Joe said.

"And what did you find out?" Harry asked intently.

"It turned out that it wasn't a gold deposit those men were protecting, but a large deposit of Lithium. It's a very rare earth metal, which still resides deep underground at the center of the crater. At current prices it is worth millions of dollars," Joe said.

"How do you know that?" Harry asked intently.

"From the meteorite that we found at the site and the survey results confirmed a large anomaly the size of the Eiffel Tower located around one hundred and fifty feet underground at the center of the crater. We believe it's the remnant of the asteroid strike that formed the crater at the site. And we believe it's a chunk of pure Lithium metal ore, and as I said before, worth millions of dollars to the right people..." Joe said.

"Go on..."

"During the night, we escaped and made our way to the river and found our boat, and made it back to Manaus. The day, Isabella and I flew back to the States, but we are still concerned about the safety of Dr. Schapiro and his daughter," Joe said.

"Yes, that's right. Your sister, Rebecca said that you may be able to help us," Isabella said. Continuing, she added,

"I'm really worried about Leo and his daughter, we owe it to them to sort this out if we can."

"Don't worry I will look into this and sort it out," Harry said. Continuing, he added, "What can you tell me about Jack Milo?"

"Not much, but he seems to run the gold mining operation, although he did say he had to talk to his boss about us, while we were there. Jack Milo is a middle age man with a weather-beaten face and a bald head about your height and build. But, to me, he gave me the impression that he had a shifty background. That's about all I can say," Joe replied.

"I think the same; he certainly meant what he said to us. Not a word about what we discovered or else. Those were his words. But, Dr. Schapiro knew the man. Apparently, Jack Milo is a well-known character in Manaus for gold prospecting in the region. Milo knew about Dr. Schapiro's daughter who works as a teacher in São Paulo. Milo's threats to Dr. Schapiro and his daughter certainly scared us all," Isabella remarked.

"And Dr. Schapiro how does he make a living?" Harry asked intently.

"Oh, he works for the local government authority dealing with oil and mineral exploration in that region of the Amazon jungle," Isabella said. Continuing, she added, "He said it was a 'backwater post', but he preferred it, now, that he was close to retiring."

"I know, how he must feel," Harry said flippantly.

Chapter 19

Isabella and Joe return to Mexico and decided they would travel again by car as the last time they had enjoyed the trip. They were both eager to see the professor again and find out what possibly made the Almecs migrate from Columbia to Mexico.

Isabella and Joe could hear the screeching birds as they flew overhead as their car approached the house of the professor. Dr. Philippe Manuel was a professor at the local university and was in charge of the archaeological department for the Mexican government in the local region. Apart from the light of the nearby street lamp, the house looked deserted and uninviting.

A dog was howling and barking as they knocked on the door.

"Glad to see you again, come in, come in…" Dr. Philippe Manuel suggested.

"Yes, thank you."

"Don't mind the dog she always barks…"

"Did you have a good trip getting here?" the professor asked.

"Yes, it was fine," Joe replied.

"Tell me more about the Almecs?" Isabella asked eagerly.

"Not much is really known about them. They are a mysterious civilization which like many before and after just disappeared from history. The large head sculptures, which are as big as a small car that you see in this region scattered all around the area depict the faces of African males and not the indigenous Indian tribes you see in Mexico. Some scientists have suggested they originally came from Africa to first Columbia and then moved up to this region of what is now Mexico. How they managed to cross the Atlantic Ocean and get to South America, I don't know?" said the professor matter-of-factly.

"Perhaps, they chose to cross the Pacific Ocean using the Indonesian Islands and island hoping until they had to cross the wide expanse of the ocean," Isabella said. Continuing, she added, "It would seem a more logical route than the crossing of the Atlantic Ocean, although a lot farther to travel, but still, a major endeavor to accomplish."

"But, there is much we don't know about them. In my view, they were smarter than we imagine. They must have been to cross an ocean and survive," the professor said candidly.

"Oh, yes, of course."

"Is this the only reason, why you have come back so soon?" the professor asked.

"Yes, there is more," Joe replied.

"We've come to learn more about the Almecs. We want to see, in situ, more of the beautiful sculptures they made. Understand their culture. And also we want to listen to what you have to say. And why do you think they moved to South America from Africa?" Isabella asked.

"Good question, but difficult to answer. We are a species that like to discover new things..." the professor replied.

"But, why do you think they chose to cross a vast ocean, whichever way they took to get here?" Isabella asked.

"It's in our blood already coded in our DNA. That's the simple answer," the professor said.

"Yes, it makes sense," Joe said.

"It's the only answer that makes any sense. The more I think about it the more I come down with the same conclusion, every time. It's in our DNA. I can see in the sophistication of the Almecs' sculpture a civilization that must have been advanced for its time. It is said that the symbols and the glyphs found around some of the Almecs sculpture are the forerunners to the Mayan writing script that they had at this time," Isabella said.

"Many ancient civilizations just vanished into thin air, probably due to climate conditions or some other catastrophic event that forced its demise as a civilization. Then they get absorbed into the surrounding environment and a new civilization takes over, until over perhaps a millennium or a few hundred years they too disappear from history. It's happened time and time again in the past, it's par for the course. It's a warning sign for our current civilization; we may be on the brink of something similar happening to our present civilization," the professor said sadly.

"What else can you tell me about the Almecs?" Isabella asked.

"Over the past twenty years or so I have studied the Almecs and have found no evidence of a warring society. They seemed to be a peaceful civilization that for some reason died out, got absorbed, into the surrounding area, and ceased to be a breeding colony. This can happen when an outsider comes into the community and brings a new disease into the local community they have not seen before and have no immunity to, thereby it decimates the population to such an extent that the population goes to the brink of extinction, literally overnight. We have seen in recent history how plagues have affected local populations around the world. Because we have a bigger world population it would take a major catastrophe to affect the current population, but if it did, we could be thrown back to the Stone Age very quickly. There are probably only a dozen or so individuals right now that fully understand how to design and engineer an integrated circuit board, and if they suddenly disappeared all that knowledge could vanish overnight," the professor said emphatically.

"I never really thought about it, that deeply before," Joe said.

"Yes, you're right, professor," Isabella said.

"Sometimes, it only takes a small pin to bust a large balloon," the professor said.

"Yep, that's all it takes," Isabella agreed.

"Tomorrow, I would like to show you both some more interesting Almec sculptures. You may be perplexed as to what they may have been used for, we shall see," the professor said.

"What's that?"

"It's a surprise, you will find it interesting I hope. I would like to hear your first views on the matter. Tomorrow, we will see," the professor said.

"Oh, by the way, I spoke on the phone with Dr. Pannee Righa in Columbia and we exchanged photos of Almec sculptures. He explained the influence of the Hindu culture on the early Almecs and he showed me pictures of sculptures there and I showed him pictures of Almec sculptures here and we agreed there was a relationship. I thank you for bringing that to my attention. It will take further investigations to fully assimilate the evidence and conclude what may have happened," the professor said.

"I'm glad we had been of some help to your research," Isabella said.

"Yes, sometimes it takes more than one person to see the relationships in a culture, especially, one with a different experience of a particular culture to see the relationship between the two," Joe said.

"If I go away from this trip with a better understanding of the Almec's culture, then it would've been a worthwhile endeavor," Isabella said.

"But, I think, Isabella was right about the Almec's motives. Who would travel across a vast ocean without being aware of what was there? I don't think you would make the journey on just a haunch. That part doesn't make sense to me," Joe said. Continuing, he added, "There must have been a map."

"You can clearly see the African faces on those carved head sculptures, that's for sure…they carved the faces of the people around them, what they saw and these people could pose and model for the carvers," Isabella said.

"There's a lot of conjecture about that issue, which is still not resolved, and probably won't be, anytime soon, because some archaeologists would like it to be their particular narrative, rather than the most likely outcome. Me, personally, I agree with you, Isabella. But there are many archaeologists who say the Almec's sculptured heads are just depictions of their gods. And were not carved to depict the everyday faces of their population, but to represent their gods. No evidence has survived to this present day to conclusively come down on one side or the other," the professor said.

"Hey, that's why such an event as a Great Flood could have washed away all of the evidence in one event," Isabella said.

"Yeah, you could be right on that score, as well," the professor said.

"Yeah, a Great Flood could have affected this region more than say, Africa," Joe said.

"Are you referring to the Great Flood in the Bible?" the professor asked.

"Uh, yes, it could be so. Isabella needs to iron down some dates, but it's possible…yes," Joe said.

"Yes, that's what I've been trying to do since I started to collect my evidence. I have created a timeline of events so I can better picture what may have happened. Here, take a look at this…" Isabella said.

"We have plotted a series of events, which have taken place on this timeline. It's easy to see what may have happened in the past. From the evidence, Isabella and I have gathered it will either prove Isabella's theory or not. But, we still have a long way to go, before we can say for sure what may have happened in the past," Joe said emphatically.

"Hold on, Joe…it's not just my theory, but many eminent scientists around the world have suggested the same…they just haven't bothered to take the time and effort to either prove their right or wrong. But, I can't let it go ever since I heard about a polar shift at university. I have been debating and arguing with teachers, students, and professors about the validity of my thoughts on the matter. Since then, I have been trying to validate my theory that a polar shift happened, not that long ago. This may have caused many of the anomalies that you see in the archaeological record," Isabella said vigorously.

"You could be right, Isabella," the professor said calmly.

***

The following day, Dr. Philippe Manuel showed Isabella and Joe a series of large spherical balls of stone as large in some cases as a small car. The professor told Isabella and Joe that the large stone balls were found all around the region and that some of them lay buried until they were discovered. The professor explained that they still had no idea what the large spherical stone balls were used for or indeed how they were carved so accurately.

"Wow! There are truly amazing."

"They are found throughout the region. We have no idea what they were used for or indeed how it was done. The craftsmanship was suburb and the accuracy was amazing; we just don't know how they were able to manage it. We don't have the tools they used, so we can't say how it was done," the professor said.

"From what you say and how many were found in the area. My first thoughts are they could have been a flood and that's why many were found in rivers and some completely buried," Isabella said.

"Yes, you could be right. We just don't know, we have no evidence to work on," the professor said. Continuing, he added, "Perhaps, one of these days we will dig somewhere and find the evidence until that happens it's just a mystery."

"It is clearly a mystery to solve," Isabella remarked.

"It's clearly is an enigma, professor, and one we may never truly understand. Why a culture goes to these great endeavors to carve such sculptures for reasons unknown is a puzzle. I hasten to add that even today master carvers would have difficulty carving such stone balls to such accuracy, I believe," Joe said dumbfounded.

"Have you tested how these stone balls were produced by using modern-day techniques?" Isabella asked.

"Yes, it would be interesting to find out how they did this."

Shaking his head, the professor said, "I haven't, but I believe other archaeologists have conducted similar studies to see how easy or not it would have been for their carvers to produce. If you go back to the ancient Egyptian culture and see how they produced such detailed carvings with such symmetry you have to wonder how this was done with such limited Bronze Age tools. The same can be said for the fine carving produced at Angkor Wat in Cambodia. And there are many other places around the world with similar fine examples of stone carving using basic tools. Our ancestors were smarter than most people think, that is for sure. I'm always amazed at what our ancestors were able to achieve without modern-day techniques and tools. Perhaps, there was a catastrophic flood that washed away all the evidence, that's for you, Isabella, to find out."

"Perhaps, that's what happened," Joe remarked.

"Well, it's certainly been an eye-opener coming to Mexico and seeing these sculptures, that's for sure. I hope we can move the needle in the right direction and figure out what may have happened in the past," Isabella said.

"You will have to let me know what your findings are and keep in touch," the professor said.

"Yep, it's certainly been an adventure to tell our grandkids when we decide to settle down," Joe said, smiling.

Chapter 20

On the drive back to America, Isabella and Joe discussed what they had found out in recent days.

"I'm still worried about Leo and his daughter," Isabella said.

"I have news about the other group of scientists; they are all alive and well. They had moved into a different area in the region. They posed no threat to the prospectors.

"What about their captain and the crew, what happened to them?" Isabella asked.

"They're alive, as well, they'd been in the jungle hunting for bush meat when we arrived and found the boat abandoned," Joe replied.

"So, we just got spooked!" Isabella said.

"Yeah, and the prospectors, they can't keep a gold deposit secret forever. The story will eventually come out," Joe said.

"I thought it was Lithium, not gold?" Isabella asked.

"Yes, Lithium, but just like gold to them," Joe said.

"Right, as I draw this timeline…"

"You can see a better picture of events. And what evidence supports each event on the timeline?" Isabella said.

"We have the woolly mammoth evidence. And then there's the Biblical Great Flood, which we have several approximate dates for." Isabella said.

"Hmm, oh, yes."

"Oh, and of course the Almecs…and the Piri Reis Map, which are interesting anomalies," Joe said.

"Yes, yes…I see, I see it!" Isabella cried out.

"And, of course…the asteroid strike, I've been able to give an approximate date, but because our field survey of the area was interrupted by those gold prospectors it is only my best guess," Joe said.

"Yes, I know, Joe, but for now it's all we have," Isabella said, smiling. She had found what she believed was the best evidence to prove her theory was right. The earth had been hit by an asteroid at such a location and angle to temporarily make the earth wobble in space. She could see it, would other scientists agree with her? The whole event may have only lasted for days and weeks not thousands or millions of years, she said to herself.

"What are you smiling about? Joe asked.

"Hmm…"

"You have a grin as wide as the Niagara Falls," Joe said.

"Yep, I have…"

"What have I missed?" Joe asked.

"Now, I have a visual picture from seeing this timeline, it's easy to see what I've been looking for all these years," Isabella said emphatically.

"What's that?"

"Well, as scientists we look for the raison d'etre the reason to be, the empirical evidence, when in reality there are none. The universe is in chaos but does show some deterministic features in some areas. It's like understanding the string theory of the universe. A series of strings vibrating at different frequencies at the quantum level is how it's described. But, of course, it's a lot more complicated than that," Isabella said emphatically.

"Are you trying to muddy the waters?" Joe asked curiously.

"We have some evidence, but a great flood would have washed away most of it, in one go, then over time the rest gets compromised, as well," Isabella said.

"And your point is?"

"Mass extinctions have occurred a number of times in Earth's history, we know of at least five major extinction events, but many more localized events have occurred for many reasons. You only have to look back over the last three thousand years and count the number of empires and civilizations that have come and gone," Isabella said emphatically.

"So, you think a polar shift occurred around twelve thousand years ago?" Joe asked curiously.

"It's my main conclusion from what evidence I have seen and a logical answer," Isabella replied emphatically.

"You and I have spent a lot of time compiling this evidence and checking its validity," Joe said.

"Yeah, I know."

"Have you heard from your friend, Rebecca, yet?" Joe asked.

"Yes, she told her brother that he's going out to Columbia this week."

"Great! At least, it's in the right hands, now," Joe remarked.

"Yes, I hope so…"

***

"That company will have to obtain a license to mine that quantity of metal ore," Joe said. Continuing, he added, "In that process, the news will eventually leak out or they will publish their findings. I would like to publish my initial results from the limited survey we conducted, at some point."

"You'll have to wait and see what her brother finds out," Isabella said worryingly.

"Don't worry, I won't publish anything until I'm given the all-clear to do so."

"Yeah, let Rebecca's brother handle it."

"I'll let Leo know what's happening by email," Joe said.

"What have you found out?" Isabella asked excitedly.

"I've been doing my own research on the Internet into that company. It turns out the company is owned by another company, which is listed on the stock market. The company prospectus lists it as a gold mining operation with several stakes in various gold deposits around the world. The company's latest accounts show it made a small loss last year and is into hundreds of millions in debt. Most of the debt is down to plant and process machinery. But, I well-timed announcement of a gold or Lithium deposit would send the shares higher in the short term. Perhaps, this is what the company plans to do…and make a quick killing in the stock market," Joe replied.

"Is this what you're planning to do…buy some shares?" Isabella asked.

"Yep, I don't see any downside, but much potential for a huge payday, at some point in the near future," Joe replied.

"It's not illegal is it?"

"No, totally above board, just me being canny with my assessment of the company," said Joe.

"Oh, I see."

"It was perhaps why those prospectors were so keen to sell us a tale about a gold deposit as they viewed the whole area as a gold mine. A properly conducted survey of the area could yield the expected finds and the cost-benefit analysis derived to see if it was economically sound. You don't have to be a geologist to work out the price of gold. The amount of Lithium in the area could be worth hundreds of millions of dollars. At this granular size, it saves a lot of processing costs. From that point onwards it's simple mathematics. A lot of people are going to make a lot of money," Joe said.

"I hope you're right."

"I've tipped my toe into the stock market and we will see what happens," Joe said flippantly.

Joe could hear the birds chirping outside in the garden. It was a welcome sound almost reassuring that nature still swings, whichever way it decided to go, he said to himself.

"Anyhow, I spoke with Harry, yesterday and I informed him of all the updates. He said, less serious than first thought. But, he said he would look into the company and some of its employees. He should be there in Brazil sometime today," Joe said.

***

On the airplane, Harry Steel wondered about his new mission as he sat there drinking his JD and coke cola in business class. Joe had given him the updated news about the lives of the other scientific group and it now appeared less serious than first thought, he said to himself.

But, he still had to investigate. He didn't know if the threats were serious or just threatening words, but just the same were insidious, biting at every minute of your existence; it was enough to induce a cardiac arrest just living day to day. Especially, for a man like Leo, the pressure would build up and bang a heart attack, the stress would have taken another life, he said to himself. This reminded him of when he was in Iraq.

It was just another day patrolling the streets of Baghdad…It was a city in turmoil with one faction fighting another; it was a civil war with the US forces trying to keep law and order, since the demise of Saddam Hussein's regime.

After a few more close calls with death, my tour of duty was over in Iraq and I got transferred back home to spend the rest of my service honing my skills at the Marine base in Louisiana. The only hassle I had there was learning to live with millions of mosquitoes that constantly attacked day and night. At least, I could relax and not be aware that a sniper may have his eyes on me, or an IDE placed by the roadside to blow up when triggered by a passing vehicle. After a while, you forget about the risks and just get on with your job. The thought of being blown up and surviving as an invalid didn't inspire me to think about it, but I saw enough of our boys blown up to realize it was a realistic chance every day we went on patrol. It got to the stage when it was difficult to know who was on our side and who was not; because there were so many factions fighting each other we were just in the middle of the chaos. And our enemies were prepared to kill innocent people just to advance their cause. Baghdad and Fallujah became hotbeds of resistance and car bombs and IDEs were exploding everywhere you went, there was nowhere safe even in the Green Zone. As soon as the Republican Guard had been defeated then civil law broke down and the civil war began with every maniac with a machine gun was out for revenge, he said himself.

"Would you like a drink, sir," the air stewardess asked.

"Yes, a JD and coke, please," Harry replied.

Harry's mind drifted back to his time in Iraq. He was cynical because he had seen the realities of decisions made by our politicians and the reasons why they make bad decisions. Our politicians think they know the answers like our kind of democracy will suit all nations, so they continue with policies that ultimately destroy lives and kill innocent people believing they are doing the right thing for this or that country, he said to himself.

For king and country and the so-called oppressed they wage their wars, he thought. But, it's not as simple as that and there are many factors why some people choose to live under a dictatorship rather than have free and fair elections under a democratic hood, he said to himself. In his view, it should be left to the people who are being oppressed to rise up in a revolution to oust the dictator and elect their own leaders, not use our politicians to make those decisions for them. It should come from the people and not from politicians thousands of miles away in another country making decisions for them. Just like we rose up in the War of Independence against British rule, where we were being governed and taxed without representation from establishment thousands of miles away. It's just as important for other oppressed people to have their revolution as it was for the American people against the British, he said to himself.

Harry Steel was on his way to Brazil to check on the safety of Dr. Leo Schapiro and his daughter and check out the mining company and some of its employees. He had Jamie a data analyst at the CIA headquarters at Langley, Virginia do him a favor and run a background check on Jack Milo of SAMO (South American Mining Operations) the gold mining company. The profile of the man was typical he had previous jobs in mining operations mostly for gold. What was it about gold that becomes a lure into the cycle of constant expectation of a major find? The lure of gold for some people was all they thought about, he said to himself. Jack Milo's boss it turned out to be a director of the holding company, which was normal. Jamie's data profiling had turned up a lot of useful leads, Harry thought.

Jack Milo was a real live one. Always into some sham or scheme to get people to part with their hard-earned savings. This is what Joe Goldstein had found out and what Jamie had provided on the company and the man, it was almost obvious they were up to no good. His first visit was to see Leo and go from there, he said to himself, as the taxi drove up to Leo's house.

"Hi, we spoke on the phone, my name is Harry Steel, and my sister told me about your situation."

"Thanks, for coming, my name is Dr. Leo Schapiro. But, just refer to me as Leo, it saves all the fuss."

"Start from the beginning and take your time," Harry said.

Leo told Harry how he got involved with the gold prospectors, which were now threatening him and his daughter if any information leaked out about what the gold prospectors were doing in the jungle.

"You can rest easy; I'll have a word with Jack Milo and his boss before I leave here," Harry said.

"Thanks, Mr. Steel," Leo said.

"Just call me Harry and don't worry I'll soon sort this out," Harry said.

***

The following day, Harry set out in the hired fishing boat which had a fast diesel engine to go up the Amazon River. Arriving at the same spot on the river, Harry and the captain of the fishing boat saw the tugboat still moored to the shoreline. Harry spoke with the tugboat's captain and crew before heading off into the jungle to find the gold prospectors.

The next day, Harry found the prospectors busy surveying the area and they were surprised to see Harry emerge from the jungle all alone.

"I've come to see a Mr. Jack Milo," Harry said to the gold prospectors.

"Who wants to know," one of the gold prospectors asked.

"I do, my name is Harry Steel."

"Take him away to see the boss," one of the prospectors said.

After a short journey through the jungle, Harry and his minders arrived at the prospector's camp.

"We found this man in the jungle, he says he wants to see you, boss," one of the prospectors said.

"My name is Harry Steel."

"You want to talk with me?" Jack Milo asked.

"Are you Jack Milo?" Harry asked.

"Yes, what do you want?"

"You threatened a friend and his daughter with their lives if any information about your mining operation got leaked to the public, is that true?" Harry asked bluntly.

"What's it got to do with you?" Milo asked.

"Everything…"

"Everything…" Jack Milo repeated.

"Yes, everything, if I don't get what I want from you and your boss, then I will have to resort to other methods," Harry warned.

"Oh, yeah…"

"If I don't get your word and your boss's word that my friend and his daughter will not be harmed in any way should information about what you are really doing here gets out, then I will have to come back and seek my revenge," Harry said.

Huh, who are you to tell us what to do," Milo said.

"You don't want to know, just tell your boss the situation. In fact, contact your boss, now. And I will speak to him before I make a visit," Harry said.

Suddenly, they could hear the distant sounds of lemurs calling their mates up in the tree canopy. For a moment, they all stood there looking up into the tree canopy surrounding their jungle camp.

"I know all about your operation here and what you may be planning and will let the authorities know, if I don't get what I want from you," Harry said.

***

Within minutes, Milo was making a call on his satellite phone to his boss in Mannus and briefly spoke before handing the phone to Harry.

"Hello, my name is Harry Steel."

"I understand from Milo what you want," the boss said.

"Do we have a deal?" Harry asked.

"Yes, but what do I get in return?"

"The ability to sleep soundly in your bed at night," Harry replied.

"It wasn't meant to be like this…one of our men went too far. They were meant to just threaten them off the site," the boss said.

"Now, do we have a deal or not," Harry asked intently.

"Yes, of course."

"When do you plan to release the information to the public?" Harry asked.

"Later, this week…"

"Good, I can tell my friends they don't have anything to worry about. Is that correct?" Harry asked.

"Yes, that is correct."

***

Later that week, Harry heard the news on the radio about the mining operation and considered his job done. He telephoned Leo and told him that he was heading home as the news about the mining operation had been made public and that he and his daughter now didn't have anything to fear from the mining company and they could now go back to living their lives in peace.

***

In Sonora, California, as the stock market opened and the news about the mining operation in Brazil had hit the news agencies the price of the mining company had more than doubled on the news about the Lithium find. Joe was just about to sell his stock in the mining company as bids dried up in the stock as buyers scrambled to own the stock.

"Just sold out of that mining company in Brazil, just in case it falls again in the following days," Joe said.

"Why, do you expect it to?" Isabella asked intuitively.

"It could, when all the initial frenzy dies down," Joe said.

"What do you mean?" Isabella asked.

"Well, at the moment, there are not enough bids to sell compared to the bids to buy, meaning it's a good time to sell into a buyer's market rather than the other way round," Joe said.

"Oh, I see, so you made a profit?" Isabella asked.

"Yes, a very handsome profit, doubling my stake and more, and now, it's the right time to sell, before the analysts have had time to work out the likely profits or not for the company," Joe said.

"I thought you said this Lithium deposit would be like a gold mine for that company?" Isabella asked.

"Yes, I did, but that was before I did my research on the mining company and found out how precarious their financial woes are," Joe said.

"How bad are they?"

"There robbing Peter to pay Paul, to put it frankly. And when the analysts and big investors do their sums and have worked out if this Lithium find is a gold mine or not to the stock then the price discovery of the stock could take a serious fall," Joe said.

"What do you mean by price discovery?" Isabella asked intently.

"At the moment, the stock is being pushed up by the initial momentum of buyers wanting to get into the stock without knowing all the facts about the Lithium find and the outstanding finance of the company. When all that information gets assimilated and assessed by analysts the price discovery mechanism in the stock market is in what they call buyers beware syndrome. When all the facts are known the true price discovery of the stock could differ greatly from its current price. So, the best time to sell is now," Joe said.

"Oh, I see…"

"Unless you happen upon another Microsoft or Google and wish to stay invested for the long run, then it's best to sell when you can bank a profit in your stock market investment. I always remember what Rothschild a member of the banking dynasty said when asked by a reporter about how he made his fortune. He said he always sold to early but always banked a profit. Meaning doesn't be greedy and wait for more," Joe said, smiling.

"How much have you invested?" Isabella asked.

"Only half of what I made in my first stock market purchase," Joe said. Continuing, he added, "Changing the subject, we were short-changed in Brazil, when those prospectors arrived, so much of the field survey will need to be done again before we can know for sure what day that asteroid hit the earth. But, my best guess with the aid of deduction analysis of isotopes and other crystals contained in the meteorite samples, it looks to be a safe bet, on this date being the likely candidate," Joe said.

"And what date do you have in mind?" Isabella asked.

"It's not set in stone but around ten thousand to twelve thousand years ago is my estimate," Joe replied.

"You can't be more specific," Isabella said.

"No, not at this time without a full survey of the area," Joe said.

"Now, I only have to prove at what angle it hit the earth, which it is then likely caused a wobble in the earth's rotation," Isabella said.

"You mean a polar shift?" Joe asked intently.

"Yes, a polar shift Isabella replied briskly.

Chapter 21

As Isabella and Joe sat out on their balcony enjoying the sunset they discussed what they had learned from their adventures around the world. Isabella was eager to inform Joe about a well-respected scientist who had first proposed the polar shift theory based on his research many years ago.

"Yes, it's what Charles Hapgood, a Harvard graduate and later a history professor proposed in some of his books. He cited that there had been at least five different polar shifts over the last one hundred thousand years. He reckoned from his research that polar shifts had occurred every fifteen thousand to twenty thousand years or so," Isabella said.

"Was he suggesting a recurring cycle?" Joe asked.

"No, just that his research suggested these sorts of time frames when cataclysmic events took place such as an asteroid strike or a passing planetary object or a passing star that caused the earth to move off its axis," Isabella replied.

"So, he wasn't sure how these polar shifts had occurred, but was confident that they had happened, is that what you are suggesting?" Joe asked intently.

"Yes, that's right...it's not always possible to hang your hat, but something happened that's for sure. Too much evidence exists that supports polar shifts had occurred in the recent past and will happen again in the near future, that's for sure. I will publish my research and findings and let the academic community peer review it."

"So, he wasn't a geologist, then?" Joe asked incredulously.

"No, you're right..."

"But, don't let that put you off," Isabella said, smiling.

301

"So, how can you base any information on polar shifts on this man's work?" Joe asked incredulously.

"Well, I don't, but he made some very interesting and astute assumptions, which I believe are correct. Our ancient ancestors, by all accounts, were great astronomers for some reason. They took great lengths to align their pyramids, monuments, and important buildings to the cardinal poles. They made sure their structures aligned to the north-south axis. By using this information Hapgood theorized and plotted the changing positions of the North Pole. He also argued that contrary to mainstream consensus most of the structures he cited were indeed a lot older than we are led to believe. For example; the Great Pyramid of Giza, Egypt we are told was built by Khufu, yet no evidence has been found of his cartouche inside or outside of the pyramid. You have to ask, why is this? If he was the builder of the pyramid you would have thought that he would have wanted his name written all over the monument. Plus, there is evidence to suggest it was built ten thousand years ago and not four thousand years ago. Ancient scholars from Greek and Arabic sources cite the Great Pyramid being built not in the time of Khufu but thousands of years before. There are many more anomalies associated with the Great Pyramid, but the most important one is its alignment, it's pointing in a completely different position to the north-south axis, as we know it, today," Isabella said matter-of-factly.

"But, the poles could have drifted since Khufu's time."

"Yes, but the margin is only around one degree every million years or so, but the Great Pyramid's alignment is off by a greater distance of many degrees compared to the current north-south axis as it is today," Isabella said. Continuing, she added, "So, if the Great Pyramid was built in Khufu's time around four thousand years ago then its north-south alignment would be aligned to the current north-south axis, but it isn't!"

"Perhaps, they just made a mistake in their alignment of the north-south axis," Joe remarked.

"No, way…"

"If they could build such a sophisticated structure as the Great Pyramid, they could accurately find the cardinal points without a problem," Isabella said.

"Yes, it does make sense, but it's still a mystery, but that's history always changing when new evidence reveals itself."

"Charles Hapgood theorized that these polar shifts could have happened almost overnight in geological terms causing cataclysmic floods, tsunamis, earthquakes and dramatic climate change, which his research using ice core samples suggested this may have happened," Isabella said.

"It wouldn't take much for a rogue planet or star passing near our solar system for the right conditions to occur for the earth to wobble and a polar shift to occur, which the scientific community would not be aware of in the recent past," Joe said.

"There are accounts in ancient writing where they talk of a time when there were two moons in the sky, which is folklore but as we know much of folklore has a grain of truth attached to it, so it's possible such an event took place in the recent past."

***

The promise of riches didn't last long for Jack Milo the boss of the Amazon jungle mining operations. Several months later, Jack Milo was arrested early one morning at his Florida home in the United States. The U.S. Securities and Exchange Commission (SEC) had warrants for Hector Rodrigues the CEO of the mining company and Jack Milo for insider trading on the stock market. Their scheme to cover their tracks had been found out. And now, they both faced real jail time.

Using their close relatives, to hide their purchases of stock they hoped to conceal the truth about their investment in the stock of the mining company, before the news broke about the colossal Lithium deposit in the Amazon jungle, which they had planned would send the shares in the mining company up in incredible value before the true value of Lithium deposit could be evaluated. Jack Milo and Hector Rodrigues hoped by hiding their investment in the mining company they could 'make a killing' in the stock market without the authorities knowing about what they had done. Only, for it to be a dawn of false hope.

***

Meanwhile, Harry Steel and his wife Susan were relaxing on their rented fishing boat on an inlet off the Florida Keys watching the sunrise as they prepared to devote a day to fishing. Harry was reflecting on his last mission for the CIA and for his sister Rebecca out in the Amazon jungle.

"What are you thinking about?" Susan asked.

"My last mission for the CIA and what I did for Rebecca's friends out in the Amazon jungle," Harry replied. Continuing, he added, "I can't talk specifics about the CIA mission as you know, but out in the Amazon jungle for Rebecca, I can talk about that."

"Whatever you want to say just go ahead."

"Well, it seems every possible scenario could happen."

"Yeah, that's life, its unpredictably," Susan said, smiling.

"Everything seems to be connected in one way or another. Since the Covid-19 pandemic, you have to ask if our politicians and governments are forward-thinking about the possible calamities that can hit our civilization without a warning. Continuing, he added, "Before I go on, let me cast our lines and see if we can catch our supper for tonight." Harry said enthusiastically.

"I'm looking forward to seeing what we can catch," Susan said.

"Me too…"

"Go ahead and tell me more," Susan stated.

"Well, at the moment, the world economy is finely balanced in feeding a population of around seven billion people, but that could change in an instant if something drastic happened to the world's food supply. The fallout from that could send our civilization back to the Dark Ages. And just imagine if there was a worldwide plague that killed off billions of people virtually overnight."

"It could happen. It makes sense!" Susan agreed.

"Now, there may be only a few handfuls of people capable of designing and engineering a computer microchip. What would happen if they were no longer around, we may end up in the Stone Age faster than anyone thought possible. It's happened many times in history where cultures and civilizations have disappeared virtually overnight. Dr. Isabella Garcia and her theory about polar shifts suggest a catastrophe could happen from multiple causes, which shows we don't live in a stable world, which we were taught at school," Harry said succinctly.

***

Suddenly, virtually overnight, Harry's paradigm had changed and the world was in a panic after a Solar Flare Ejection (SFE) from the sun sent an EMP (Electromagnetic pulse) straight at the Earth. It was the start of things to come, a possible polar shift, and nowhere to hide and nowhere to run.